Books by Emma Miller

PLAIN MURDER

PLAIN KILLING

PLAIN DEAD

PLAIN MISSING

PLAIN CONFESSION

Published by Kensington Publishing Corporation

PLAIN CONFESSION

EMMA MILLER

KENSINGTON BOOKS
www.kensingtonbooks.com

KENSINGTON BOOKS are published by

Kensington Publishing Corp.
119 West 40th Street
New York, NY 10018

All Kensington titles, imprints, and distributed lines are available at special quantity discounts for bulk purchases for sales promotion, premiums, fund-raising, educational, or institutional use.

Special book excerpts or customized printings can also be created to fit specific needs. For details, write or phone the office of the Kensington Sales Manager: Kensington Publishing Corp., 119 West 40th Street, New York, NY 10018. Attn. Sales Department. Phone: 1-800-221-2647.

Kensington and the K logo Reg. U.S. Pat. & TM Off.

BOUQUET Reg. U.S. Pat. & TM Off.

eISBN-13: 978-1-4967-0649-2
eISBN-10: 1-4967-0649-8
First Kensington Electronic Edition: April 2018

ISBN-13: 978-1-4967-0648-5
ISBN-10: 1-4967-0648-X
First Kensington Trade Paperback Printing: April 2018

10 9 8 7 6 5 4 3 2

Printed in the United States of America

Chapter 1

Rachel Mast stepped out on the back porch of her parents' farmhouse. She wore a calf-length dark-blue dress, a black apron, thick black stockings, and black leather shoes. Her hair was twisted up into a knot at the back of her head, and over it, she'd tied a dark-blue scarf. From head to toe she appeared Amish, wearing a borrowed dress of her mother's and her sister's shoes and stockings. In the clothes she felt Amish, but she wasn't. At least, technically, she wasn't Amish anymore. Although, today, her old life called to her with poignant whispers that tugged at her heart.

The house was crowded with people, all Old Order Amish except for one out-of-place Methodist minister who'd come to pay his respects. He'd then stayed for the chicken and dumplings, the Dutch apple pie, and the sweet-and-sour coleslaw, for which her mother refused to give out the recipe. This was a funeral gathering, and as always, the Amish turned out to lend their support to their own. The newly deceased was Daniel Fisher, a member of their church community, the victim of a tragic hunting accident.

That morning, Daniel had been laid to rest in the Amish cemetery, and due to the small size of the family house and the circumstances of the sudden death, Rachel's parents had offered their home for the gathering. Rachel wasn't certain how many mourners had come back from the cemetery, but vans and buggies had been arriving for the last hour. One preacher or another was offering prayer and consoling words in the parlor; children played quietly on the stairs or, frightened by the weeping, crept under tables to press close to their mothers' legs. Babies were passed from hand to hand, rocked, nursed, and jiggled, and plates of food and soft chairs were produced for the elderly and infirm.

Amish women and teenage girls prepared and served food nonstop. The hall and sitting room tables were stacked with pies, cakes, cookies, and sweet muffins. Kitchen counters barely contained the baked hams, sausages, fried chicken, and roasted turkeys. Casseroles, bowls of canned peaches, and kettles of soup and gravy covered two stove tops and spilled over onto a desk.

It was because of the turkey that Rachel had ended up wearing Amish clothing instead of the simple black pantsuit that she'd arrived in early this morning. Ida Mae Hostetler had been coming in the back door with a tureen of turkey gravy and giblets, just as Rachel had been on her way out to the springhouse for another pitcher of buttermilk. A cat had been attempting to sneak into the house, lured, no doubt, by the kaleidoscope of enticing scents drifting from the kitchen. Ida Mae, a small woman, had the mischance to tread on the tabby's tail, and the resounding screech had been so startling that she had lost control of the container of gravy and thrown it into the air. Rachel, being at the wrong place at the wrong time, caught the bulk of the contents down her pants, blouse, and jacket, not to mention in her hair. Thus, she was forced to don the only clothing available, Old Order Amish garb.

Dressing this way didn't feel as uncomfortable as it should have, Rachel decided as she wandered out onto the porch and rested a hand against a turned wooden post. Outwardly, she'd left her Amish home and way of life as soon as she'd turned of age. She'd desperately wanted to see more of the English world, and she'd wanted an education, something frowned upon by the *ordnung,* the code that Plain communities chose to live by. She'd turned her back on the family heritage and friends she loved, leaving the peaceful valley and the small town of Stone Mill to become part of the mainstream American society.

Alone, possessing only a rudimentary eighth-grade education, she'd worked, acquired her high school diploma, her bachelor's degree, and finally an MBA from Wharton. She found that she had ambition, a knack for numbers, and the imagination to use them to make people's lives better. But success in the world of finance didn't bring the personal happiness she had been seeking. So she'd resigned from a high-paying position and returned to her home to open a B&B in a wonderful old brick house that had been teetering on the brink of collapse. She'd reunited with her family and come to the conclusion that she would forever be caught somewhere between the Amish and the English worlds.

"I've come full circle," she murmured to no one in particular. All those years of being away, and she could now put on an Amish dress, pin up her hair, and almost become the girl who'd run barefoot through these fields and struggled to learn to churn a pound of butter.

Rachel stared out into the farmyard, her gaze unfocused, not really seeing the lines of gray and black buggies or the groups of black-coated men in wide-brimmed wool hats standing out of the wind. The ground was wet, the gravel and dirt churned up by the horses' hooves and the running feet of children. Little was left of the two inches of snow that had fallen the previous day. Most had melted when the temperature rose, making the area around the barn particularly messy.

A middle-aged Amish couple approached the back porch, the red-cheeked woman dressed in black, balancing a four-layer coconut cake. "We've come to pay our respects, Rachel," the man said solemnly in *Deitsch*.

The wife nodded.

Rachel returned the greeting in the same tongue. Among her people, *Deitsch,* mistakenly called "Pennsylvania Dutch" by outsiders, was the language of choice, although all but the youngest children also spoke English fluently.

"How is Mary Rose holding up?" the woman asked as she came up the steps.

"Doing poorly," Rachel replied. "It was a shock, losing Daniel that way. Especially with the new baby."

"God's ways are not always easy for us to understand," the husband remarked. "He was a fine young man, devout and hardworking."

"Always mindful of his elders," the woman added. "Bringing groceries to the shut-ins. A credit to his parents."

Rachel motioned toward the door. "I think Mary Rose is with the bishop in the parlor. Kind of you to bring the cake."

"A small token," the woman intoned. "We'll remember the widow in our prayers."

Her husband opened the door and held it for her. He was a stocky man of medium height with graying hair, a broad German face, and light-blue eyes. "We pray for the whole family," he added.

For a moment, the sounds of the gathering drifted out onto the porch, and then were muffled again as the door to the house closed behind the couple. Rachel pulled her mother's shawl tighter around her shoulders. It was a raw day, above freezing, but still cold with a damp chill. She wasn't ready to go back inside yet, though. There were too many people there, too much talk, and too few open windows. Unlike her immediate family, some in the conservative community hadn't adopted the English habit of using deodorant, and the multilayers of winter wool clothing didn't mask the body odor.

Rachel knew her mother needed her, and standing there

with idle hands wasn't encouraged. But she'd been on her feet since dawn and she needed to catch her second wind. Hard work didn't bother her; she'd been raised to appreciate it. But it lifted her spirits to step away from the communal grief and listen to the wind whipping down off the mountain and the shriek of a red-tailed hawk high overhead. Just another few minutes, she promised herself, and she'd be ready to plunge back into the controlled chaos again.

On the side of the barn, in the shade of the overhang where snow still lay, Rachel caught sight of something red. She studied it. What was it? A mitten a child had dropped? If so, small fingers might grow cold on the way home. Rachel went down the steps off the porch and, taking care to avoid the puddles, she walked across the yard toward the object.

As she grew closer, she realized her mistake. It wasn't a mitten but a bird, a cardinal lying sprawled in an unnatural position on the white snow. Odd that she hadn't noticed the brilliant red feathers against the white when she first stepped onto the porch. She wondered if the bird had died of illness or flown into the barn wall and broken its neck.

Evan was an accomplished bird-watcher, outfitted with expensive binoculars, telescopes, and membership in multiple birding organizations. He could recognize hundreds of species of birds, often just by their song. But cardinals were common enough that she'd recognized them since she was a small child. She had rarely seen a dead one in all her years on the farm. She decided she would move the poor thing and get one of her brothers to bury it. No sense in leaving it for children to see.

But, to Rachel's surprise, as she neared the dead bird, it suddenly revived. It shuddered, shook out its wings, hopped, and flew up, fluttering over the top of the barn in a flash of crimson, vanishing from sight. Not dead, then, Rachel decided, but only stunned. Alive and strong enough to fly.

A pity poor Daniel Fisher couldn't have done the same, she thought. What would his widow have thought if Daniel had abruptly sat up from his bier and walked? Not dead as everyone supposed, but only stunned and suffering some sort of coma? That was the sort of wondering best kept to herself or shared with Evan. Her parents wouldn't understand and take her musing as disrespectful to the deceased.

Rachel turned back to the house and then remembered the buttermilk she'd come out to retrieve. As she turned toward the springhouse, she met two of her distant cousins on the path. One carried a pitcher of milk, the other a wheel of cheese.

"Such a pity it had to happen to Daniel," the oldest was saying in only slightly accented English. "And him so full of life and vigor."

"And so cute," her sister replied. "He had a way with him, you know?"

"You can say that again. Even sweet to—Rachel?" The girl's eyes widened and she nearly lost her grip on the container of milk. "You're wearing Amish dress. Have you . . ."

"Turned Amish again?" Rachel chuckled. "*Ne.* Just an unwanted encounter with a pan of turkey gravy."

"It suits you," the older girl said. "Better you come back to the faith now, my mother says. And not marry that Englisher policeman."

In her late teens, the girl was tall and thin as a rake handle with small eyes and not much of a chin. Poor thing, Rachel thought. It was what came of a closed society intermarrying over so many years. She hoped that Uncle Juab would give her a piece of land and a few cows to attract a suitor. She was a clever girl and deserved a husband as much as her prettier sisters did.

"Best we'd all get inside and help," Rachel suggested. There would be a lot of dishes to wash. Maybe she'd volunteer. She didn't mind washing dishes. She was free to think because her hands knew the tasks. It wasn't like having to make conversation about the natural appearance of the deceased or conjectures about how such a terrible accident could have happened. A hunting accident. Daniel had inadvertently shot himself.

Rachel took a deep breath of the cold air, retrieved the buttermilk, and returned to the kitchen. As when she'd left, the kitchen was packed with busy, chattering women and one who was loudly weeping. Rachel's mother, a fussy granddaughter balanced on one hip, saw Rachel and gestured for her to take a serving tray from the edge of the sink.

"I wondered where you were," her mother said, making her way through the crowded knot of women to her side. "Apple cider and lemonade. And that box of tissues. Could you take it into the parlor? And see if anyone wants coffee or water."

The baby girl, Rachel's brother Paul's youngest, was dressed in traditional Amish garb in a long gown, old-fashioned cream-colored baby cap, and black high-topped shoes. In her tiny mouth was a pink pacifier shaped like a flower secured by a pink ribbon and pinned to the front of her baby gown. Pins on clothing were supposed to be straight pins, but since it was attached from the inside and both Rachel's mother and her sister-in-law were sensible, Rachel suspected a safety pin inside the child's clothing.

"Shouldn't you sit down for a while?" Rachel suggested as she picked up the tray of drinks. "The doctors said you shouldn't overdo." Her mother's color was good today, and her eyes were bright, but Rachel knew that she didn't have her full strength back yet after being treated for breast cancer. Her hair was growing back from the chemo, and it seemed thick and healthy in appearance, but it was still very short for an Amish woman. Today, her *mam* wore her traditional *kapp* instead of the scarf she'd been wearing for the last six months. And the pins on her dress and apron were definitely straight pins.

"Don't worry so much." Her mother smiled. "I am *goot*. Save your compassion for Mary Rose. How she will manage without Daniel, I don't know. When I think what he's done for that family since he married her. Not that I fault poor Ernst. So long Mary Rose's father was in that wheelchair before the Lord took him home. And her brother, Moses, being the way he is." Her last word held a certain *tone*.

Moses Studer was considered odd by the Amish. It was Rachel's guess that if he had lived among the English, he would have been diagnosed years ago with Asperger's. Instead, his friends and neighbors simply remarked on his occasionally strange behavior and his way of talking and interacting with others. The good thing was that he was completely accepted by the Amish and cherished as another soul, blessed by God.

"But how many bridegrooms would take responsibility for a failing farm, a mother-in-law, and a twelve-year-old boy when he married?" Rachel's mother continued. "Without Daniel, the family would have been—"

"Esther." Rachel's Aunt Hannah bustled through the throng, interrupting. "Your Samuel wants to know where his old Bible is, the one with the worn cover given to him by his great-uncle. Preacher Harvey has a cousin in Bird-in-Hand who repairs old books. He says that if those loose pages aren't fixed, the whole volume is in danger."

"In the cabinet under the stairs," her mother answered. "Wait. Can you take this one? If she needs her diaper changed, there's a stash in the big bathroom closet. I'll get the Bible. Samuel couldn't find a fly on the end of his nose."

Rachel waited for an opening to carry in the tray of drinks, but instead of thinning out, the crush seemed to get worse as more food was being passed into the living room, where more tables had been erected. Mary Byler, who was sitting near the woodstove, fanned herself with a copy of the magazine

Family Life and motioned to her. "Rachel! Are you going to have the wedding at that English church in town?" she called.

For such a small woman, her voice carried easily above the murmurs, and Rachel involuntarily winced. This didn't seem the time or place to be talking about her impending wedding. "We are," she answered quietly.

"What? I can't hear you! Shh, I'm trying to hear Rachel," Mary said to the two nearest matrons, who were talking about the new widow's eldest brother.

Rachel knew who they were discussing because she'd heard Arlene Troyer say, ". . . It was Daniel that got him that good job at the mill."

"Come over here, Rachel." Mary motioned with her makeshift fan. "I want to talk to you. Hear all the details."

Rachel offered a quick smile. "Sorry, fetching for my mother," she called back, and then to her aunt, she said, "Excuse me. *Mam* wants me to take these drinks into the parlor."

"Rachel?" the old woman called after her. "Where are you going?"

Rachel plunged into a divide in the black bonnets and wiggled her way through to the narrow hallway without losing her glasses of cider and lemonade. She'd have to go back for the tissues.

Aunt Hannah followed close on her heels with the baby on her hip. "Why don't you want to talk about your wedding? Are you having second thoughts? Because if you are, there's no shame in it."

Rachel shook her head. "I'm not having second thoughts. I just didn't want to talk about it today. I feel so bad for Mary Rose. Talking about my wedding seems almost . . . well, almost like boasting about my blessings."

Rachel's niece stared at her with large round eyes. She was a pretty child; Rachel didn't know if she'd look like her mother or her father. Babies, at least young ones, always looked alike to her. She liked babies well enough, but she was wary of them, especially when they cried. This one was vigorously sucking on her pink pacifier and didn't show any signs of bursting into tears.

Aunt Hannah shook her head. "Honestly, girl, you do get the strangest notions. Is it a pity about Daniel? Of course it is. A sweet boy, always good to the older people. Never missed worship. But people die. That's life. People, even good people, die. Women become brides and they become widows. And some, like Mary Aaron . . . well, we don't know how that will end, do we?"

Rachel's throat tightened. Mary Aaron had been at the grave site, not in Amish dress as her mother wanted, but wearing one of Rachel's outfits, gray pants and jacket with a white blouse. And a pair of her heels. Rachel didn't want to get into that hive of bees with her aunt, so she ignored the comment about her cousin.

"Life goes on," Aunt Hannah continued. "And you shouldn't feel bad because a new part of yours is opening. There's enough sadness and grief in this world without feeling guilty about being happy. And you are a good person. You deserve to be happy. Do you understand what I'm saying?"

Rachel nodded. Aunt Hannah was a dear, but always full of advice. And Rachel wasn't sure that she wanted to get into a discussion of life here in the midst of the funeral gathering. Instead, she said, "I love you, Aunt Hannah. You're the one with the good heart." And, balancing the tray, she leaned over and kissed her plump cheek.

"I hope I do have a good heart," Aunt Hannah answered. "Now, I'm going to see about finding a fresh diaper for this little one and you see that our bishop gets his lemonade. He always takes lemonade."

Rachel moved on, gave her father a glass of cider, asked Beck Beiler if she could take her dirty plate, and made an appropriate comment to Mary Rose's mother, Alma Studer. She found the widow with the bishop and one of the deacons in the parlor and passed out all her glasses. A squeal of childish voices and a pounding of feet came from the stairs to the second floor, and Rachel excused herself and started to go up the steps to see if anyone was watching over the kids. Everyone expected children to be children, but running inside and making too much noise at an after-funeral dinner was outside the bounds of proper behavior.

The front door opened behind her, and a gust of cold wind whipped against Rachel's legs and arms and down the back of her neck. She turned to see her fiancé, Evan Parks, just inside the doorway. He was wearing his trooper's uniform and looked as out of place among the Plain folk as a penguin in a flock of robins. "Evan," she called to him.

He looked up, saw her, and did a double take.

Rachel glanced down at her dress and realized what had startled him. "I'll explain later. Are you off work already?" she asked, unable to look away or fail to see how handsome he was. He always looked taller and broader in the shoulders in his uniform with his hat and knee-high boots and the huge handgun in its holster.

He shook his head. "Can I speak to you?" He was wearing his official expression, and Rachel wasn't certain if it was because of the occasion or that something was wrong. "Outside," he said, tilting his head in the direction of the door.

"All right." She'd seen Evan at the cemetery, but he'd been on traffic duty and they hadn't had a chance to speak. She'd thought he wouldn't be off for a few hours, but they were planning on seeing each other later. If he was here, there must be a serious reason.

"There's a problem," he said, when they were alone on the porch.

She hugged herself for warmth; the temperature was quickly dropping. She wouldn't be surprised if it snowed again tonight. "Okay."

"It's Daniel Fisher." A wrinkle appeared on his forehead

and he folded his arms over his chest in that way he stood when he had something unpleasant to deliver.

Rachel shivered in the raw wind. "What's the problem?"

"We just got the preliminary report from the medical examiner. His death wasn't an accident. It looks as if he was murdered."

Chapter 2

"Murdered?" Rachel glanced around to see if anyone was near enough to overhear them. But that was foolish. What would anyone be doing on the front porch? Everyone else was coming and going through the kitchen. The front door was only used to carry out the dead or to welcome a bride. Well, she reconsidered, it was used by teenagers wanting to slip in or out of the house unnoticed. And for state troopers bringing bad news.

She stared at Evan. "Are you serious?"

"I wouldn't be here if I wasn't." Evan's normally pleasant face with its square chin and dimple was grim.

He took his job seriously, so seriously that he'd given up his position as a detective with the Pennsylvania State Police to be a trooper again. Evan liked helping people and he felt that he was of more use on the road, performing the mundane work of a policeman, than sitting at a desk.

Some, including his friend and fellow officer Lucy Mars, considered what he'd done to be career suicide, but Rachel hadn't. She realized that it was important to Evan that he serve where he felt most needed and the most comfortable. He'd been a good detective, but his heart wasn't in it, and she'd seen more of the old Evan since he'd returned to the work he loved. She knew a little something about making choices that didn't seem completely rational, and she'd decided long ago that peace of mind meant more than a higher income or more prestige.

"I need you to help me speak to the family," Evan said, pulling her out of her thoughts. "Actually, Detective Sharpe will be providing the information. He's the one who took over my old position, but he's from Philadelphia. He hasn't had any experience with the Amish community—knows nothing about them. Sharpe asked for me to be there when he speaks with the immediate family, and I want you as well. Will you help me?"

Rachel grimaced. Since she'd returned to Stone Mill, she'd often found herself acting as a go-between when the Englisher police needed to communicate with the Amish. The Plain community was a closed one to the modern society. *Keep apart from the world* was the motto they lived by. They didn't like or trust Englishers. And they didn't like Englisher police in particular. Amish who didn't want to cooperate with law enforcement or with state or national officials could suddenly lose their ability to speak or comprehend English. A violent confrontation with authority in the old country two hundred years before had taught them caution and suspicion. They didn't always trust her because she'd left the order, but at least she understood their ways.

"Please, Rachel. This will go easier if you'll help us out," he urged.

"What can I do?" She looked at him and shrugged. "I don't know what's going on."

"Just be there in the room. These people trust you. The family will know we mean them no harm if you're there to reassure them."

"Okay. Sure. I'll do what I can," she promised. "But why does the medical examiner think Daniel's death wasn't an accident? It's not unheard of. A hunter drops his gun or catches the trigger on a branch and shoots himself. Remember John Knepp up the valley? His rifle went off when he was crawling under a fence. One blast, and it was over. Why not Daniel? What makes them think he was murdered?"

He glanced over her head, one hand on his wide leather gun belt. "I can't discuss details, but they're sure someone else killed him."

"But maybe it was still an accident, even if Daniel didn't do it himself. There are always hunters in the woods during hunting season. Someone might have accidentally shot him and never known it." Of course, there had been cases of the Amish murdering, but not like this. The Amish were a peaceful people; besides, everyone had liked Daniel Fisher. Who could have possibly had a big enough problem with him to shoot and kill him?

Evan's features softened. "It would be best you heard this from Detective Sharpe. I, *he*," Evan corrected, "needs the immediate family. Just Mrs. Mary Rose Fisher, the mother-in-law . . . what's her name?"

"Alma. Alma Studer."

"Mrs. Studer, and Mrs. Fisher's two brothers, Moses . . ." Evan paused. "He's what, early twenties?"

"Twenty-four. At least that's what I heard someone say at the funeral," Rachel confirmed.

"And . . . Lemuel, isn't it?"

"*Ya*, Lemuel is the younger. But he's a child," she reasoned. "Thirteen . . . fourteen at the most. Is it necessary to include him? This has to be so confusing for him. Amish kids aren't like the English. Lemuel's probably never seen television, and he certainly hasn't seen any violent movies or any cartoon superheroes. My people shelter their children from violence."

Evan shook his head. "Detective Sharpe was clear. He needs to speak to everyone who lives in the household."

"I don't understand, then. Moses doesn't live at home. He has a job at the mill, and he lives there. Apparently, he's doing so well that the miller is considering apprenticing him. My aunt said that Daniel got the job for him."

Evan considered what she'd told him. "Maybe I misspoke.

Maybe Detective Sharpe didn't say anyone who actually lives in the home." He exhaled. "Moses needs to be there."

"Does it have to be today?" Rachel pressed her hand to her forehead, fearing she had a headache coming on. Her migraines were coming on more frequently and she wasn't sure why. She didn't think she was stressed, planning the wedding, but maybe she was. Something like this happening in the community was certainly stressful. "Mary Rose just buried her husband, Evan. Surely you could give her a day or two?"

"Rachel, this wasn't my idea, and it's not my case. I'm only trying to make things easier for everyone concerned." A static sound came over the radio attached to his uniform. A voice. He ignored it. "And the sooner the investigation starts, the sooner we'll find out who killed Daniel. Maybe it was someone he knew, maybe not. But if it was a random murder, then others are at risk." The radio came on again. He tapped it and it went silent. "This isn't my call or yours. There are procedures, and Detective Sharpe is the one who decides when and where to start. Either he can speak to the family here and now, or he could insist they all come down to the troop. I thought that having you here, it would be easier on the family. Translate for them if they're not following. Is it possible for you to find a private spot for him to talk to them?"

"*Ya*, I can do that," she conceded. "Let me speak to my *dat*. It's his house and he will be the one to say the detective can have this meeting and where it can be done."

He frowned. "I thought the house was your mother's domain. Didn't you tell me that most Amish wives rule the home?"

Rachel shook her head. "It's not that simple. Ordinarily, you're right. My mother would have the final say. But there are elders here, a bishop or two, and I don't know how many preachers." She sighed. "There is an image to maintain. Most Englishers believe that ours is a male-dominated society."

"And that's not true?"

"Well, it is, and it isn't. In most of the families I know, the wives control the checkbook. Men usually make the big decisions such as where to live and when to buy or sell land, but the rest is either a joint decision with their wives or weighted in favor of her opinion." She shrugged. "Other than with my Uncle Aaron. He likes to think he's in charge."

"But the women can't be bishops or preachers or . . . what's the other position that's important in the Amish church?"

"Deacon. They are the enforcers. Nothing like the mob, but they keep order. If anyone breaks the *ordnung,* it's the deacon who would be the first to speak to the person who's committed the transgression." She gave him a quick smile. "Back to what you were asking about women's roles, you also have to remember that the women have an equal vote in church business, and they have most of the raising of the children. Amish society is pretty equal as far as men and women go."

Evan had lived in Stone Mill all his life. They'd been engaged for several years, and he'd known lots of Amish personally. If he didn't understand, how would this Detective Sharpe, an outsider, hope to?

"I think you've lost me. I still don't know why you don't ask your mother if there's somewhere the detective can speak to the Fisher family."

Rachel moved a few steps to the left to get out of the path of the raw wind and the scattering of sleet that was now wetting the floor of the open porch. "Because if I go to my mother for permission, then it will look to others as if she rules the house."

"Which she pretty much does."

"As I said, it's complicated. If I go to *Mam, Dat* will lose face. I think that's the best way to put it. She would go along with any of his decisions. And it will look as though he's in charge. A proper, Old Testament family."

Evan held his hands out to her, palms out. "Whatever. Please just make the arrangements. Detective Sharpe is ten minutes out. Either we have something set up when he gets here, or he'll ask the family to come down to the troop."

She clasped her hands together, shivering. "Fine. But it's cold out here. Come inside and wait while I hunt up *Dat*. I'm sure he can arrange something."

Exactly ten minutes later, Rachel's father showed Detective Sharpe and Trooper Lucy Mars into the front parlor that minutes before had held the elders and church leaders. The mourners still crowded the hall, the living room, and the smaller parlor and kitchen, but they'd been gingerly ushered out of the main parlor. Seated in the chamber were a red-eyed Mary Rose and her mother; both her brothers remained standing, behind the women. Rachel and Evan waited near the fireplace.

Detective Sharpe, who Rachel hadn't yet met, was a stocky bulldog of a man in a navy-blue suit, carrying a small notebook. Sharpe's graying hair was neatly trimmed in military style, and he had brown eyes, a high forehead, and a strong nose that showed the effects of at least one break. With an air of self-confidence, he strode, back rigid, to a settee across from the Amish, and sat down. Trooper Lucy Mars, whom Rachel knew well, took a position just inside the closed door.

For a few long seconds, the two opposing camps, the Englisher authority figures and the distinctly anti-authority Amish, stared at each other. Mary Rose's mother slipped an arm around her daughter's shoulders and handed her a handkerchief. Mary Rose cradled her sleeping baby and blew her nose. Lemuel, a thin, undersized boy with wispy blond hair, bad acne, and gray eyes, looked frightened. His brother, Moses, assumed the blank, emotionless expression that often puzzled Englishers or made them assume the Amish person wasn't particularly bright.

Moses's shaggy hair was several shades darker than his brother's, and he was of medium height with gangly limbs. His face was long with eyes much the same color as his brother's and sister's, but there was something unsettling about Moses's flat gaze.

Quickly, Rachel made the introductions, then explained in *Deitsch*, "Detective Sharpe has something to tell you." She looked from Alma to Mary Rose. "And . . . and he may have questions for you concerning Daniel's death." She repeated what she'd said, this time in English, so the police knew what she was telling the Studer family.

"Sorry for this intrusion on the day of Mr. Fisher's funeral," Sharpe delivered in a raspy smoker's voice. He was overloud in the quiet room and Rachel had to make an effort not to flinch. He reminded her of a drill sergeant addressing new recruits. Not that Rachel had ever been to boot camp, but she had seen movies and TV.

Mary Rose sat up straighter and clutched her sleeping baby. Her mother, a hollow-cheeked woman with a small chin, gray hair, and glasses, closed her eyes and then opened them and fixed her gaze on the floor. Lemuel gripped the back of his mother's chair.

"It's my duty to provide you with unpleasant and disturbing news," Sharpe continued. "I'm sorry to inform you that Daniel Fisher did not meet his death as was first assumed. He didn't die accidentally by his own hand, as you were first told. Someone shot him. We believe he was murdered."

Rachel repeated what he said in *Deitsch*, but didn't repeat it in English because now she was just translating directly.

Sharpe studied the family and then looked to Evan. "Do they understand English?" he asked. "Is it necessary for Ms. Mast to translate?"

Mary Rose, her brothers, and mother made no response. Sharpe might have just announced the weather report.

"They understand what you're saying," Rachel said. "They'd

just prefer hearing the information in *Deitsch*. You're going to get more information out of them, if they have any information, if you let me ask the questions."

Sharpe turned his attention to her, looking her up and down. "I thought you were here as a translator."

"More of a cultural translator," she supplied.

Sharpe grunted and Rachel thought to herself that while he might be an excellent detective, he had all the personality of a rusty hammer. He seemed to be regarding her and Daniel's family as if they were aliens from Mars. Her first inclination was toward resentment, but then she reconsidered. She had a tendency to make quick judgments of people sometimes, too. It was human nature. Maybe if she gave Detective Sharpe a little time, he'd prove himself competent.

"You must have questions," Sharpe said.

Rachel looked at him. "What makes you think Daniel was shot by someone else? I assume it was something in the autopsy report."

Sharpe looked at Rachel, then Evan.

"Rachel," Evan said quietly.

"What? How can they have any questions if they haven't been given any information?"

"Right now, I think we're just fact finding. I think what Detective Sharpe is saying is that if they have any information that might help him find who did this, now would be the time to speak up." Evan then pointed, indicating she should repeat the information to the family.

Rachel exhaled loudly, then spoke in *Deitsch*, repeating what Evan had just said.

Mary Rose tightened her grip on the baby and shook her head rapidly.

"No," Rachel said in English. "She doesn't."

"What about her brothers?" Sharpe asked. "Either of them have anything to tell me? Anything I should know? Any questions?"

Lemuel shook his head. Moses said, "*Ne,*" in a barely audible voice.

"What did he say?" the detective asked.

"No," Rachel translated. "He says, 'No.' "

Sharpe looked from one impassive face to the other. "Mrs. Studer? Does anyone have anything to add? Any thoughts as to who might have a grudge against Daniel? Any physical confrontations? Heated arguments with a neighbor?"

Again, Rachel translated, even though she knew very well the family understood every word the detective had spoken.

Mary Rose shook her head. "*Ne.* Daniel . . . He . . ." She choked up and buried her face in the handkerchief again.

"Everyone liked him," Alma said in *Deitsch.*

Rachel translated again, and the room went silent.

After a minute or two, Sharpe announced, "This meeting doesn't seem very productive. I may need to speak with all or some of you later." He stood. "My condolences. I'm sorry for your loss." His delivery seemed rote and as unemotional as Moses's face.

"Can we go?" Alma asked Rachel in *Deitsch,* her expression unreadable.

"She wants to know if they're free to go," Rachel repeated in English.

Detective Sharpe made his way out of the room and the house without commenting.

"That's all for now," Rachel said softly in *Deitsch.* Then Evan, Lucy, and Rachel followed Sharpe to his unmarked car, which he'd left locked and running.

"What do you make of that response, Trooper Mars?" Sharpe asked as he opened the driver's door with a key. "Nobody seemed surprised. Did they know he'd been murdered?"

"I don't think so, sir," Lucy answered. "No matter how shocked they were, they wouldn't have shared their surprise with us. I've seen similar reactions when dealing with the Amish. Some of these people are more isolated from our world than we realize. I imagine they were frightened." She went around the car and got into the passenger's side and fastened her seat belt.

"Or in shock," Rachel suggested, although she had been troubled by the family's response as well. She looked at the detective. "Trooper Mars is right. The Amish are a private people. They don't demonstrate emotion in public, especially to outsiders. And they're all grieving. Mary Rose just buried her husband this morning. And the suggestion that Daniel died from unnatural causes would be extremely upsetting to all of them. To all of us."

"To the state of Pennsylvania," Sharpe said, turning the heater on full blast. "Thank you, Ms. Mast."

"Rachel. Please call me Rachel," she replied, forcing a tight smile. "Especially in front of the Amish. They don't approve of titles. I'd suggest that if you interview them, they'll feel more at ease if you use first names rather than Mrs. or Mr."

He glanced up at her, one hand on the steering wheel. "I've been with the Pennsylvania State Police seventeen years. I have my own code of conduct. Our procedures are done according to rules, not cult preferences."

Rachel knew that her reaction to the word *cult* must have shown in her eyes because Evan gave her a quick look that contained a silent plea for forbearance.

"Trooper Parks," Sharpe said, "I believe you have duties." The detective closed the car door and drove out of the yard.

"Charming fellow," Rachel quipped. She looked up at Evan, one hand on her hip. "Are you having second thoughts about surrendering your detective's badge?"

"Not on your life," Evan said. "This is the kind of case that I hate."

"But you had a knack for getting to the truth."

"Maybe you do," he answered quietly. He met her gaze. "Now, you get in the house before you catch pneumonia. The detective is right, I need to get back on the road."

Rachel pressed her lips together, hugging herself for warmth. "Do you really think Daniel was murdered?"

Evan considered. "There's obviously evidence or Sharpe wouldn't have come."

"What evidence?"

He shook his head slowly. "I don't know. The detective didn't say when he asked me to come out."

"And you didn't ask?"

"Rachel—"

"I know. I understand," she said, feeling bad for having pushed him. She knew the police followed procedures and there was, undoubtedly, a procedure as to how information on a case this new was disclosed. Because of the Amish belief that a body needed to go into the ground as soon as possible, preferably without embalming it, the case had already been rushed. Now that they suspected foul play, it made sense that they would take their time.

"Look, Rachel," Evan said, not seeming to be annoyed with her. "The real investigation is just starting now. Even if the victim died at the hands of another person, it could have been accidental. It's too early to make the determination that he was murdered."

"But Sharpe *said* Daniel was murdered."

Evan motioned with one hand. "Just give us a few days. Okay? We'll find out what happened."

She hesitated. "Okay." He looked as though he needed a hug, but this wasn't the time or the place. "Will I see you after you get off work?"

"I'll call you," he promised. "It all depends on what happens on the road." He flashed her a genuine smile. "Love you, babe."

"Me, too," she answered. "Be safe out there among the Englishers." She blew him a kiss and dashed back toward the warmth of the house, her head full of unanswered questions.

*   *   *

"You're sure you don't mind staying long enough to handle the check-ins this afternoon?" Rachel asked her neighbor, Hulda Schenfeld. "I don't want to put you out."

Hulda glanced up from the computer screen. She was settled into a leather office chair, her sheepskin-lined boots resting on a footstool. Her white leather jacket with the silver trim and her designer jeans would have been perfect for a skiing weekend at some resort, but Hulda, in her nineties, was long past such strenuous sports. "Sorry, dear," the elderly woman said. "I was checking out Coach purses. Christmas isn't too far off, you know." She tapped one hearing aid. "Say again."

Rachel repeated her question. Hulda filled in for her or Mary Aaron in the office several half-days a week. Hulda was a whiz on the computer, and she was perfectly capable of handling any routine guest reservation, check-in, or checkout. And if anything went wrong, she had no trouble solving the issue.

"It's just that I don't know how long the fitting will take," Rachel explained. "It's in State College, that little bridal shop off Main. I think the street is Redwood, Red something."

"Redwick," Hulda corrected. She removed her round wire computer glasses, put on her regular glasses, and regarded her with bright, intelligent eyes. "What time is your fitting? You don't want to be late. You've already missed how many? Three fittings."

"Two," Rachel argued. "Only two. That time you fell—"

"Could have taken myself for the X-ray."

"You could not have," Rachel countered. "And the other time I missed it when that pipe broke."

"Your final fitting," Hulda mused. "I know the gown will be lovely. You've kept that nice boy waiting far too long. If you'd married him the first time you agreed to, you might have a baby in the stroller by now. You're not getting any younger, Rachel."

Rachel chuckled. "Thanks for reminding me."

Hulda patted Rachel's hand. "Don't take it as an insult, dear. You know I want the best for you. But I call it as I see it." Hulda's snowy hair was close-cropped in a stylish pixie cut, a change from her normal finger waves. Tasteful diamond studs twinkled in her earlobes. "You aren't to worry about a thing here at Stone Mill House. Two couples expected: the DeSalvos and the Martins. The Martins are repeat guests and they always get the second-floor corner suite."

"Thanks. You're a lifesaver. You know I like to greet incoming guests, but I want to be certain they fixed the neckline on my dress. If I showed myself in that, my mother would stop speaking to me again."

"You'll make a beautiful bride, no matter what you wear. But, yes, I do see you in a traditional white gown, none of this peekaboo, see-through nonsense. Why any young woman would like to show her bosoms and her belly to the world in a house of worship is beyond me. You cannot believe the dress my grandniece Rebecca wore last spring. Fifteen thousand dollars for an ugly gown that didn't cover half of what it should have." Hulda shrugged. "She called it blush, but it was purple, if you ask me. But what would you expect from a bride who dyed her hair blue and wore high-topped sneakers under her dress?"

Rachel nodded sympathetically. She wasn't about to dive into the rough seas of Hulda's relative's sense of fashion. Smiling, Rachel changed the subject. "Ada just left, and the girls have finished cleaning. Mary Aaron's not back yet, but I expect her soon, and she can take over when she gets here."

Her cousin had been living on and off at the B&B for the last year. Mary Aaron had a natural head for business and was wonderful with the guests, but lately, her heart hadn't been in her job. The time for deciding whether she'd leave the Amish faith or be baptized into the religion was growing short. Rachel didn't know what Mary Aaron was going to choose, and she didn't think Mary Aaron knew, either.

It was a serious bone of contention between her and the Amish community, not to mention her relatives. Uncle Aaron and a lot of others believed that she'd *put ideas into Mary Aaron's head*. She'd tried to explain to her cousin how difficult the decision was, and even now, after so long among the English, she sometimes longed for the Plain life she'd known as a child. Maybe some could walk away and not look back, but Rachel wasn't one of them. And she didn't believe Mary Aaron was, either. Once an Amish girl, always an Amish girl, Rachel thought. You could put on the jeans and the leather jackets; you could cut your hair and wear makeup, but there would always be a yearning deep inside for the things you relinquish when you move away from your family and community.

"I worry about that child," Hulda said. "Mary Aaron. I don't know if she'll ever be happy out here, among us Englishers." The older woman smiled wryly at her own quip. "She's such a special girl."

"I know," Rachel agreed. She loved Mary Aaron like a sister. She was so full of life, overflowing with joy. And her faith was bedrock deep and sky high. If Mary Aaron asked her, which she hadn't, she would have told her that she believed she was well suited to the Amish way of life and that abandoning it would be a grave mistake. For her own part, she'd come too far to go back, but Mary Aaron was different. Most Amish young people experimented during their *rumspringa,* their *running around time*. Most got their rebellion out and adhered to tradition and remained solidly in the faith.

It was Rachel's hope that her cousin would be the same, even if it took her a while to figure things out. But Mary Aaron could be stubborn. Rachel had decided months ago that the harder she pushed her toward baptism, the harder Mary Aaron fought against it. Until then, Rachel was glad to offer her cousin a place to stay and space to make her own life choices.

"Will you go, already," Hulda urged. "Look at the time. You'll be late for your fitting, or worse, driving too fast on that twisty road over the mountain."

"You're sure I'm not imposing," Rachel said. "Asking you to cover things here *and* borrowing your car." Mary Aaron had borrowed her Jeep, but Rachel had expected her back an hour ago.

"Pfff." Hulda grimaced. "I offered. And what would I do at home? Watch one of the shopping channels on TV? My sons have forbidden me to set foot in Russell's this week. They say it's inventory, and I make the new manager nervous." She peered over her jeweled glasses again. "And just because I want things done properly. Barred from my own store."

Rachel patted the desk. "I'll be back as soon as I can. Oh, Bishop's shut upstairs in my apartment. Don't let anyone let him out. One of the guests is afraid of cats, and she says Bishop is stalking her."

Hulda chuckled. "That Siamese is too fat to chase a mouse, let alone a guest, but he does stare at people, I'll give you that. And he's just a little cross-eyed. That probably makes them nervous."

"He's just watching over the house," Rachel defended as she tugged on her good coat and gloves. "And Ada left you a dinner plate. Roast beef."

"Go, already," Hulda ordered.

Rachel made it as far as her back porch. She was just about to step out into the yard when Mary Aaron pulled in and jumped out of the Jeep.

"Rae-Rae!" Mary Aaron called. "I was afraid I wouldn't catch you before you left. You've got to come!"

Rachel noticed that her cousin was wearing Amish clothing, down to the *kapp*. She'd been sure Mary Aaron had been wearing jeans and a sweater when she'd left the B&B after breakfast. "I can't go anywhere," Rachel protested. "I have a dress fitting. Remember?"

"You have to come," Mary Aaron insisted. "That police detective is at the Studer farm. He's trying to question Moses. And it's not going well."

Chapter 3

Mary Aaron slowed the Jeep when they turned onto the gravel road that snaked up the mountain to the Studer farm. Because her cousin was driving, Rachel had been able to change her clothing. Matters always went more easily with the Old Order Amish if Rachel dressed modestly, and she kept a long denim skirt and one of Mary Aaron's tops in the vehicle, along with a navy wool head scarf and a traditional women's coat. Rachel wasn't attempting to disguise herself as Amish. Everyone knew who and what she was, but if she wore her English clothing, some of the Plain people would refuse to talk with her. And in a delicate situation like this one, Rachel thought she needed all the help she could get.

She'd tried to reach Evan on his cell phone, but he didn't answer. She knew he was on duty again today, but his not picking up meant that he couldn't talk. He might be in the middle of a highway stop, or he could be in the presence of superiors. Unless he was already here at the Studer farm . . . She hoped he was here, but she wasn't counting on it. And if he wasn't here, since he hadn't asked her to come, she might be in trouble with him for interfering in official police business again. They hadn't argued about that hot potato in a while, and she'd like to keep it that way. Of course, Evan had asked for her help two days ago, so maybe this would be all right with him. She doubted that Evan would ever grasp why she felt so compelled to help the Amish in dealings with mainstream authority, a world they didn't understand.

The Jeep hit a buggy wheel rut and both Rachel and Mary Aaron were thrown against the seat belts. "It might be better if you slow down a little," Rachel suggested.

"The person who called me said that there was one police car already at the house and a second coming up the road with lights flashing and sirens blaring." Mary Aaron shifted into first gear to take a particularly steep incline and gripped the steering wheel as if it were trying to escape. Mary Aaron wasn't a bad driver, considering this road and the short time she'd had a license, but from her expression, Rachel suspected that her cousin still thought of a motor vehicle as an adversary rather than transportation.

The Studer farm sprawled on a relatively flat section of land on the side of Blue Mountain. The gravel road the property was located on was practically impassable in bad weather. Rain tended to cause washouts, and it was low on the county's priorities for snowplowing. There had once been a half dozen homes here, some going back to the earliest days of English settlement. Now, there were only roofless stone hulks, fallen outbuildings, and one working farmstead, making the Studer family an isolated one.

"Who called you?" Rachel asked, gripping the armrest for support.

"Rosh Hertzler."

"The old one or the teenager?" Hertzler was a common name in the valley, and Rachel knew of at least two Rosh Hertzlers.

"The younger."

"Young Rosh has access to a phone?" Rachel guessed him at twenty years old, old enough to be kicking up dust, but young enough to still be under his father's roof. Rosh's father was conservative, not someone who would condone his son possessing a cell.

Mary Aaron shrugged. "He's *rumspringa*. A friend of the Studers."

"But too young to be in Moses's gang." Her time in the English world always made her wince when she used the word *gang* in connection with Amish youth, but it was innocent enough, and the best translation of the word they used. Kids of the same age group in school tended to bond, and they stayed close friends as they married and raised families of their own. In many ways, Amish friendships were stronger than most Englishers', almost as tightly knit as blood kin.

"*Ya,* but Rosh's steady, a good head on his shoulders. He told me he was going down the road when he saw the patrol cars in the barnyard. He thought I should know." Mary Aaron braked to turn sharply onto a wooded lane, scaring up two pheasants that exploded into flight a hand span from the front bumper.

"This had better be an emergency. This will be the third dress fitting I've missed."

"Rosh said there was trouble," Mary Aaron repeated, hitting the gas hard and sending them both back in their seats. "He said to come."

Rachel grimaced. Mary Aaron was her dearest friend, but she wished she'd insisted on driving. She was definitely driving home. "So where was Rosh that he could see that there was already one police car there? Because I can't see the house yet." Branches were brushing the top of the Jeep as they pulled onto the dirt driveway. It was late fall, so the trees were leafless, but in the other seasons, this lane must have felt like driving through a shadowy tunnel.

"He didn't say."

The trees behind them, Rachel could see open pastureland and grazing cattle on either side. Ahead sprawled a two-story house built of gray fieldstone, a huge barn, and several outbuildings. She counted two marked police cars parked near the house. An Amish woman stood near the police cars, waving frantically toward a smaller structure between the house and stables.

Mary Aaron brought the vehicle to a stop, and they both got out. Rachel saw that the woman in the blue dress was Daniel's widow, Mary Rose. She had a black shawl thrown over her shoulders and was wearing a pair of men's knee-high muck boots. Despite the oversized clothing and her frightened expression, Rachel was struck by how young and attractive Mary Rose was, far too young to be a widow.

"Mary Aaron! Rachel!" Mary Rose gestured toward the open shed stacked with cords of wood. "Over there!" she shouted in *Deitsch*. "The woodpile. I'm afraid for Moses. You must do something."

A woman came around the shed. It was Lucy Mars, tall in her trooper's uniform, boots, and hat. She stopped abruptly and gestured. "Rachel. Can you come and see if you can talk to this boy? I'm afraid we've got a situation here. I'm pretty certain he understands what we're saying, but he's not responding when we ask that he put the ax down."

"He's got an ax?" Rachel asked incredulously.

"Sounds to me like someone's cutting wood," Mary Aaron interjected.

Rachel and Mary Aaron followed Lucy to the back of the building where Detective Sharpe and another trooper stood. Rachel didn't know the second man well, but she thought his name was Lincoln.

Mary Rose came behind them. "Moses, don't be scared," she said in *Deitsch*. "You haven't done anything wrong."

"I'm going to ask you one last time to put that ax down and answer my questions," Sharpe barked.

Moses seemed not to have heard him, because he didn't respond or even glance in the detective's direction. The young man set another section of oak on top of a chopping block and brought the ax blade down to neatly divide the chunk in half. Without pause, he picked up another piece of wood, placed that on the block, and drove the ax head down with more power than Rachel would have thought he possessed.

Rachel glanced over at Lucy. Her expression gave nothing away, but Rachel knew that she was concerned . . . and maybe even a little scared. Sharpe and the craggy-faced Lincoln were tense; the trooper's right hand hovered above the butt of his holstered pistol. Lincoln's face was pitted with scars, probably the result of a bad case of acne when he was a youth, Rachel supposed. But it made him appear fierce and threatening.

Mary Rose tugged at Rachel's arm. "Do something," she begged in *Deitsch*. "They will hurt him."

Sharpe glanced at Rachel and Mary Aaron for the first time. "What are you doing here?" he demanded. "This is a police matter."

"What's the problem, Detective?" Rachel asked.

Alma Studer hurried toward her. "I've told them to leave," she said in *Deitsch*. "This is still my property. I don't want them here upsetting my children, frightening Mary Rose." She was wearing a man's barn coat and muck boots similar to her daughter's. She had a scarf tied over her head in place of a bonnet. She scowled at Sharpe. "Moses has nothing to say to them. He did nothing wrong. They should go."

"Calm down," Rachel soothed in the same dialect. "The police are just doing their job. Don't you want to know what happened to Daniel?"

"What are you saying to her?" Sharpe asked. "Speak English."

"But they've upset Moses," Alma said, ignoring the detective, "and Lemuel's gone to get his hunting gun to run them off."

Mary Rose gave a little cry of alarm and clapped a hand over her mouth.

Rachel looked at Mary Aaron, who'd heard every word, and then back at Alma. "You have to stop Lemuel," Rachel said. "If Lemuel comes out here with a gun, they'll either shoot him or arrest him or both. You, too, Mary Rose. If you care for your brother's safety, you have to keep him inside."

Alma hesitated for a few seconds and then turned and trotted toward the house. Mary Rose looked from Moses to her mother's retreating back.

"Go with her," Rachel urged in *Deitsch*. "And don't let Lemuel out of that house with a gun."

"Where's she going?" the detective demanded as Mary Rose dashed away. "What did you say to her?"

"I think her baby needs her," Mary Aaron told him in English.

Rachel glanced at her and Mary Aaron shrugged.

Moses attacked another section of log with the ax and chunks flew. From the body language of the policemen, Rachel was afraid the situation was about to go from bad to worse.

"Should I go with Alma and Mary Rose?" Mary Aaron asked, again switching to the Amish dialect.

"*Ne*," Rachel said. "Stay here with me. I need you here." Adding Mary Aaron to the mix of agitated women and a frightened boy with a gun was more than she wanted to risk. "Can we all just take a breath, here?" Rachel then said in English.

"What did you say to them?" Sharpe asked Rachel a second time. When she didn't respond, he nodded toward Moses. "Tell him to put that ax down and answer my questions. Either that, or I'm going to place him in cuffs and he's going to jail for interfering in the investigation of a murder."

Rachel stared at the detective. "So you're definitely calling Daniel's death a murder? What—"

"We are," Sharpe interrupted. "And Mr. Studer isn't helping himself by this bizarre behavior. He acts as if he doesn't hear us, but he does."

"Please," Rachel said, holding up one hand to Sharpe. "Give me a minute." She took a few steps toward Moses. "Could you put the ax down, Moses?" she said quietly in *Deitsch*. "You're making the Englishers nervous."

He paused and lowered the ax. "Why? I don't want to talk. I'm cutting wood for the stove." His expression was strained, his lips taut and pale. He seemed totally baffled by the response by the police.

"Moses." She slowly moved closer to him and purposely put herself between him and the police. "You have to speak to them or they'll think you had something to do with Daniel's death. Your mother is upset. You don't want her upset, do you?"

"It's them," Moses replied tersely, not making eye contact with her. "They should go. We don't need them Englishers here on *Fader*'s farm."

"But, Moses, it's the law," Rachel explained. "We don't get to choose. There's nothing to be afraid of."

"I'm not afraid. Daniel is dead." Moses suddenly swung the ax and sank it into the chopping block, no doubt startling the police.

Rachel glanced over her shoulder. Sure enough, Lincoln had released the leather strap from his sidearm. "It's okay," she called to the police. "Just give me a sec." She turned back to Moses. "They just want to talk to you," she told him in English.

He switched to English. "No need for talk. Daniel is dead." He looked at the detective. "I killed him."

She was so startled that it took her a moment to react. She threw up both hands. "*Ne,*" she said, speaking to the young man urgently in *Deitsch*. "Don't say such a thing. The police think Daniel was murdered. You didn't *murder* him. You aren't a *murderer*."

"Yes," Moses announced in accented English. "I am the one who shot Daniel."

Rachel's breath caught in her throat. "Moses, listen to me. Don't say anything more." She glanced back at Sharpe. "Something's wrong here. He doesn't understand."

"I understand your English," Moses said flatly. "I am the one you want." He raised his hands in surrender. "I am Daniel's killer."

"Read him his rights," Sharpe ordered the male trooper. "Put the cuffs on him." And then turning back to Moses, he said, "Moses Studer, you're under arrest for the murder of Daniel Fisher. The officer will read you your rights."

Evan found Rachel in the garage-turned-barn, a solid field-stone structure now occupied by four goats. She hadn't wanted goats, hadn't planned to raise the animals. But she had acquired them in a crazy turn of events and had since become fond of them. She'd promised herself that she'd either build a real garage or put the goats in the old barn by the millpond, but there never seemed time to make it happen. Thus, winter was fast approaching, and her vehicle was parked in an open shed.

"Rachel."

By Evan's tone, she knew that he'd learned about what had happened at the Studer farm and about her part in it. He also knew where she *hadn't* gone today.

It was almost dark, and she'd just slipped outside to make certain there was water and enough bedding for the goats because the weather forecast was calling for low temperatures that night. She was forking hay into the manger when he entered the garage/barn. She kept at her task. It was easier to concentrate on feeding the animals than start an explanation of why she'd been forced to skip another wedding gown fitting.

"Rachel, could you put down the pitchfork and talk to me?" he asked.

She glanced back at him over her shoulder. "Would you scoop out the goat chow? Three scoops. Level scoops."

Evan had changed out of his uniform and seemed much more approachable in his jeans, Timberlands, and old winter jacket. He wasn't wearing a hat. Evan hated hats, and she always had to remind him to put one on when it got really cold and the wind whipped down off the mountain.

"Why not four scoops?" he said. "I see four goats."

"Three scoops," she repeated. She began to move some straw with the pitchfork. She wanted the goats to be warm and cozy tonight. A warm goat was a happy goat. And happy goats or any farm animal seldom got sick with the proper care. Her *dat* had taught her that.

Evan measured out the goat food and poured it into the feed bin.

"How did you know?" she asked him.

"About your missed fitting or the fact that you were there when Moses was arrested?" He shrugged and his brow wrinkled. Evan had such an expressive face, open and youthful. He couldn't hide anything from her, and she loved that about him. "Babs called me. From the dress shop. Sharpe talked to me end of shift. He wants me to *get my woman under control*."

Rachel was tempted to laugh; instead, she frowned. "I called and left a message at Babs's. I didn't just not show up. I'll reschedule." She hung her pitchfork back on the wall. That was another of her *dat*'s rules. Tools went back in their proper places. That way you can find them next time, and no one trips over them. "I don't think it was necessary for her to call you," she added.

"Were you going to tell me?"

"Of course. I didn't get a chance. I tried to call you when we were on our way out to the Studers'."

He folded his arms over his broad chest. He was being so reasonable, so calm. It set Rachel's teeth on edge. It would have been better if he just came out and said he was upset with her. She wondered if all weddings were this stressful.

"I can't believe how the whole thing went down with Moses." She stole a glance at him. "Something's definitely off. He wouldn't do that. He couldn't. He's an odd guy, but he's no killer." She pushed her navy scarf back. It was sliding down over her forehead, threating to fall over her eyes. "I wish you'd been there. Three policemen? Lucy was there. Lincoln and Detective Sharpe. And I'm beginning to be sorry you gave up the badge, because that man has no idea how to deal with people."

"Let's talk about your fitting, first. Three times? You've missed three fittings? I'm beginning to wonder if . . ."

"Don't be silly. I had a perfectly good reason. Every time. Was I supposed to leave Hulda lying on the floor in pain? Let the house fill up with water?"

"You're sure you're not getting cold feet again?" His voice was husky, deeper than normal, and she knew he was concerned.

"*Ne,* Evan, I'm not. Of course not. I love you, and I want to be your wife. It's just that stuff . . . well, my life is complicated."

He held out his arms, and she walked into them. She closed her eyes and laid her head against his chest as his hug tightened. "I'm sorry," she whispered.

"I love you so much, Rachel. I just don't want anything to go wrong, this time."

Emotion made her stomach go all fluttery. "It won't," she assured. "And I'll get the fitting. Everything will be fine. I promise."

He tilted her face up with two fingers and tenderly brushed her lips with his. "I'm holding you to that," he murmured.

Rachel breathed in the scent of him. She was doing the right thing. She knew it. Before, they'd put a hold on the wedding because she didn't know if she was ready to fully commit to him, but she didn't feel that way now.

She and Evan had been through so much together, and she could depend on him. He understood her, and best of all, he made her happy. "I had to go today," she whispered. "It could have gone bad. I mean, it could have gone worse. He was just ignoring their orders, swinging an ax. I think he had them spooked." She stepped back out of his embrace. "Evan, I'm not convinced that Moses is the one who killed Daniel. It doesn't feel right."

Evan considered her statement. "How well do you know this young man?"

"Not well, hardly at all. But Mary Aaron knows him. She's pretty sure he has Asperger's syndrome, which is why his behavior might have been . . . different today. But she doesn't think he did it, either."

Evan shook his head. "Hardly evidence. The law is concerned with facts, not hunches. I'll admit, you've had some good ones, but this time, I think it's best if you let the system do its job."

"And if Moses *is* innocent?"

"If he's innocent, why did he confess?" Evan asked.

"I don't know." She threw up her hands. "They wouldn't let me talk to him after they arrested him."

He thought for a moment. "I'll talk to Lucy. Get her take on this. If she was there, she must have thoughts on how the boy acted, if his confession seemed genuine. She's a good cop."

"So are you," Rachel said. "And you know that sometimes the truth isn't what it first appears." She pushed her sliding scarf up again. "And you're the one who got me involved in this when you asked me to be there when Sharpe spoke to the family."

"That didn't go too well, did it?" Evan grimaced. "I know how hard it is for you, but try. For my sake. Don't push into official police business, unless you're asked." He gave her a half smile. "And if you're so worried about Moses, make sure he gets a public defender now rather than later. Unless the community is willing to pitch in for a paid lawyer. A good defense attorney is expensive, and I wouldn't guess that the Studer family has the money."

"I'll make some calls first thing in the morning," Rachel promised. She switched off the lights, said good night to her goats, and they were just closing and latching the door behind them when a big Chevy van pulled into the yard.

Rachel recognized the driver, Tom Perkins. He was a

postal worker who'd retired in Stone Mill with his wife a few years previously and earned extra money by driving the Amish. Sitting beside him in the front seat was a woman in an Amish bonnet and cape. "I wonder who this is," she said to Evan.

The passenger's door opened and Alma Studer climbed down. "Rachel Mast," she called in her usual abrupt manner. "I need to talk to you. It's about Moses."

Chapter 4

"*Ya.*" Rachel hurried across the driveway. "Of course. Won't you come inside? I can make us a pot of tea." If Alma objected to her jeans and work coat or even noticed her very un-Plain clothing, she gave no sign of it, but nodded. Rachel glanced at Evan.

"Let me see if Tom would like to come in for coffee," he suggested. "You and Alma can go into the small parlor where it's private."

Rachel offered him a grateful smile. He understood that whatever Alma wanted to tell her about her son, there was little chance that she'd say anything in front of Evan or the driver. "Perfect," she assured Evan. "There's sweet potato pie in the pie safe in the kitchen. There may be some raisin left as well."

She hadn't eaten supper yet, and she doubted that he had, either. There was corn chowder and ham in the refrigerator. Her amazing housekeeper always left something yummy. But, considering Evan's appetite, she didn't think it would hurt him to have dessert first and a meal later. Knowing him, he'd likely finish the evening off with another piece of pie.

Rachel motioned toward the house. "Please, Alma. Let's get out of this wind. I don't know about you, but I could do with a hot cup of tea."

As the older woman started for the house, Evan moved close to Rachel and whispered, "Are we okay?"

Rachel nodded. "We're good. Better than good. I'll reschedule that appointment tomorrow. Well, Monday if she's not open Saturdays." She shivered in the wind. It was getting colder, but she'd always loved the brisk autumn, the scent of wood smoke and the crunch of fallen leaves underfoot.

Love you, he mouthed silently.

"Love you, too." She hurried after Alma, caught up with her, and led the way up onto the porch. "I'm so glad you came," she said to the older woman.

She wondered what was so important that Alma would go to the trouble to hire a driver in the evening. It might be that she simply was uncertain as to what was happening with Moses and wanted her assistance. Or, it could be that Alma knew something about Moses's reason for confessing to murder. In any case, Rachel wanted to hear what she had to say.

Inside, they took off their coats, and Rachel showed Alma through a narrow hallway to a tiny parlor in the oldest part of the house. Kindling had been laid in the fireplace, and although the room had electric heat, Rachel used a long wooden match to start the fire. "That will make it cozy in here," she said, making small talk in *Deitsch.* "Please, sit down. Make yourself comfortable while I put the teakettle on."

The tea would provide a relaxing atmosphere. The Amish had their ways; Alma jumping into her purpose for coming would be considered rude. Rachel would learn nothing from Alma by being hasty.

Rachel turned on the candles arranged on the mantel and end table. She loved the soft glow of candlelight reflecting off the stone walls. She'd grown up in an old house, using propane, kerosene lamps, and lanterns, but she had a dread of fire. Battery-operated wax candles were one Englisher invention she adored.

"How is Mary Rose?" she asked Alma.

"Mourning her husband, of course."

"Of course," Rachel murmured. "This has been a terrible shock for her, I'm sure. And the baby?"

"Well, thanks to God. Poor, fatherless babe."

"We had a good turnout for the funeral. The bishop's words must have been comforting to the family. I'll be right back." Rachel excused herself to heat the water and prepare tea and a dish of cookies. Patience was not her strong point, so it seemed as if it took the kettle forever to heat, but she knew Alma couldn't be rushed.

Evan was just coming into the kitchen alone as she picked up the tray to return to the parlor and Alma. "Tom didn't want coffee?" she asked.

"He had to pick up something for his wife at the drugstore. He said he'd be back in an hour. Don't worry about me." Evan motioned in the direction of the parlor with his chin. "She say anything about Moses?"

"We didn't get to that yet," she explained. "Coffee's hot in the dining room. Mary Aaron just made it." There was always a fresh pot and refreshments available for the guests at Stone Mill House six a.m. until nine p.m.

"Don't worry about me," Evan assured her. "I can find it."

Balancing the teapot, mugs, cream pitcher, and sugar on the tray, Rachel returned to her visitor. Alma sat in the same spot, hands folded in her lap, features composed. Her mouth was pursed, her eyes wary behind her glasses. Across from her on an antique Windsor chair sat Mary Aaron. She was wearing a plaid skirt, a blue cotton sweater, and gray Ugg boots. Her wheat-colored hair was braided and pinned into a crown on top of her head. And over that, she had tied a blue-and-white kerchief. Rachel was grateful for the head covering. Alma didn't seem to be disturbed by Mary Aaron's English dress, either.

As Rachel entered the parlor, Mary Aaron got gracefully to her feet, her hands clasped together at her waist. "I'll leave you two to talk alone," she said softly in *Deitsch*. "I just wanted to know if Lemuel was all right. And Mary Rose, of course. What happened today, with the Englisher police, it had to have been frightening."

"*Ya*," Alma agreed. "But you stay, if you want. What I say, you can hear."

Mary Aaron glanced at Rachel. "Are you sure?" she asked.

Rachel nodded, and Mary Aaron sat down again. For several moments, the only sound in the room was the crackling of the kindling on the hearth. Mary Aaron rose, used the poker to stir up a flame, and added several larger pieces of wood. Alma commented on the weather. Rachel made the appropriate reply and mentioned the likelihood of a cold winter this year. Alma agreed.

"The woolly bear caterpillars have been darker than usual this fall," Mary Aaron remarked.

Alma agreed and again there was silence.

Rachel stirred sugar into her tea. The fire crackled soothingly. The logs were apple wood and sweet smelling. "If there's anything I can do for you . . ." Rachel began.

"*Ya*," Alma said. "There is. I know the two of you helped Hannah Verkler. It was a *goot* thing you did for that girl, a brave thing."

Rachel and Mary Aaron exchanged glances. Hannah was the Amish girl they'd gone together to New Orleans to find some time ago, the girl who'd been held prisoner by wicked human traffickers. To this day, no one in the Amish community talked about that.

Hannah had returned home and put her life back together. Among the Plain people, any mistake could be corrected, any sin forgiven. Hannah didn't live in the valley anymore, but Rachel had heard that she and her new husband had a baby, that they were happy. Rachel wondered if Hannah was really happy, if she could ever forget what had happened to her. She hoped Hannah *was* all right. She deserved a storybook ending, if anyone did.

"I want you to investigate my son-in-law's death and prove to the Englisher police that Moses didn't murder Daniel," Alma stated in *Deitsch*. "Show them that he could never do such a thing."

"I'm not a detective," Rachel protested weakly.

Scoffing, Alma pointed a finger. "You found Hannah. When everyone said she was lost to us, you found her."

"*Ya*, I did. We did, Mary Aaron and I." The conversation continued in *Deitsch*. But . . ." Rachel wanted to say that they'd been lucky, that getting back a woman who'd been tricked into the underworld of human evil was a stroke of luck. But luck wasn't a word that the Amish lived by or even used. They lived by faith. "It was God's will that she came home to us," Rachel said. "Mary Aaron and I . . ."

"We were only His tools," Mary Aaron supplied. "It was God's mercy and Hannah's own prayers that saved her."

Alma nodded, folded her arms, and leaned forward, her voice strident. "So, if the *goot* Lord uses you once, He may do it again. You ask what you can do to help. This is what you can do. My Moses is a *goot* boy, but he doesn't always think. Not like us, at least. He would do anything to protect his family."

"You mean he might tell an untruth?" Rachel asked. "He might confess to a crime he didn't commit?"

Mary Aaron moved to stand beside Rachel. "Why would he do such a thing?"

Alma raised a finger to silence her. "Hold your tongue, girl. It is Rachel who knows these tricky Englisher police and their laws. You may listen only, you who are putting on hair dye and maybe face paint. If you were my daughter, *rumspringa* or not, I would give you a piece of my mind. What next? Teeny bikini?"

Mary Aaron frowned and shook her head. "No makeup. I don't wear makeup. And I'm covered."

"Then there is hope for you," Alma acknowledged. "I will not tell your father how you dress. I know you will come to your senses soon and be baptized." She reached for her mug of tea. "I only say this to you because I fear for your soul."

Rachel's thoughts raced as Alma and Mary Aaron exchanged words. Moses had confessed. Who was she to insert herself in this murder case? Evan would be totally against her doing so. She had a business to run, a wedding to get through. She was marrying a Pennsylvania State Trooper. What if something she did got Evan in trouble? It sounded as if Detective Sharpe was already annoyed with her.

"Rachel," Alma said, turning back to her. "Moses is my son. A mother knows what her child will do. He would not kill."

Alma's plea touched her. The woman was truly frightened for her son. She believed him innocent, and Rachel wasn't so naïve to think that only the guilty were convicted of crimes. Moses Studer had no idea how the outside world worked. "Alma," she began. "It's not that I don't want to help you, only that . . . I don't know what I *can* do."

The older woman's hands trembled so hard that tea splashed out of the cup. Tears rolled down her weather-aged face. "You must help me," she urged. "You went out there among them English. If you don't help my Moses, who will?" She placed the cup on the tray and covered her face with her hands. "Why would Moses want to kill Daniel? It is Daniel who saved us from ruin."

"Maybe there was an accident," Mary Aaron suggested. "With a gun. I'm sure Moses didn't mean to hurt Daniel."

"*Ne.*" Alma shook her head. She took her hands away from her face and stared straight at Rachel. "If he did such a thing, he would tell me. He would tell our bishop. Moses wouldn't want such a terrible thing weighing on his soul. *Ne,* my Moses is a devout boy, not a killer. You must tell those Englisher police he didn't do it."

"Alma," Rachel answered gently. "The police won't take my word for it that Moses didn't do it. He told them he did. I . . . We'd have to have proof."

The older woman met Rachel's gaze. "Then find proof he didn't do it."

Mary Aaron gripped Rachel's arm. "Maybe you could . . . we could, you know, ask some questions. See if anyone saw anything or knows anything about someone who would want to hurt Daniel."

"I don't even ask that you find his killer, only that you show them police my boy didn't do it," Alma pleaded.

Rachel struggled with her conscience. From the beginning of her romance with Evan, her becoming involved in police matters had been a sore point between them. Now, she'd given him reason to think she was trying to delay their wedding again, something that wasn't true. It wasn't right to do this to Evan just before they were to be married. But Alma's tears cut her to the quick. Rachel could only imagine how terrified, how worried, the older woman must be. First the death of a dear son-in-law and now her eldest son a suspect.

"Rae-Rae?" Mary Aaron squeezed harder.

"I guess I could go to the jail and see if they'll let me speak to Moses," Rachel said hesitantly. "Maybe now that he's there, now that he sees what jail is, he'll want to recant." She looked at Alma. "Tell them it wasn't true what he told them. Tell them he didn't really kill Daniel."

Alma smiled through her tears. "Thank you," she whispered.

As Rachel entered her mother's kitchen the following morning, she could hear the murmur of voices coming from the parlor where the quilting circle had gathered. But she wouldn't have had to hear her mother's friends to know the gaggle was here; seven buggies stood in the yard and unfamiliar horses hung their heads over the pound fence. Her father was nowhere to be seen; Sally and Levi were in school, and her older siblings who still lived at home were likewise absent. Fresh loaves of raisin bread stood on the stove, and the delicious smell of bubbling lamb stew filled the air.

Ada had sent a butterscotch pie, and Rachel placed it on the counter next to her Aunt Hannah's raisin crumb pie and what looked like a pumpkin pie. A tray of Dutch apple tarts rested on a side table. None of the members of her *mam*'s quilting circle would go home hungry today, that was for sure. They'd all leave with extra food to take home or drop off for a neighbor.

Most of the quilters were members of her parents' church community, but several came from adjacent Amish groups. And her sister-in-law Miriam, married to Rachel's eldest brother, Paul, would be here. Miriam's quilts took prizes at the fair. Rachel suspected her sister-in-law of bringing the apple tarts. Miriam had a delicate way with piecrust that few of the older women could best. Rachel thought that she was a perfect match for the family and considered her another sister.

A tall covered stainless-steel pot of hot chocolate stood on the warming side of the woodstove. Rachel ladled herself a mugful and added square homemade marshmallows. As a child, she'd loved walking home from school on a cold day to find that her mother had made hot chocolate. It warmed the children and made the whole house smell delicious. And there were always leftover biscuits and a jar of honey for healthy appetites. Her *mam* was never far from her kitchen and it was always spotless. Rachel often wondered how she managed with nine children. Her *dat* always said you didn't need plates. You could eat off her *mam*'s floor.

As Rachel made her way to the parlor, she overheard snatches of conversation. Apparently, Daniel Fisher and his untimely demise were the primary topics.

"Where would the family have been without him?" some-one remarked in soft *Deitsch*.

"Good Lord sent him when they needed him most."

"Hard to believe. That Moses, I wouldn't think he could do violence. He found the Troyers' calf caught in that barbed-wire fence one night and cut himself up getting it loose. Joe Troyer said he was crying like a *kinner* when he carried the calf to the house." That was Aunt Hannah.

Rachel hesitated in the hallway, keeping out of sight. She wasn't exactly eavesdropping on her mother's friends, which would be rude, but she was listening for information that might help her help Moses. Or at least help Alma and Mary Rose find acceptance in what had happened. That made it all right, didn't it?

"I never heard why Moses left home to go work for Joe Troyer. Why didn't he stay home and help Daniel work the farm after Daniel married his sister?" That sounded like Sadie Peachy to Rachel. She was a jolly neighbor who was famous in the valley for her blackberry jam.

"He and Daniel never got along, so I heard," Aunt Hannah explained. "As my Aaron says, there can only be one man in the house, one head of the family."

"Well, all I can say, is"—that was the older woman's voice Rachel couldn't identify—"he never appreciated Daniel. That farm was going to wrack and ruin when he started courting Mary Rose. If Moses was going to cause trouble under his mother's roof, better he went elsewhere to sow his wild oats."

"Always a strange one, that Moses."

"Never a smile."

"I don't think Moses got along with Daniel all that well," Miriam said. "At least Paul didn't think so. Daniel was young, and it was probably hard for him, too. He and Mary Rose were still practically newlyweds."

"You know what they say about two young stallions in a field," Rachel's mother added.

Rachel had too many questions to remain where she was for long. She entered the parlor and greeted her mother and the guests. To her surprise, her sister Amanda was there, sitting at the end of the quilting table, needle flying, not saying a word.

"Pull up a chair," their mother insisted. "We can always use another pair of hands."

"*Ya,*" Aunt Hannah agreed. "Sit here by me." Plump and good-natured, Mary Aaron's mother was a favorite relative of Rachel's. Aunt Hannah had always made her welcome in her hectic household, and her explosive humor and big heart had made up for Uncle Aaron's stern manner.

"*Ne,*" Rachel protested. "You don't want my help in this. It's too beautiful for me to touch it. You know how awful my stitching is."

The quilt was a Bethlehem, done in dark, rich blues and deep, vibrant reds. Unlike with most modern quilts, the needlewomen were working every stitch by hand. When finished, it would be exquisite. They'd found a buyer for the quilt even before it was finished. And the proceeds would go to assist in the hospital bills for an Amish family with premature twins in a neonatal unit in a Harrisburg hospital.

"I'll be glad to stop a minute and visit with you, though, if you don't mind," Rachel added.

"We're happy to have you," Aunt Hannah pronounced. "But I warn you, we're going to pester you for news about the Studer boy. Such a pity. Is it true he confessed to killing his brother-in-law? I just can't believe it myself."

"Me, either," Rachel's mother agreed. "Alma and her late husband are good people. They taught their children right from wrong. I don't believe Moses could spill his brother's blood."

"Brother-in-law," Anna Lapp reminded them. She was small and thin with bright blue eyes and a tiny cupid mouth. "And he and Lemuel and Mary Rose aren't full brothers and sister. Moses was from Alma's first marriage. He was a Studer, too. As I mind, he was killed in a lumbering accident. A tree kicked back and did him in. They couldn't have been married six months when he died, but long enough for poor Alma to be left in the family way. She was young, too, real young."

"So much sadness to bear." Dora Eby tied off a thread and snipped it with a pair of tiny, worn scissors that Rachel thought might have come from the old country.

Dora was a square, practical woman who could always be counted on to lend a hand in time of trouble. The mother of eleven children, she'd readily taken in five more nephews, including a toddler with cerebral palsy, after tragedy struck a cousin's family. So kind and loving had she been to the new nestlings that few in the community could now remember which had been born to the Ebys and which had come on a rainy August night.

"Alma will be assured a place in heaven," Dora went on. "One husband lost to an accident, another to a long, crippling illness, three babies stillborn, and now, a son-in-law killed, maybe by violence, and one of only two living sons accused of killing him. Pray for her, is all I can say. Pray for Alma, for Mary Rose and her baby, and for Moses."

"Every word is the truth," Aunt Hannah agreed. "Daniel is safe with the Lord, and it's the living who need our help now."

"So, it was Alma's second husband who owned the farm?" Rachel asked.

"I should say so," Dora confirmed. "Alma and her first husband didn't own anything but one skinny horse and the clothes on their backs." She took up another square and eyed the pattern before beginning to stitch it onto the backing. "It was a love match, so everybody said. And they were both hard workers. If he'd lived, they would have made a living, that's for certain." She passed the needle to Rachel. "Thread that for me, will you? My glasses need changing for some stronger."

Rachel took the needle and Dora went on. "She married some kin of her dead husband a year after they buried him. The first husband, not the second. He died, what, two years ago?"

"Something like that," Rachel's mother supplied.

"So, the farm should go to Lemuel, or maybe split between Mary Rose and Lemuel," Dora went on. "But if it hadn't been for Daniel, they all might have starved to death before Lemuel got old enough to leave school and do a man's work."

"I don't know Moses that well," Rachel admitted, handing the threaded needle back to Dora.

"He's strange, that one," Miriam said. "Doesn't talk much and doesn't take well to authority, my Paul says. But he's not the kind you'd expect to do anything like that. Unless, maybe, it was a hunting accident."

"I suppose a lot of people were hunting that day," Rachel said innocently. "It being the first day of the season."

"Moses for certain," Aunt Hannah said. "And the man he works for. And our Uncle Aaron and our John Hannah. They came home to tell us Daniel was gone."

Rachel's mother nodded to her. "Your brother Benjamin took Danny with him hunting that morning, but I don't expect they were anywhere near the Studer farm."

Miriam looked up from her sewing. Her stitches were so small and even that Rachel would have thought it had been done on a sewing machine. "Paul went, too. He was gone all day. I don't know who went with him or where they went. Didn't get back until after dark."

Sadie chuckled. "Probably half the men in this valley went hunting that day."

And I probably need to talk to them all, Rachel thought as she rose to excuse herself. But first she needed to go and see Moses at the county prison, because Alma's insistence that her son was innocent might be wishful thinking. *Maybe there's no need for me to play detective, no need to ask questions of anyone. Maybe, in spite of what his mother believes, he really did do it.*

Chapter 5

❦

"Make this brief," Evan said. He was at the wheel of his SUV, driving her over the mountain to Bellefonte, where Moses was being held at the Centre County prison. "You'll get to talk to him in one of the rooms used by lawyers and clients," he continued in a brisk, officer-of-the-law tone. "Obviously, you're not an attorney or a cop, so I had to call in some favors to get you inside."

"I know that, and I appreciate it," Rachel said, looking at him. She didn't care that he was being curt with her this morning. His tough exterior didn't work with her. She could always count on him to be supportive. He might grumble and try to argue her out of one of her plans, but in the end, he came through for her. He was a fantastic guy, and it was always a marvel to her that they'd found each other and that he truly loved her, in spite of all the baggage she dragged behind her.

Evan grunted noncommittally. He was wearing his uniform, although it was Monday and his day off. He'd already told her that he'd need to be present when she spoke with Moses, since, technically, she had no business there.

"I understand that, with Moses's confession, there isn't much that can be done," she said, "but I promised his mother that I'd speak with him."

"You need to convince him that he has to have legal counsel," Evan replied, keeping his eyes on the road. "Even a guilty man needs legal assistance in our justice system. If his family can't afford an attorney, the court will appoint one for him."

"Right. You said." She grimaced. "Public defender. Not the best option for someone who says he killed a man. And not the best for an Amish man. A court-appointed lawyer might have no experience with the Amish. And then with the way he is—"

"The way he is?" Evan asked.

"You know . . . odd. I told you, I'm no expert, but my guess is that he has Asperger's syndrome. He doesn't respond to things the way we expect a person to respond."

"Hence the ax."

Rachel almost laughed at Evan's dry joke, but the matter was too serious for laughter. It was easy for a man like Moses to be mistreated in the justice system; there weren't enough people trained to deal with men and women who were different from the average Joe. And without an official diagnosis, any request for special treatment would be denied.

"Anyway," Evan went on, "any public defender is better than having no attorney."

She pressed her lips together and puffed out her cheeks, but stopped short of blowing a raspberry. He was right, but the idea of some just-out-of-law-school do-gooder or overworked, stressed-out lawyer just going through the motions worried her. Even if Moses was guilty, he deserved to be treated fairly.

She glanced over at Evan. He'd shaved this morning, and she caught the faint whiff of aftershave lotion. His campaign-style trooper hat rested on the backseat, and she noticed that he must have stopped for a haircut on the way to pick her up because the line along the nape of his neck was militarily precise.

Chet's Barber Shop opened at six thirty sharp six days a

week, and if a regular was ill or elderly and unable to get out of the house, Chet would stop by in the evening or on Sunday to give a trim. He'd been cutting hair in Stone Mill since Rachel was a little girl, and unlike some no-frills, unisex haircut places, Chet knew how to give a man's haircut.

Evan slowed the SUV behind a mammoth motor home lumbering ahead of them. The road surface was pocked and uneven due to potholes caused by falling rocks, and the guardrails on the outer side of the highway didn't inspire confidence. The slow-moving RV had a Florida license plate, and it was obvious to Rachel that whoever was driving didn't have much experience on narrow mountain roads. At least they were behind the RV and not descending the far side of this mountain with the big vehicle breathing down their necks.

"I really do appreciate you doing this for me," she said, looking at him again. "I know this sort of thing is outside your comfort zone."

"I'm not happy about it," Evan repeated for at least the third time since they'd left her house. "You shouldn't be involved in this at all. Sharpe told me that you were lucky that he didn't bring charges against you for interfering at the Studer farm. He complained that you were speaking to them in *Deitsch* and wouldn't tell him everything being said."

"Thus the *get your woman under control.*"

He didn't even crack a smile.

She sighed. "But you understand how it is with my people. If I'd spoken English to them, they might not have listened to me. Detective Sharpe may not realize it, but I prevented more trouble than I caused." She thought about fourteen-year-old Lemuel and his threat to get his shotgun and she winced. That wouldn't have gone well, but it wasn't something she wanted Evan to worry about, either. Some things were better not brought up.

As if he guessed that there was more to the story than

Sharpe had realized, Evan raised a hand in protest. "I don't want to know about it. I can't be involved in this. You can't be involved. Have you forgotten that we're trying to plan our wedding?"

"*Ne,* I haven't forgotten. Of course I haven't forgotten," she said with enthusiasm.

Truthfully, the wedding was fast becoming a headache. Not marrying Evan. She wanted to marry him, but the wedding itself was stressing her. There was so much to do. *Food.* First there had been a caterer; now her mother was preparing the meal. *Flowers.* She hadn't known what to choose and the arrangements had seemed expensive. *A wedding dress.* Appointments to be made and missed. An Amish wedding would have been so much simpler. She would have chosen an ordinary dress, and they would have had the entire community helping prepare and serve the food. But that wasn't possible, since neither of them was Amish.

"I need you to help me decide what we're doing on our honeymoon," Evan said. "We have to make reservations for the good stuff."

She smiled at him. "Turks and Caicos. Seven days." She'd never been to the Caribbean before, and it sounded wonderful. Warm. Palm trees and sand. Blue ocean. It had been Evan's choice, and she couldn't have chosen better. He'd researched the various islands and given her three destinations to pick from. But she'd guessed from his enthusiasm that he really wanted her to choose Turks and Caicos. "Whatever you decide will be fine with me," she assured him. "I trust your judgment."

They'd reached the crest of the mountain and had begun the steep descent on the far side. The brakes on the motor home ahead of them were grinding. Traffic was backing up behind Evan and Rachel because this was a no-passing area for the next several miles.

"How about scuba-diving lessons?" Evan suggested. "It's

something neither of us have done before. I've read that you really can't appreciate the beauty of the island without seeing the fish and . . ."

Rachel knew she should be paying attention to Evan, but she kept thinking of the expression on Moses's face when he'd said that he'd shot Daniel. He'd sounded desperate, but, to her, he hadn't sounded guilty . . . at least not guilty of murder. A hunting accident was probably the most logical answer, but if so, why not explain it that way? And it bugged her that she didn't know why the authorities were so certain that Daniel hadn't killed himself. Suicide wasn't unknown among the Plain people, although it was abhorrent to their beliefs. Of course, Daniel could have been depressed or mentally ill. Why did the investigation point to—

Abruptly, Evan's tone jerked her out of her thoughts.

"Rachel? Are you listening to me?"

"I'm sorry." She struggled to remember what he'd been saying. "You wanted to know if I think we should take scuba lessons?" She glanced around, realized that they'd moved onto a larger road, and that the annoying RV was nowhere to be seen.

"We moved on from that. I was telling you about this evening cruise I've made reservations for. A sailing ship. Dinner on the boat. It's supposed to be very romantic, couples only. I think we get free champagne because we'll be newly-weds."

She wasn't much for champagne or any sort of alcoholic beverage; the Amish didn't drink. Against Evan's mother's protests, there would be no champagne toast at the wedding reception. She smiled anyway. "It sounds great."

"But not great enough to hold your interest."

"No, really," she insisted. "It will be the trip of a lifetime. I'm looking forward to it."

"I hope so," he said. "I want it to be special for you. For both of us."

"And it will be," she promised. "I'm sorry. I didn't mean to zone out. I don't want to mess this up for Moses." She offered Evan an apologetic smile. "I'll feel better after I talk to him."

"And then, that will be the end of it?"

"Definitely," she said. "Well . . . probably."

The room was small and windowless, no more than eight by eight, the walls painted institution gray to match the cement floor. There was one table, secured to the floor, and two plastic chairs that had seen better days, also immovable. Beneath the table, on the floor, was a metal ring; there was another attached to the table. The rings, she suspected, were to secure wrist and ankle cuffs of violent or dangerous inmates. No pictures on the walls, not even any graffiti. The décor was definitely lacking in charm. She'd seen more style in Amish outhouses.

It was warm in the tiny room, despite the cool temperatures outside the prison. It smelled of disinfectant and hospital floor wax. Rachel wondered how long they'd been waiting. Fifteen minutes? Thirty? She'd left her cell phone in the SUV and never wore a watch. Evan had come in with her, but now he was outside in the hall speaking with one of the guards. She hated prisons. Hated them. The sound of metal doors closing behind her always gave her the creeps. It was such a sad sound.

Rachel thought about what would have happened if something had kept her from meeting with Moses Studer. If she were forbidden to talk with him, what would she say to his mother? She couldn't imagine a young man who was used to fresh air and quiet being imprisoned in this gloomy tomb with all the other inmates. Unable to sit still, she rose from the chair and began to pace. She hated being cooped up in tight places, without a window . . . without being able to see the sky. The air seemed stagnant, and she was conscious of the sound of her own breathing.

How long would they have to wait?

She paced the room, from one side to the other, five more

times, and then at last, the door opened and Moses walked in. He was wearing an orange jumpsuit and looked as out of place here as a live lamb in a supermarket. Fortunately, he was not in handcuffs or ankle chains.

Evan peered in. "Make it short," he said before the door closed behind Moses. "We've got to be out of here in twenty minutes."

She nodded and motioned to the table and chairs. Moses sat down and she took the seat across from him. He appeared frightened and didn't seem to know what to do with his hands. He stared down at them, then hung them at his sides. By the time she'd straightened in her chair, Moses had laid his hands flat on the table, flexed them, and dropped them limply into his lap.

"Hello, Moses," she said. "I don't know if you remember me. I'm—"

"I know who you are," he said, reverting to *Deitsch*.

He didn't make eye contact with her, which was a little awkward in such a small room.

"I'm not stupid," he added.

Rebuffed, Rachel took a deep breath and tried again. "Your mother sent me."

He didn't respond, just stared down at his hands. His thin lips were drawn tight.

She'd never known an Amish person with Asperger's, but she'd worked with a brilliant accountant, Travis Crane, who never looked at anyone directly, and he was straightforward to the point of rudeness. As she remembered, Travis was socially awkward in much the same way as Moses seemed to be. Everyone in the office had said Travis had Asperger's syndrome.

"Moses, to keep it straight between us," she said, "I never thought you were stupid."

It took him a moment to respond. "Some people do."

"I'm not some people. I care about you and your family, Moses. And I'd like to help you, if I can." She clasped her hands on the table in front of her. "But you have to help your-self. You know that you're in a lot of trouble, don't you?"

Again, it took him a long time to answer. "*Ya,* I know that." His gaze moved from his lap to a spot on the wall to her left.

"Your mother and your sister and your brother are wor-ried about you," she said.

He closed his eyes. "I worry, too. About them."

She studied him for a moment. With Travis, it had always been better to just get to the point of her visit to his office or her phone call. There was no exchange of pleasantries. "Moses, did you shoot Daniel?"

"I said that I did."

Rachel leaned forward in her chair. "Moses, you don't seem like a bad person to me. Was it an accident? If you shot Daniel, did you mean to shoot him?"

He glanced at her, and for just the fraction of a second, she saw desperation in his eyes. He looked away. "He's dead. Daniel will go to heaven. He's better off there. Isn't that what the preachers say?" He sounded as if he were reciting from rote memory. "Heaven is a better place. We should be happy for him."

"The preachers also tell us that it's a sin to lie. Are you lying, Moses?"

"What is a lie?"

Confused, she shook her head. "You know the difference between a lie and the truth. I know you do." She hesitated. "Are you telling the truth when you tell the police you killed Daniel?"

"I had to."

"You had to what? Kill Daniel or confess to killing him?" she asked, starting to get impatient with him. "Was what you told the police the truth?"

Moses hesitated and then said, "There can be different truths."

She closed her eyes for a moment. This wasn't going anywhere and they were running out of time. And she hadn't even broached the subject of a lawyer yet. But something definitely didn't feel right. As odd as he was, Moses didn't seem like a killer. "Why would you confess if you didn't do it?"

He spread his hands on the table again. "I lost my hat. I don't know where. Do you think I should have my hat on?" He ran fingers down the back of his head. "They say hats aren't allowed, but I should cover my head."

"I don't think God will mind," she answered. "You're inside. I think He will understand." She tapped her fingers on the scarred Formica tabletop to get his attention. "Moses, you didn't answer my question. Why would you confess to a murder you didn't do?"

He smiled, a sad smile. "Why do men do any of the things they do?"

She exhaled loudly. "I don't think you're the one who killed Daniel. Am I right?"

He murmured something under his breath.

"I didn't hear you, Moses. Please, look at me," she said beginning to feel a little desperate. Moses's behavior wasn't going to bode well at a hearing. Not if a judge tried to speak to him. "I want to help you. If you know who I am, you know that I would never do anything intentionally to harm you or your family."

"I think you mean well, Rachel."

He said it while staring at the wall, and his observation startled her. "I do mean well. I can't abide injustice. And if you are convicted for something you didn't do, that would be the worst kind of injustice. Is it true that you've refused a lawyer?" When he didn't respond, she went on. "Moses, you have to have an attorney. Even if you did shoot Daniel, you need someone to ensure that you're treated fairly. If it was an accident, and you shot him, it's different than if you deliberately—"

"Only God can judge," he interrupted.

"Not in a court of law. And a lawyer wouldn't judge you.

He or she is only there to protect your rights. Even if you did . . . if you did what you say you did, you have a right to a fair trial. Every American has that right."

"Englisher law."

"*Ne*, Moses, *American* law. And even Amish men and women are Americans. Remember, our ancestors came here from the Old World to find those rights. You have to ask for an attorney. If it's money you're worried about, don't be. I'll think of something, and I'll find a lawyer for you, a good one."

He shifted in his chair, looking at his fingernails. "I'm supposed to be at work."

Rachel wasn't certain what to say to that, so she said nothing.

"I am. I'm supposed to be at work. I don't like to be late."

"You can't go to work if you're locked in here."

Moses seemed to consider that. "My mother needs my pay. I give her my pay. Not all. Most of it. Some I keep for lunch. For soda pop on Saturday. Just Saturday. They cost a dollar twenty-five at Wagler's Grocery. I get a grape soda pop and a submarine sandwich. Every Saturday. That costs six dollars. The rest goes to my mother. She depends on it." He folded his arms and rocked back and forth in his seat. "I think I should have my hat. My *mam* would want me to wear my hat."

"It will be all right," Rachel said. "She'll understand."

Moses didn't seem to hear her. He was quiet for a minute or two, and then he said, "It wasn't an accident." He was looking over her head now, and he'd clasped his hands together as if in prayer. "I don't think so. I don't think it was an accident that Daniel died. But he's in heaven now, so it's all right."

"How do you know?" she pressed. "How do you know it wasn't an accident? Were you there?"

"I confessed." He smiled again, that same sad smile.

The shadow of a beard showed on his thin cheeks. She'd have to remember to see that he had the means to shave if that was permitted. "I don't believe you're telling the truth, Moses," she said softly. "I don't think you killed Daniel."

"Why do you say that? You don't know me. Maybe I could have done that. Maybe I could have pointed a rifle at him and pulled the trigger."

"Can you look me in the eye and tell me you did?" Rachel asked.

Moses blinked back tears. And then, slowly, he shook his head from side to side.

"So you're telling me that you're innocent?"

"If the police ask me, I will say I did it. I will."

"Why? Who are you trying to protect?"

An insistent rap came at the door. It opened a crack. "We have to go now," Evan said.

She looked back at Moses. He'd lowered his head to the table and was silently weeping. His arms hid most of his face, but she was touched by his trembling shoulders. "You have to have a lawyer," she repeated. "Your mother wants you to have a lawyer. Don't make this even harder on her."

Moses said nothing.

"I'll take that as a *ya,*" she said. "I'll come again, if I can, and I'll pray for you, Moses. I will pray for you."

Moses said nothing more and Rachel allowed Evan to lead her out of the room. She said nothing as she followed Evan back through the metal doors and checkpoints. She didn't speak as they walked to his SUV; he unlocked and opened the passenger's door for her. She kept her silence as he drove away from the forbidding prison.

"Will he accept an attorney?" Evan asked as he pulled onto the highway and accelerated.

"I think so. He didn't say that he wouldn't."

"What *did* he say?"

She looked at him. What had Moses said? What had he meant? "I don't think he did it, Evan."

"Did he tell you that?"

"Not directly," she answered.

"So you didn't learn anything, and you're not sure if he'll agree to have a lawyer?"

She thought about what Moses had said about Daniel's death not being an accident. Did he mean he knew who did it, or did he mean he had done it accidentally? She groaned inwardly. She'd believed that coming to see Moses would put her conscience to rest, but it hadn't. She was more confused now than she had been before she'd entered the prison. "I think he was trying to tell me that he didn't shoot his brother-in-law," she said, not answering his question.

"But he gave a confession to the police."

"Yes, he did."

"And now he's saying that he's innocent."

"Not exactly," she admitted. "But that's what he meant. At least, I think that's what he meant." She laid her hand on his arm. "It was a cry for help, Evan. I can't just walk away from this. Not now."

"The thing is . . ." Evan hesitated as if searching for the right way to explain his thoughts. "The thing is, Rachel, once someone makes a confession, justice takes a certain path. He said he did it, so they believe him. I know you don't want to hear this, but it's more likely he's lying now."

"I know that." She glanced at the window, watching the scenery go by but not really seeing it. "But I'm telling you," she said softly, "Moses didn't kill Daniel."

Chapter 6

"Moses is definitely different," Rachel said to Mary Aaron as she dropped into her recliner and pulled off her boots. "But he doesn't seem like a killer to me. He seems . . . I don't know, sweet." She reached for her sheepskin slippers, her favorite winter footwear, at least when she was at home.

"Sweet?" Her cousin wrinkled her nose.

Rachel wasn't certain what Mary Aaron meant by that observation. The two of them were shut away in Rachel's suite on the third floor of Stone Mill House. Mary Aaron was perched on the corner of the bed, tossing a toy mouse for Bishop. The big Siamese would fetch for Mary Aaron but not for her. Odd, since Bishop was her cat. Sometimes, Rachel thought the animal only tolerated her, but to others he could be quite affectionate.

"You don't think Moses is sweet?" Rachel asked, bringing her own thoughts back to the matter at hand. "Do you know him well?" She was familiar with most of the Amish families in the valley, but some she knew only by hearsay. "Are you friends with Mary Rose?" Rachel didn't know any of the Studers well. She'd rarely seen Moses's mother or sister in town, and of course, she didn't attend Amish worship service anymore. She couldn't remember Daniel at all, other than as another German face in a straw hat and suspenders.

Mary Aaron unpinned her *kapp* and shook out her bun. She placed the head covering on the quilt and combed out her hair with her fingers. "I don't think anyone knows Moses well," she said as she began to plait her hair into one thick braid. She was wearing her own jeans, new running shoes, and a pale-pink cotton sweater.

Mary Aaron had recently begun running seriously and was doing thirty miles a week. Rachel was glad to see her testing the bounds of her culture, but she hoped her cousin wasn't running just because it was something Rachel did. Or at least, she hoped that Mary Aaron enjoyed running. Rachel had had little enough time for it the past year, and she was afraid that her endurance was slipping.

Rachel didn't say anything about Mary Aaron's attire. Some days her cousin wore traditional Amish dresses; others, casual English clothes; and often a mixture of the two. Rachel wished she would make up her mind because the suspense was worse than knowing—and because Timothy, Mary Aaron's faithful admirer, kept asking her when Mary Aaron was returning to the fold. As if Rachel knew . . . anything.

Although Mary Aaron was at an age where most Old Order Amish women had already been baptized into the faith, she hadn't made the commitment yet. The decision was up to each individual, but it was a choice rather than an absolute. Waiting didn't jeopardize her place in the community, but it did upset a lot of people, especially her parents. In spite of that, Mary Aaron was still permitted to attend worship and was welcome in her family's home. Had she been baptized and then reconsidered her dedication to being Amish, she would have been shunned and that meant almost everyone she knew and loved would turn their backs on her.

The house phone rang and Rachel checked the caller ID. She grimaced. It was the bridal shop. They were anxious for her to make another appointment to have the last fitting on her gown, but she didn't want to commit to a particular time because what if she couldn't make that one, either? The dress had seemed to fit well enough the first time she'd tried it on. Okay, so it needed a little letting out in the waist. Just a little. Bridal gowns all seemed to come in size 6 or 4, and she was definitely an 8 . . . or maybe more of a 10. But she wasn't vain. And she was no one's idea of a fairy-tale princess. Making her look like someone she wasn't for one day didn't seem as important right now as trying to help Moses Studer save his life.

Rachel let the call go to voicemail; she'd call the bridal shop back later. "I don't think he did it," she told Mary Aaron.

Mary Aaron got up and put her *kapp* on the bookcase near the door. "But he confessed," she said. She glanced at her reflection in the oval antique mirror that hung on the wall. "I think I should dye it back to its original color," she said. "The streaking looks silly."

"I don't think it looks silly, but if you ask me, your hair doesn't need streaking. It's lovely as it is," Rachel remarked. She heard her cell phone, lying on a table, vibrating. She ignored it and glanced at Mary Aaron.

Her cousin's hair was wheat-colored, thick and shining. In the summer, the sun tinted it with golden highlights, and in winter, it darkened a little and became a rich honey hue. With her rosy complexion, even features, sparkling eyes with their thick lashes, and a faint scattering of freckles across her nose and cheekbones, Mary Aaron's face was fresh and charming. Personally, Rachel had always thought that Mary Aaron had a classic girl-next-door face, and that she was someone who would retain her natural beauty into her eighties. Rachel would have said so, but she knew that Mary Aaron would be embarrassed by the compliment. It would be too *English*. Not Amish.

Mary Aaron looked into the mirror again and grimaced. "I wish my hair was either strawberry blond or butter yellow or as dark as Evan's."

Rachel chuckled. "If wishes were horses." Though younger, Mary Aaron was as close to her as any of her sisters—closer. She was her dearest friend and usually had better sense than most women twice her age. But her cousin's venture into *rumspringa* was sometimes trying. At least she hadn't taken up smoking tobacco or drinking alcohol like some Amish young people did during their running around time. And it was Mary Aaron's common sense and her rock-solid faith that Rachel was certain would set her right eventually.

"Do you think Moses is the type of person who could point a gun at someone and shoot him?" Rachel asked, bringing the subject back to what was troubling her.

Mary Aaron shook her head. "*Ne,* but I've been wrong before, haven't I?" She dropped onto the bed again. "You aren't going to let this go, are you?"

"Do you think I should?"

"I don't want to talk you into something that will cause you trouble. Have you prayed on it?"

Rachel nodded. "On my knees. But I'm not sure He heard me because I haven't . . ."

Mary Aaron's eyes widened with concern. "He always hears us, but we don't always hear Him when He speaks to us. What does your conscience tell you to do?"

Rachel didn't hesitate. "To do something. To ask questions. To see that Moses has legal representation that will look out for his best interests."

Her cousin sighed. "Then that's what you have to do . . . what we have to do. It won't hurt anything if we talk to his family and to men who might have been out hunting in that area that day. People who might have seen or heard something."

"That's what I thought." She got up out of the chair and crossed the room to her desk. Mounted on the wall beside it was a large whiteboard. Using an eraser, she wiped clean the list of chores she'd planned for the B&B that week.

She took several dry erase markers from a pottery cup on her desk. Picking out a teal marker, she printed Daniel Fisher's name at the top center of the board in all caps and underlined it in red. Beside his name, she wrote *deceased* in cursive, low-ercase. Then, a few inches below, on the left side, she printed *FAMILY* in caps and underlined the word. She listed all the members of Daniel's immediate family: Mary Rose Fisher, Baby Eliza Fisher, Alma Studer, and Lemuel Studer.

Below, boxed in red, she printed Moses's name. And be-side it, in cursive, lowercase, she wrote *confessed*.

"Moses didn't actually live with Daniel," Mary Aaron pointed out.

"Right, but he's family."

Directly below Daniel Fisher's name and to the right of *family*, Rachel printed *HUNTERS* in caps. And then, to the right of *HUNTERS*, she printed *ENEMIES*. She glanced over at Mary Aaron, who was now on her feet and standing an arm's length away. "I don't need to tell you that anything you see here is just between the two of us."

Mary Aaron rolled her eyes. "Seriously? Do you think you need to remind me of that? When have I ever let slip some-thing that was supposed to be private between us?"

"You're right," Rachel said. "I'm sorry." She took a green marker and printed across the bottom of the whiteboard, *ACCIDENT or MURDER?*

"It might not have been either," Mary Aaron suggested. "It could have been self-defense or maybe a struggle that . . . you know. Something else?"

Rachel considered that and then carefully erased *or MUR-DER*. "You're right," she agreed as she erased the question mark and put it immediately after *ACCIDENT*. And then, below the word, she wrote a single sentence.

Why a false confession?

Rachel looked back at Mary Aaron to see if she'd missed anything.

"*Goot* start." Mary Aaron nodded. "But there were probably a lot of hunters and I don't know of a single enemy, so maybe you should have given more room for the hunters."

Rachel dropped the markers into the cup and stepped back to look at the board. "That's what we're going to find out. But first, I'm going to call a few attorneys."

"You think the Studers can afford a lawyer?" Mary Aaron asked. "The community may not want to pay for one since Moses said that he did it. I know *Dat* wouldn't. He said so this morning. He doesn't believe in lawyers anyway. He said God will protect the innocent and punish the guilty."

Rachel shrugged. "He wouldn't want to pay for one anyway. You know that he wouldn't accept one for himself. I love Uncle Aaron, and I know he's your father, but he is set in his ways."

"*Ya,*" Mary Aaron agreed. "That he is. And he's influential with the community. You can't count on financial help for Moses. They'll pray for him, but I doubt they'll open their wallets."

"I know," she answered. "I was thinking of asking Ell to help. Part of her inheritance from her father was that charitable fund for emergency assistance here in Stone Mill. I'd offer to pay for the attorney myself, but I have no idea how much we're talking about. The will stipulated that the needs of the traditional communities were foremost. And I know they helped to pay for Eli Beiler's son's kidney transplant last year."

"It might not cost anything if Moses tells a judge he's guilty."

"Even a guilty man needs a lawyer," Rachel explained. "To be sure his sentencing is fair."

"That makes sense." Mary Aaron shrugged. "Maybe Ell would be willing to help. Unless his confession makes her believe he's guilty. I don't understand why he'd say he killed his brother-in-law if he didn't."

Rachel grabbed the red marker and drew a line under *confessed* on the board. "That's a good question. I did some research on the Internet. I'm not sure what people did before so much information was so easy to find. Anyway, it happens more often than we realize. False confession. There are several reasons. The first is that many suspects are questioned over long periods of time by the authorities. They may be mentally unsound, frightened, or they simply want to please. Others confess for the attention they think it will bring them, or just to get away from the police because it's suggested they'll be released if they confess. Many suspects don't understand the consequences."

"Moses wasn't . . ." Mary Aaron seemed to search for the English word. "*Intimidated* by the police, was he?"

"I don't think so. He confessed right in front of us. The police's response to him was based on his behavior. Tea?" Mary Aaron nodded, so Rachel switched on the electric teakettle. She had a small refrigerator where she kept milk and snacks for the times she didn't want to walk down multiple flights of stairs for a cup of tea and a piece of fruit or some cheese and crackers. She felt as if they needed a cup of tea right now, to calm their minds and steady their thoughts. "More confessions than you'd think are false confessions, and a lot of people are behind bars who are innocent. I read that one of the primary groups DNA testing has helped is those convicted due to false confessions."

"That's awful."

"It is. Evan didn't really want to talk about the possibility of Moses being innocent, but I finally got him to open up a little. He said that once someone confesses to a crime, it's difficult to get law enforcement or anyone in the judicial system to consider the suspect might be innocent. And it's almost impossible to have a suspect released on bail once he's confessed, even if he withdraws his statement. Everyone chalks it up to the criminal regretting telling the truth."

"But if the wrong person goes to jail, the dangerous person is still out there. And the police aren't even looking for him."

"Exactly." Rachel sighed. "The other reason a person might give a false confession is obvious to me: to protect someone else."

"Right. Someone who Moses cares about more than himself? That makes sense to me."

"It's possible," Rachel admitted, "but we can't guess. We have to find solid facts if we want to convince the police and the judge that Moses was telling a lie when he confessed."

"Do we know if there's any evidence that proves Moses did it?" Mary Aaron asked. "Anything other than him telling the police he did it?"

Rachel shook her head. "I don't know anything yet. As I said, Moses was sticking to his story yesterday when I saw him. But, guilty or innocent, he still deserves an attorney. So that will be my first task, to see that he gets one."

"What can I help you with?"

"Maybe you could ask around, talk to anyone you can locate who was hunting on Blue Mountain that day."

"I can ask my brothers. They were hunting with *Dat*. Not in that area, I don't think, but they'll know who was," Mary Aaron said.

Rachel rubbed her cheek thoughtfully. "I'm not saying that the hunters are necessarily suspects, although they would all have had guns. And he was killed by a gunshot; that's why the police originally thought he accidentally shot and killed himself. They thought maybe he dropped his gun and it went off or he fell from the tree stand and the gun went off on the way down."

"Do they know what kind of gun killed him?"

Rachel shook her head slowly. "If they do know what it was, they aren't saying. Evan said ballistics can be slow to come back. Especially now that there's been a confession."

"Then how did they know he was murdered and it wasn't an accident?"

"I don't know yet. I'm going to see what Evan can find out. If he'll try to find out. In the meantime, we should talk to as many Amish hunters as we can."

"And the family," Mary Aaron said.

Rachel walked back to the board and tapped the heading that read *FAMILY*. "Absolutely. We're going to start right here."

Fourteen-year-old Lemuel met Rachel and Mary Aaron in the barnyard outside the Studer farmhouse. He was carrying a large box of empty quart canning jars. "My mother and sister are in the kitchen," he said. "I guess it's one of them you came to see."

They followed him into the house. Alma was standing at the stove stirring what smelled like a large kettle of applesauce while Mary Rose washed jars at the sink. "Come in," Alma called. "Mary Rose, pour Rachel and Mary Aaron some coffee." She glanced at her youngest son. "Are there more out there?"

"Another two cases. And I know there are more empties in the attic," he said. Lemuel set the box of jars on the table. "Want me to bring 'em in?"

Alma nodded. "We'll need at least another dozen, maybe more." She was wearing a white apron that had seen better days, and a navy scarf that covered most of her hair. "You'll have to excuse me," she said, still stirring. "This batch is nearly ready, and if I don't watch it close, it will burn."

Mary Rose poured two cups of coffee and carried them to the table. "Milk and sugar?" she asked shyly. She looked tired, but unlike the last time Rachel had seen her, she didn't appear to have been crying.

Rachel smiled. "Please."

As Mary Rose placed the creamer-and-sugar set on the table, Rachel noticed a bruise on the young woman's wrist.

"You okay?" Rachel asked, indicating the mark.

"Clumsy," Mary Rose said, pushing down her rolled sleeve.

"Those jars ready yet?" Alma called to her daughter. "Nearly ready for them."

"Coming," Mary Rose told her, returning to the sink.

Rachel glanced around the kitchen as she added milk and sugar to her cup. The space was smaller than her mother's and badly in need of painting. A single multipaned window over the sink let light into the room. It was one of the old-fashioned, swing-open, wooden-framed windows that you rarely saw anymore. There was a wide wooden windowsill, but no pots of live herbs as her *mam*'s kitchen had. It was a stark room, speaking of poverty and hard use.

Rachel shrugged off the impression. Maybe she was reading more into the austere room than she should. The bubbling applesauce, the fresh coffee, and Alma's smile of welcome belied the sense of heavy sorrow. The kitchen was certainly clean enough. She didn't spy a single spiderweb or smudge of dirt on the walls or ceiling, and the round wooden table with its soft patina and worn surface was spotless enough to meet her mother's standards. Housecleaning was never one of her own strengths, but Rachel could appreciate the hours of work it would take to maintain a kitchen without electricity or modern aids for canning, ironing, cooking, and washing clothes.

A baby's wail came from the interior of the house. Mary Rose glanced at her mother, as if for permission to go to her child.

Alma nodded impatiently. "*Ya,* go on. Our guests won't mind. She's probably thrown her lamb out of the crib again."

With a relieved expression, Mary Rose hurried from the room.

"She's a good mother," Alma said hastily. "Needs to trust her own instincts more. Worries over that babe like a cat with one kitten." The older woman used hot mitts to push the kettle to the back of the stove and turned off the flame. Wiping her hands on her apron, she picked up another cup off the counter and joined them at the table. "How's my Moses? Is he all right?" She pulled out a chair and settled her weight into it. "We've been praying for him."

Alma's eyes were heavy-lidded behind her glasses. Dark circles under her eyes made her look seventy, although by the ages of her children she must be a decade younger, Rachel thought.

"He's not come to harm in that English jail, has he?" Alma asked.

"No," Rachel answered. "I haven't spoken with Moses today. There are rules about phone calls. But my . . . Evan, the man I'm going to marry, he called a friend and checked on him. He's well, your Moses, at least as well as he can be under the circumstances."

Alma set her cup heavily on the table. "He didn't do it. I know he didn't. I don't know why he'd say he did, but I know my son." Her voice cracked with emotion. "He can't even cut the heads off our chickens. I do it, or sometimes Lemuel. Neither Moses nor Mary Rose have the belly for it." She rubbed at her jaw absently, making Rachel wonder if she had a toothache.

Mary Aaron sipped her coffee in silence. Alma's daughter came back into the room and stood by the doorway, hands behind her back like a child. She appeared younger than her years and at a loss for words or maybe just lost, Rachel thought. And who could blame her? Widowed in such a brutal way and left with a baby girl to care for alone.

"I've called several attorneys," Rachel said, patting Alma's arthritis-twisted hand reassuringly. "I should have someone to represent Moses by tomorrow. Your son didn't say he would refuse counsel, so I believe he will accept. I tried to impress on him just how important it is to have a lawyer."

"Moses is a strange boy, but his heart is good," Alma answered. "I don't care how much it costs. I will pay this English man of the law. I'll find the money somehow. I don't know why they had to lock him up. He's innocent, and he wouldn't run away. He'd never do that. Moses likes to be close to home."

"But he left home to go out and work," Mary Aaron said. "Didn't you have enough for him to do here on your place?"

Alma looked down at her cup. "Daniel thought it would be best if Moses brought in money regular."

"So, he helped out with the family," Rachel said, even though she'd already gotten this information from Moses. It was always good to let people talk when they wanted to; she'd learned that a long time ago. "Even though he didn't live here?"

"That's right." Alma nodded. "Money's been a problem for us since my husband passed. Moses knew that and he always did his share. Now, he's the one who needs help."

"I don't want you to worry about paying the lawyer," Rachel insisted. "I think I know someone who may be willing to help. There's a special fund to—"

"I don't want charity," Alma interrupted. "We pay our way. We may not have much, but we pay what we owe."

"It wouldn't be charity," Mary Aaron put in. "It would be no more than you helping a neighbor who'd lost everything in a fire. A good person left money in a will to help Amish families in our valley."

"It's just for situations like this," Rachel explained.

"And we do need help," Mary Rose said quietly. Her voice was sweet and high-pitched like a child's, but not jarring. "We won't make it through the winter if we don't get more wood chopped. We heat with wood up here, and our woodshed's not half full."

Alma folded her arms. "Daniel was a good woodchopper. Anybody who knew him would say that about him. I've never seen a man enjoy cutting firewood like he did."

"Almost like it was a prayer," Mary Rose said. "He'd split logs by the hour, sometimes until it got too dark to see." She went back to the sink and finished washing the two quart jars still in the dishpan. "Lemuel is really stepping up with the chores, but he can't fill Daniel's shoes. We need Moses home. We need him bad."

"I'll mention it to *Dat*," Mary Aaron said. "We'll get some men and boys from the church to come and help."

"No need to trouble your father. He has his own wood to cut," Alma replied. She raised the cup to her lips but didn't drink. "Cold," she said. "I can't abide cold coffee."

"It's the least we can do for you," Mary Aaron insisted. "It might be a while before Moses can come home. And you have enough to worry about."

"Thank you," Mary Rose said softly. "We would appreciate it."

Rachel looked at Mary Aaron and tugged inconspicuously at her earlobe. Mary Aaron nodded. "We were wondering," she said, "was Daniel hunting alone? That day that . . ."

"That he was shot?" Alma's mouth grew firm. "I wouldn't know. Mary Rose?"

Mary Rose turned from the sink, her hands dripping water on her apron. "I don't know. It was the first day of rifle season. A lot of hunters out there. I do know he was going to our old orchard on the edge of our property. Why does it matter who he went with?"

"If somebody was with him, they might have seen something or someone," Mary Aaron said.

Rachel sipped her coffee. "Did Lemuel go with him?"

"I don't know," Mary Rose said.

"I don't see why it matters." Alma got up from the table.

Rachel met Mary Aaron's gaze, then looked at the door. She wanted to talk to Lemuel, but she wondered if maybe it made more sense to speak with him alone. He might be more forthcoming without his mother present. Most teen boys were.

Mary Aaron took a big gulp of coffee. "Could I top off my coffee? It's delicious."

"Don't see why not," Alma answered, walking to the sink to retrieve several clean jars. "Mary Rose?"

"I'm just going to go outside for a second," Rachel said, getting out of her chair. "Something in my car," she muttered. "Be right back."

Mary Aaron engaged the women in a discussion about the length of the apple season as Rachel slipped out the door. She went out to her vehicle and pretended to look for something on the seat. When she looked up, Lemuel was coming across the barnyard with another box of jars. "Could I speak with you a moment?" she asked.

"Guess so." He stopped and waited for her to approach. "Moses didn't do it, you know," he said. "He wouldn't. He shouldn't be in jail."

"Which is why I'm trying to help him." Rachel glanced in the direction of the house, then back at the boy. She didn't like being sneaky. "It would help me if you could tell me, were you hunting with your brother-in-law the day he was killed?"

"*Ne.*"

"Do you know who was?"

Lemuel shook his head. His nose and bare hands were red with the cold, and his jacket looked thin. Rachel decided to ask her mother if she had any outgrown boys' coats that would fit him.

"You think Daniel was hunting alone?" she pressed.

"Probably." Lemuel shrugged noncommittally. "But I don't know for sure." He looked down at the ground. "Sorry."

"That's all right." Rachel smiled at him. He didn't smile back. She pressed her lips together. "Did you hear the shots?"

"*Ne.*"

"Did you . . . do you know who found Daniel?"

He shook his head and looked away and she felt bad for having asked a child such a thing. It was just that she was trying to piece together what had happened in the woods that day. The chain of events from the time Daniel left until the paramedics carried his body away.

She studied the teen. "Lemuel, did you like Daniel?"

It took him a long time to respond before he looked up. "Does it matter?"

Chapter 7

"He was your sister's husband," Rachel said, thinking his response was a little odd. But what teenager didn't have difficulty speaking to adults. "You lived in the same house. I was just wondering if you got along well with him."

Lemuel stood there with the canning jars in his arms looking as if he'd never considered the subject. He shrugged. "I'm sorry that he's dead. It'll be hard for *Mam* and Mary Rose without him to do the heavy work . . . unless Moses comes home to help." He shifted his weight from one foot to the other. "Winter's coming. I'm worried about them . . . if they can . . . if we can pay the bills and make it through until spring. With the stock. You have to buy feed and we don't have much money, I don't think."

Rachel nodded. "I can see that you're concerned. But I don't want you to worry. I'm doing all I can for Moses. As for your family, you know the community will chip in. Your mother and sister and the baby won't do without."

"Cows . . . pigs and horses need to have grain and it's expensive. And I guess a lawyer for Moses will cost a pretty penny, too."

For a boy who'd appeared so reserved, Lemuel spoke well and seemed intelligent. She offered him a faint smile. "None of you will go hungry," she promised. "And I'm doing all I can to get Moses home to help you. But you could help me by telling me everything you know about the day Daniel died. Did he leave the house alone?"

Lemuel hesitated, then shook his head.

"Who went with him?"

He glanced away. "Me."

"I thought you said he hunted alone. That you weren't with him."

"Hunters don't always hunt together," Lemuel responded, looking at her again.

"Okay. So you left the house together that morning?"

He nodded.

"Was he upset? Did you notice anything unusual about him?"

Lemuel shook his head and his gray eyes shuttered. "*Ne.*"

The wary teenager was back, and the fragile connection Rachel had felt between them a few seconds ago seemed to dissolve. "Did you two go out alone or was someone with you?"

"Left alone, but . . . there was going to be a drive."

Rachel nodded. In a drive, hunters organize. Some walk through the woods and fields making noise to frighten the deer and drive them toward other hunters in the group. A drive often resulted in multiple kills, and the meat was shared among all the hunters.

"And who met you for the drive?"

Lemuel seemed to ponder the question. He shifted one foot, digging his heel into the dirt. "Moses and Joe."

"Joe who?" she asked softly. It was important to know which Joe, when the valley contained as many as it did red roosters.

"Troyer. The man Moses works for. Joe and Moses were going to do the driving. And me and Daniel were going to do the shooting. Daniel was the best shot of any of us."

She was a little confused because he'd first told her they didn't hunt together. But maybe he'd misunderstood the question. She was sure now. "How about you? Are you a good shot?" He must be, she thought, if the men had chosen him to bring down the deer.

"I s'pose. Better than Moses. *Mam* thinks he needs glasses." He glanced toward the house and shrugged. "I already told the Englisher police all this. When he died."

"Please," Rachel pressed. "It's important that I hear it all firsthand." She pulled her coat a little closer against the wind. It came down sharp off the mountain here, cold and crisp and smelling of fall leaves. "And did it happen like that?" she asked. Daniel had fallen from a temporary deer stand in the woods. That was where he was found. "Did Joe and Moses do the drive?"

Lemuel shook his head. "*Ne*. Moses and Daniel got into it about whether to hunt the slopes or the old apple orchard. When Joe put his two cents in, backing Moses, Daniel told Joe that he'd best hunt his own farm."

"Was there an argument?"

He didn't answer. The faintest shadow of a mustache was beginning to sprout above Lemuel's upper lip, but he was still so much of a child. Rachel felt a rush of pity for this boy who had no father to guide him.

"So, then what happened? After Daniel told them they should hunt on their own?"

"We split up."

"You split up, meaning Moses wasn't with Daniel?"

"Lemuel!" Alma hollered from the back doorway. "I need those jars today."

"Coming, *Mam*."

Rachel watched the boy stride away toward the house, feeling as if she knew less now than she'd known before she came.

At her request, Rachel dropped Mary Aaron at her parents' home. She and Mary Aaron had both worn Amish clothing to speak to Daniel's family, so in the long dress, even without a prayer *kapp,* Mary Aaron blended in with her sisters as they drove the milk cows up the lane to the barn for evening milking. Rachel returned home alone, mulling over the conversation she'd had with Lemuel.

At this point, Moses's case seemed a hopeless one. Moses said he killed Daniel and nothing his brother or his mother had told her would prove otherwise in a court of law. Even if Lemuel testified that Moses hadn't hunted with Daniel, that wouldn't be enough to convince the police that Moses's confession was false. The sensible thing for her to do would be to find him an attorney and then step back from the whole investigation.

Sensible, yes, but could she just walk away? Doubt nagged at Rachel. It wasn't just Moses who was odd; the entire family was strange. No one had a negative word to say about the deceased, yet his widow and her family didn't appear to be all that heartbroken at his death. Something just didn't add up.

She wished she knew why the authorities were so certain that Daniel's death hadn't been a simple accident. If it wasn't an accident, it had to have been deliberate, and murder wasn't common among the Amish. If the shooter was Amish, he would believe that the act doomed him to hell. In a culture that believed that the next life was far more important than this mortal one, it would take a compelling reason for someone to trade hope of eternal life for the alternative. Of course, maybe it hadn't been an Amish man who shot him. The killer could be English. But who would have such a grudge against Daniel—a man reportedly without enemies—that they would deliberately take his life?

Dusk was falling when she reached Stone Mill House. Her neighbor, Hulda, clad in a hot-pink down ski coat, snow boots, and a fur hat, was in front of the inn, sweeping leaves from the sidewalk. Rachel pulled into the driveway, stopped the Jeep, and got out. "What are you doing?" she demanded.

Hulda believed she was invincible, but no one in their nineties was invincible. Rachel shuddered to think how easy it would be for her elderly friend to fall and break a hip.

"Planting turnips," Hulda shouted back and then laughed. "What does it look like I'm doing? If it rains, these leaves will make the brick walk slick. Someone could fall and you'll have a lawsuit on your hands."

Rachel crossed the lawn to her friend. "I'm not arguing with you about the leaves," she said. "I meant to do something about these this morning and I forgot. I'm asking why you're out here doing the sweeping."

"I'm sweeping a few leaves. I'm not up on the roof cleaning out the gutters, and I'm not washing the upstairs windows, although they could use it. But I'm not in my coffin yet, and until I am, I intend to do pretty much as I please."

Rachel grimaced, properly chastised. "But I worry about you."

"And I worry about you, all this running back and forth, involving yourself in murder investigations, but I don't ask you to sit in a rocking chair and knit." She removed a tissue from her jacket pocket and dabbed at her nose. "And speaking of upstairs windows, the woman in the middle room is complaining about the squirrels. She claims they're scratching on her window. Staring at her. She wants you to chase them away."

"Mrs. Morris." Rachel rolled her eyes. "Last time she stayed with us, it was a giant cardinal pecking on her window. And before that . . ." She chuckled. "A suspicious number of barn swallows."

"She's right there. There were a lot of them," Hulda agreed. She blew her nose and tucked the tissue back into her pocket. "Sounds like a case of ornithophobia to me. Not sure what her problem with the squirrels is. Don't know if they've got a name for that."

Rachel sighed. "I'll speak to Mrs. Morris, reassure her that the squirrels are only searching for food. For someone who's so unhappy with our wildlife, she comes here a lot."

"Is she the one who takes the lightbulbs from her room when she leaves?"

Rachel shook her head. "No, different peculiar guest. Mrs. Morris just complains about the wildlife. I think she's lonely and wants a reason to come down and talk with whoever's on the desk."

"Maybe." Hulda leaned on the broom. "Retirement isn't all it's cracked up to be."

Rachel chuckled again. "You're hardly retired. You still control the store and your house, not to mention that you're treasurer of the historical committee and still serve on how many boards?"

"Don't be impertinent. We were talking about Mrs. Morris, if I recall," Hulda reminded her.

"Right. Well, there's a concert tonight at our Methodist church with refreshments after. Evan was supposed to go with me, but I got a text from him that he's got to take a double shift. Maybe Mrs. Morris would be interested in going with me."

"Someone sick?"

"No. Trooper's wife is in the hospital. First baby. Apparently, she's in labor. Anyway, since Evan can't go, I'll ask Mrs. Morris if she'd like to join me. Maybe you'd like to come. The violinist is really good, and the coffee and dessert table following the program aren't to be missed."

"Thanks, dear, but not tonight. It's my standing date with my grandson. One of those foolish TV shows about the end of the world. Might be some zombies involved. He loves it, and I can't understand for the life of me what's going on. But we eat bowls of popcorn and drink cocoa with marshmallows. I can put on my pajamas and crank up the gas fireplace. The boy will never be the financial success his grandfather was, but he's a lot sweeter. Any other evening and I'd be happy to come. But I don't want to disappoint him."

Rachel took the broom from her. "I understand. And I can't thank you enough for helping out again today, but from now on, when you want leaves swept, call me or one of the girls. You aren't Superwoman."

Hulda chuckled. "I'm not? And just when I—" She broke off in mid-sentence as Rachel's cell rang.

"Excuse me," Rachel said. She looked at the caller ID. She didn't recognize it; she took the call. "Rachel Mast. Good evening."

"Hi, this is Irene Glidden. You called my office yesterday. I apologize for calling after hours but it's been a crazy day."

Glidden. The name suddenly registered with Rachel. "Could you hold on just a second," she said, pressing the phone against her coat to muffle the sound. And then, to Hulda, she whispered, "It's an attorney. I told you I've been trying to get one to take Moses's case."

Hulda waved a hand. "Take your call, honey. I was about to wander on home anyway. See you tomorrow. And good luck finding someone to defend that boy." The older woman stood on tiptoes to deliver a peck to Rachel's cheek and then headed next door to her own house.

Rachel returned to the Jeep. "Ms. Glidden? Sorry about that. Thank you for returning my call."

"Call me Irene. My father's a Quaker, and . . . well, let's say I'm more comfortable on a first-name basis. Have you found anyone to represent Moses Studer?"

"No, I haven't. I was hoping that you'd consider taking the case."

"I'm setting up an appointment with Mr. Studer first thing tomorrow morning. Provided, of course, that he still needs representation."

"Oh, he needs it, all right. You come highly recommended." Rachel pulled the car door closed behind her. She must have left the door open when she'd gone to speak to Hulda on the lawn because one of the barn cats was curled up on the passenger's seat beside her. She couldn't blame the cat. The heater was a good one, and it was rapidly getting nippy outside.

"I come highly recommended because of my record or because my grandparents were Amish?" Irene chuckled. "A private joke. I represent a lot of Plain people, Amish and Mennonite, that is. Truthfully, most of my practice is real estate and civil matters, but I have an extensive record, first as a public defender for the state of Pennsylvania, and then as associate and partner in a prominent law firm in Harrisburg before I moved home and opened my own office. I'm not promising that I'll take the case. I want to speak with Moses first."

"That's wonderful news," Rachel said. "But I have to be honest with you. I'm working on securing funds for Moses's defense, but it may take some time. The family may not be in a position to pay you."

"We can work out something later if I definitely come onboard. My Amish grandparents? Just between us, their farm is an amazing source of natural gas. It paid for my education, my brothers' and cousins' educations, and it continues to provide the foundation for my law practice. God has been good to my family, and I do my best to share some of those blessings."

Rachel took a deep breath. "Irene, I think you may be the answer to my prayers."

"If an old Quaker hippie can qualify as that." Irene laughed. "Now, give me a quick rundown on Moses's problem."

The two talked for another twenty minutes and then Irene said she had another call coming in. She promised to get back one way or another, and the conversation ended on a friendly note. *Please, God,* Rachel prayed silently as she got out of her Jeep. *Let this woman be the one we're looking for.*

Rachel was halfway to the house when her phone rang again. Thinking it was Irene with another question, she answered without checking the caller ID. It was Babs from the bridal shop.

"You are impossible to catch up with," Babs jabbered, never letting Rachel get beyond hello. "I call both your phones and leave messages. I text but you never get back to me except to tell me you'll get back to me. And that Hostetler girl isn't any better. I've got an opening, a cancellation, really. Tomorrow morning at ten. Can you make it?"

"Tomorrow morning?" Rachel tried to remember if she had anything else scheduled. "I think so."

"You have to make it or my seamstress can't promise that the gown will be finished on time. Tomorrow, Miss Mast. Please don't disappoint us again. You wouldn't believe how many December weddings we have. Our schedule is jammed. Be here tomorrow at ten sharp."

"Love you, too," Rachel murmured after she disconnected and slid her phone into her pocket. She was beginning to wish she had just convinced Evan to elope.

Inside the kitchen door, she took off her coat and scarf. She hung them on the hook and glanced into the dining room to see if any of her guests were in there.

All seemed quiet, so she opened the refrigerator to see what Ada had left for her. She wanted to take time for a long, hot shower, and she wanted to check the computer for the new guests coming for the weekend before she tracked down Mrs. Morris and invited her to the concert.

A turkey sandwich, cranberry sauce, and German potato salad waited on a blue-and-white pottery plate. Perfect, Rachel thought. Ada might be as prickly as a porcupine, but what would she do without her?

Rachel poured a tall glass of milk and took her meal into the small parlor where she'd spoken with Moses's mother. The supper smelled marvelous, and she'd spied an apple pie standing on the counter in a Siamese-proof glass cake dish. Not that Bishop would deign to eat people food. Roasted chicken hearts and canned tuna were his only deviation from the premium dry cat chow he favored. But her housekeeper was a cautious woman who was suspicious of all indoor cats.

Rachel had just lit the fire on the hearth when Evan's ringtone made her smile and dive for the cell phone.

"Hey, hon, how's it going?"

"It's going. How about you?" she asked. "Safe and sound?"

"Safe and sound. A quiet evening, so far. Sorry I won't be able to make the concert tonight."

She smiled. "I'm sure you are." Evan's taste ran to country and western, rather than violins and piano, not to mention flute. "But I understand. Work has to come first. Did the baby arrive?"

"Not yet, not that I've heard."

"You'll be pleased to know that I have an appointment for my fitting tomorrow morning at ten a.m."

"I'll be pleased when you tell me you showed up for the appointment," he replied dryly.

"I do love you."

"Love you more."

"I love you the most," she responded. "The lawyer called. Irene Glidden. The one you suggested. She hasn't agreed to take the case, but she's going to talk to Moses tomorrow."

"Pit-bull Glidden? She actually called you back? I told you that was a long shot. She's a tough lady, a legend. I can't tell you how many judge appointments she turned down. She's getting on in years, but if anyone can help Moses, it will be her."

"Thank you for suggesting her."

"The kid deserves good counsel, even if he's guilty. And my motives aren't entirely altruistic. I was thinking that if you get someone of the caliber of Irene Glidden to represent Moses, maybe we can get on with our wedding."

Rachel curled her foot under her and leaned back in the easy chair. "I am getting on with it," she said. "I'll be wearing a white gown when I walk down that aisle, and not an Amish dress that would double as my funeral shroud."

"Pleasant subject. Where did that come from?"

"It's the custom. At least in our church . . . my parents' community and many of the Old Order groups I know. A woman's wedding dress is a plain dress, usually blue, but it can be a different color. After her wedding day, it's packed away for her to be buried in."

"I don't want to think about the dress you're going to be buried in. Not on our wedding day and not today."

She smiled. "And you won't have to, because I'm wearing an English bridal gown."

"When will I see this amazing dress?"

"When I walk down the aisle. Not before."

"It can't come soon enough for me," he said.

"Or for me."

"Oops, someone's in a big hurry. Got to go, Rachel. Duty calls."

She heard the wail of a siren. "Be safe," she warned. "I love you."

She suddenly felt a chill. Why Evan loved being on the road, she didn't know. "Be safe," she whispered again into the empty room. "And God watch over you."

On the way home from State College for her gown fitting the following day, Rachel made her way to Joe Troyer's farm and lumber mill, where Moses had lived and worked. Joe's property was outside of her mother's church community, but not far as the crow flies, backed up against a section of state forest land. As she drove up the lane, she glanced to her left at the mill, where stacks of freshly sawn lumber cured under open sheds and mountains of logs waited the sharp bite of steel-toothed saws. A tractor-trailer stood in the process of being loaded, and trucks and Amish buggies were parked along the driveway.

Rachel continued on toward the main house and barns on the crown of a hill. Whitewashed wooden fencing lined the lane, enclosing pastureland where dairy and beef cattle grazed. Huge round bales of hay were covered in plastic and the stubble from a cornfield stretched off to the right. No tepee-shaped shocks of corn adorned the field. This had been cut and harvested by machine. From all accounts, Joe Troyer was a modern farmer with enough acreage, financial stability, and knowledge to earn a tidy living from the farm. Pennsylvania soil was some of the richest in the world, and Joe's family had made the most of it for two hundred years. And if they, like many of their neighbors who'd come here when this was wilderness, had shed precious blood to claim this land, they cherished the land all the more for the high price their ancestors had paid to settle here.

She found Joe on the telephone in a small building near the barn. Like many Amish businessmen, he'd obtained permission from his bishop to possess a phone, so long as it was a distance from the house. He saw her, nodded, and quickly wrapped up his conversation.

He came toward her, a chubby, middle-aged man of medium height with a curly red beard and lively brown eyes. "A buyer for some prime walnut we've had seasoning in the barn loft," he explained once they'd exchanged names and greetings. "A custom furniture manufacturer in Albany, New York. I hate to part with it. Old timber, really nice boards."

Rachel nodded and smiled as Joe went on at length about the walnut and the history of the tree he'd harvested it from. For all his successful ventures, Joe was a farmer. No business could be contracted without allowing for the courtesy of a pleasant exchange of conversation. Finally, when the weather and scarcity of wild turkeys so far this year had been covered and Joe was assured of the improving health of Rachel's mother, he said, "I suppose you've come to ask me about Moses."

"I have."

"Not a lot to say. Good worker. Kept to himself. Not what you'd call a bushel of laughs, but a young man who was a credit to his upbringing."

"A young man facing serious charges," Rachel said.

He thought on that for a moment. "I find it hard to believe that Moses could do such a thing. Terrible, losing Daniel that way." Joe hooked a thumb in his coat pocket. "Loss to the family. But . . ." He shook his head. "Not Moses Studer. Too much like his father."

"But Moses is . . . different."

"Like his father. *Grossfader,* too, so I heard. But I never knew old Jonah. Ernst, I did know. And he was much as Moses, maybe a little easier around strangers. But Ernst held hard to his faith, despite his chronic sickness and being in the wheelchair. Rarely missed church service. Different the Studer men might be, but they aren't killers." He waved Rachel to a bench in the sunshine, out of the way of the wind.

She sat down. "You were going to be part of a hunt the day Daniel died, weren't you?"

"I was." Joe settled onto the bench beside Rachel, keeping a decent distance away from her. He spread his legs, planted his boots squarely on the gravel, and folded his arms. "But it didn't work out that way. I'm sure you've heard we decided not to do a drive."

"I'm guessing I only got part of the story. I understand that it was a disagreement over where to hunt," she suggested.

Joe shook his head. "*Ne.* Who told you that?" When she didn't answer, he went on. "Me and Daniel. We exchanged hard words."

"But not over the hunting?"

"*Ne,*" he muttered under his breath. "When I got there, Daniel already had his dander up about something. I saw him slap Lemuel on the back of the head. Said the boy was disrespectful, something of that sort. No big deal; I've got sons of my own. They can say things they shouldn't. But the way I see it, you don't train up a child like that. Horses, dogs, or boys, there's a right way. It doesn't take the weight of a man's hand to teach right from wrong."

"So, you said something to Daniel? About hitting Lemuel?"

Joe nodded. "I understand that the Bible tells us not to spare the child. Bend a tree and all that. But Daniel was young and new to being a father and that to a baby girl. He didn't know much about dealing with growing boys. He took on a lot when he married Mary Rose and accepted responsibility for the family and the farm. Lemuel and Moses were Daniel's brothers-in-law, not his children. I have a habit of speaking my mind, and Daniel didn't care for the advice. Things were getting a little heated when Moses broke up the fight. Not physical, you understand. I didn't raise a hand to Daniel, nor him to me. But we both probably said more than we should have. And not all of it what a godly man should utter."

"So," she said, "Moses actually was a peacemaker. He ended the argument?"

"In a manner of speaking. We all went our separate ways, and that was that."

"Did you hunt with Moses and Lemuel? Did the three of you stay together all day?"

Joe removed his hat and placed it on his knee. She saw that he had a growing bald spot on the crown of his head with thick brown hair springing all around it. "I've thought about that a lot since I heard that Daniel had been killed. I went over and over it in my head, and I've prayed about it. I expected those Englisher policemen to come ask me about it, but they haven't so far."

She waited.

"I want to say *ya,* we were together all day, but I can't. You're not a hunter, but the men in your family are. They can tell you, hunters often separate. Not a big deal. I can't tell you that Moses and I stayed close all day. What I can tell you is that Moses didn't kill Daniel."

Chapter 8

"You're not the first person to say that," Rachel said. "But there's no getting around the fact that Moses confessed to shooting Daniel."

"I don't know what to say to that. I'm just giving you my honest thoughts." Joe rose to his feet.

"Can you tell me who else was hunting that day? Anyone else you saw?"

"Lot of people hunting. First day of the season." He glanced away, then back at her. "But nobody hunting on Blue Mountain. Folks tend to stay away from there."

"Why's that?"

"That *narrish* Englisher. The Studers' neighbor. He's always running people off." He rose from the bench. "I need to go. Got a buyer down at the sawmill I need to talk to. You're welcome to come back another time, but I really don't have anything else to tell you."

He walked her back to her car. An Australian shepherd appeared and fell in beside her. When Joe stopped, the dog sat at his side. He leaned down and patted the dog's head, and the animal wagged its tail.

Rachel opened the driver's door and stood there for a few seconds. "I appreciate your help," she said. "Just one more question, if you don't mind."

Joe's weathered face creased in a smile. "You're as bad as my wife. There's always one more thing."

She smiled, then narrowed her gaze, looking up at him. "You know Moses pretty well. Why do you think he would say he killed Daniel if he was innocent?"

The Amish man shook his head. "Can't say. But I'll repeat my belief that he isn't a killer. I've gotten to know him pretty well. Seen the boy around animals and seen him around children. Moses might not always know what to say, or how to act with people, but he's got a kind heart. I hope you can help him." He paused, then went on. "And if you get a chance to talk to him, you tell him that he's got a job here on my place whenever he wants it."

"I will." Rachel nodded. "If you don't think that Moses shot Daniel, who do you think did?"

Joe shrugged. "I wouldn't want to say. Not right to say, me not knowing for sure."

"Please? Just between us? I can see you're a canny man. You must have some suspicion."

Joe stroked his beard. Gray strands were beginning to pepper the deep russet, and both of his thick eyebrows were sprinkled with white. "I was you, I'd talk to that neighbor of Daniel's with the high fences and the cameras. He and Daniel have been eyeball-to-eyeball ever since Daniel married Mary Rose and took over the farm."

Rachel picked up Mary Aaron at her parents' farm and the two of them spent several hours catching up on the chores at Stone Mill House. Once the maids finished the general housekeeping and Rachel had consulted with Ada about the number of guests who would be in residence over the weekend, Rachel and Mary Aaron set off in the Jeep to talk with Daniel's widow again and let her and Alma know that it looked like they might have an attorney for Moses.

"I spoke at length with Alma and Lemuel yesterday, but Mary Rose didn't have much to say," Rachel explained to

Mary Aaron as they bumped along the country road. She'd already filled her cousin in on her visit to Joe Troyer's place and the phone call with the attorney, Irene Glidden. Rachel was waiting to hear from her once she spoke with Moses, hopefully with good news.

"Cover your hair." Mary Aaron handed Rachel a green wool scarf. Since they were going back to the Studer farm, both wore Amish clothing. The scarf matched the Lincoln green dress Mary Aaron's mother had sent over for Rachel. "*Mam* says that your blue dress was too plain for Stone Mill. She didn't want you to shame the family."

"Has she seen what you wear when you stay at the B&B?" Rachel teased, thinking of the jeans and thin red sweater she'd seen her cousin wearing the other day.

"*Ne,* and she's not going to." Mary Aaron stared out the window at the wind-blown fields and straggly pine trees. "Winter's coming soon. Weatherman said there might be snow flurries tonight."

Rachel slid the scarf onto the dashboard; she'd put it on when she reached the Studer farm. "Did you say anything to your father about Alma and Mary Rose needing more firewood?"

"*Ya,* I did. He promised to send a load from our woodshed. You know *Dat,* he's always got enough wood stored up for two winters. Whenever one of the boys does something he doesn't like, he sends them to split logs."

"Be sure and tell Alma. She shouldn't have to worry about heating the house in the next few months. She has enough to worry about."

"*Dat* and your father are going to get some of the young men together to take turns helping the family out through the winter. Taking wood, splitting it, caring for livestock, mending fences, whatever's needed. It's enough that Mary Rose has lost her husband," Mary Aaron said. "She shouldn't fear that she won't be able to care for her baby girl."

"I agree," Rachel answered. Ahead of them, a pheasant

crossed the road. It was a male with beautiful plumage. She smiled. She hadn't seen one for a while. "I want to get Mary Rose alone to talk to her. I might need you to distract Alma. Tell her that an attorney went to the prison to speak with Moses and we're just waiting to hear if she'll take the case. If Moses has agreed to allow her to represent him."

"You don't think it would be better to just wait until we know it's going to work out with the attorney?" Mary Aaron asked. "We don't want them to get their hopes up."

"I don't know. I think Alma will want to know what's going on."

"Mary Rose didn't seem too interested in the case against Moses," Mary Aaron pointed out.

Rachel shrugged. "I think she's still in shock. A timid woman like her, she's probably overwhelmed."

"Okay, that's fine. I'll speak to Alma. It will give me a good excuse to get her away and let you talk with Mary Rose for a minute. Alma can decide what and when she wants to tell Mary Rose."

As it happened, there was no need for Mary Aaron to pull Alma aside. Daniel's widow opened the door and timidly welcomed the two of them in. "*Mam*'s not here," she said, cradling her swaddled infant against her chest. "She and Lemuel went to the Hertzlers'. Joanne fell and hurt her arm."

"Joanne is Rosh's mother," Mary Aaron explained to Rachel. "Neighbors."

"*Ya.*" Mary Rose nodded. "Joanne and *Mam* are good friends, and she wanted *Mam*'s advice on whether she thought it was broken or just sprained. Before they made the trip to the emergency room. She'll be sorry she missed you. Is there news about Moses?"

"*Ne,*" Mary Aaron replied. "Rachel sent an English lawyer to speak with him this morning, but we don't know how that went yet."

Mary Rose waved them to seats at the kitchen table and offered coffee. When Mary Aaron said she'd love some,

Mary Rose placed the baby in a bassinet near the radiating warmth of the cookstove. "She's such a good baby," the proud mother declared. She hurried to pour coffee and cut slices of gingerbread. "Eat, please. Friends have brought so much that we'll never eat it all before it goes to waste."

Rachel waited until Mary Rose joined them at the table. "I'm sorry to bother you again. I just have a few more questions," she said. "I'm trying to get information that could possibly help Moses," she added.

Mary Rose passed around cream and sugar. She didn't take any herself, nor did she pour herself coffee. Instead, she sat with her hands in her lap, waiting. "I don't know what else I can tell you," she murmured. "But I want to help my brother. Of course."

"Did your husband have any enemies that you knew of?" Rachel asked, adding a spoon of sugar to her coffee.

"Enemies? Such a hard word. I would hope no Amish man or woman would have enemies," the young widow said.

"You're right, not a good word," Rachel agreed, trying to make eye contact with the young woman. "What I mean is, did anyone have anything against Daniel? Did he have any ongoing arguments with anyone?"

"*Ne,* of course not. Everybody liked him."

Rachel stirred her coffee. "You can't think of *any* disagreements that he had recently? With anyone? Amish or Englisher."

Mary Rose looked down at her hands. "*Ne.*"

Rachel thought for a moment, then went on. "I know that it couldn't have been easy for the two of you. You've not been married that long," Rachel ventured. "Daniel must have been under a lot of stress, what with the farm and the new baby. Did you see that?"

Mary Rose looked down and a hint of a blush tinted her cheeks. "He was a strong man, a good provider."

"And he never spoke to you about any specific problems with anyone?" Rachel pressed. She wanted to ask if the mar-

riage had been a happy one, but that would have been stepping too far over the line into the young widow's personal
life.

"He wouldn't do that." Mary Rose bit at a cuticle on her
thumb. "Daniel put his faith in God. If he had worries, he
took them only to his Lord."

Mary Aaron leaned forward. "Do you know if Daniel was
hunting alone that day?"

"Lemuel went with him. He told me yesterday."

"He told me, too, but I mean did he . . . they go with anyone else? Friends? Neighbors?"

Mary Rose shook her head. "You asked me that before. I
don't know. They went out together, Daniel and Lemuel. I assume they hunted together. Of course—" The widow took a
deep breath. "They didn't come home together."

Rachel met Mary Aaron's gaze, then returned her attention to the widow. "I've been told that Daniel was going to
be part of a drive that morning, with Moses, Lemuel, and Joe
Troyer. But Daniel and Joe had words. Did you know anything about that?"

"*Ne,*" Mary Rose said softly. She looked down at her
hands.

"I understand that Daniel was unhappy with your brother
Lemuel, that Daniel smacked or hit Lemuel that day."

Mary Rose raised her head sharply and her face paled.
"*Ne,* I don't. I mean . . . I didn't know that."

"That's what I was told," Rachel said.

"By Lemuel?" Mary Rose asked. "Lemuel said that Daniel
struck him?"

Rachel shook her head. "Not Lemuel. It was someone else.
Maybe he was mistaken. The person who told me."

"*Ya,* maybe mistaken," Mary Rose repeated.

"Can I ask you who came to the house to tell you about
Daniel?"

"It was Rosh." She pressed her lips together in a tight smile.
"He's always so kind to me." She stood up and went to look

down at the sleeping baby. "So young to lose her father," she said. "Such a shame."

"It is a tragedy," Rachel agreed. She took a sip of the coffee. It had cooled, but it was too weak for her taste. Gamely, she took another drink. "So, you don't know of anyone who would wish your husband harm . . . no one he might have argued with recently?"

Again, Mary Rose shook her head. "Everyone liked Daniel," she repeated. "Everyone. Just ask the church group. He had no *enemies*."

"None at all?" Mary Aaron pressed.

Mary Rose started to shake her head again, but hesitated. "Not unless . . ." She picked up the sleeping baby and cradled her gently. "Maybe, maybe you should talk to our neighbor." She glanced across at Rachel. "He frightens me, that Englisher. Maybe him you should question."

"Not much new from the widow," Mary Aaron said a short time later as she and Rachel drove away from the Studer farm.

"No," Rachel mused. "Although I didn't know that Rosh was the one who told her about Daniel." She glanced at Mary Aaron. "You know, the day Moses was arrested, when Rosh called you to tell you about the police, he said he saw them from the road. The police in the yard. Only he couldn't possibly have seen them from the road where he said he was."

Mary Aaron shrugged. "Maybe I misunderstood." She thought for a moment. "I think it's interesting that Mary Rose referred to Charles Baker."

"That makes two people to bring up his name." Rachel gripped the wheel. "His property borders the road here, doesn't it?"

"Yup." Mary Aaron pointed ahead toward a narrow, rutted dirt road that ran toward the mountain. "There's his driveway."

Rachel took her foot off the gas and the Jeep slowed. Both of them stared at the driveway. Three strands of wicked-looking barbed wire on top of a rickety fence blocked the way. A boldly lettered sign reading *NO TRESPASSING! KEEP OUT!* was nailed to one of the fence posts.

"Maybe we should go and see if anyone is home," Mary Aaron suggested, not sounding entirely sure of herself.

"Right . . ." Rachel pressed down on the brake, rolling to a stop. She stared at the barbed wire. "But I think I'd better talk to Evan first. Make sure it's safe. From what I've heard around town, this Charles Baker is a scary guy. Some kind of doomsday prepper."

"A what?" Mary Aaron asked. "A preppy?"

Rachel smiled. "A *prepper*. Sort of a recluse who hides away and thinks the world's coming to an end. He's preparing for the end of the world as we know it, preparing to survive."

"Oh," her cousin replied with a shrug. "And I just thought he was another crazy Englisher."

Back at the inn, Rachel found Ada just leaving for the day. "The cleaning is done as well as the laundry," the housekeeper assured her. "The air has a nip in it so I made you a nice chicken vegetable soup. There's plenty to go with it."

"*Danke*," Rachel said, slipping into *Deitsch*.

Ada pursed her lips in disapproval.

In Rachel's experience, most big-boned and rotund Amish women that she knew were jolly. Not Ada. She had a good heart and could be depended on, and she had an army of female relatives that she summoned regularly to clean and do laundry for Stone Mill House—helpers that she insisted be paid well and that she ruled with an iron hand. But Ada considered herself a judge of her fellow humankind, and most had been judged and found wanting. She was a treasure with a perpetual scowl and a sharp tongue. And like many older Amish, she considered *thank you* and *please* to be fancy English adaptations. The words that came so easily to outsiders were supposed to be expected behavior among the Plain people and not necessary to say aloud.

Rachel had gone over this many times with Ada and didn't care. "I appreciate everything you do for me," she continued. "I couldn't run the B&B without you."

"*Ne,* you couldn't," Ada agreed as she hung up her work apron. "Not an ounce of sense between your ears. You must be a great disappointment to your mother."

Evan couldn't understand how Rachel put up with such an employee. But for a woman who managed the housekeeping and most of the staff without a wrinkle, not to mention one who could cook an endless supply of delicious food, Rachel knew she could bear up under a great deal of criticism. Ada came and went according to her own time clock, she demanded top wages, and she wouldn't touch a telephone or check out a guest, but Rachel thanked God for her every day.

"I'll be in the gift shop," Mary Aaron said after greeting Ada and one of her granddaughters, who was sweeping the kitchen floor. "There's a box of pottery to unpack and price and the shelves to be dusted."

Mary Aaron had taken over much of the day-to-day chores with the crafts and artwork that the B&B offered for sale. Quilts, wooden toys, baby cradles, and jams and jellies: Everything was Amish-made other than Rachel's watercolors of local scenes.

Her latest painting was of a one-room schoolhouse in autumn. As in all of her artwork, the teacher and children were seen from the back so that no faces were ever represented. The watercolors sold well from her shop and at galleries in State College, but Rachel was reluctant to sign her work. Instead, the only identification on the paintings was the initials *A.D.* for *Amish daughter.* The only ones who knew the identity of the artist were Evan and Mary Aaron, and both could be trusted never to breathe a word.

Rachel went first to her office and checked her email for any inquiries or cancellations. There was a reminder for a charity event at church and a notice about the upcoming school board election, but nothing from any potential guest or returning one. She turned from the keyboard to her guest registry and looked over the names of her current visitors. *Mrs. Eloise Morris* stood out.

She'd invited Mrs. Morris to go to the church concert the previous evening, but the woman had said she was tired. Why she came to Stone Mill, Rachel wasn't certain. She spent most of her time in her room and had more than her share of silly complaints. Rachel hadn't seen her in the dining room this morning, though, which was unusual. Even though Mrs. Morris rarely left the house, she always came down in the morning for coffee. Rachel wondered if she'd left her room at all today.

She went down the hall to the gift shop, where Mary Aaron was rearranging a display of hand-sewn baby dresses and infant caps. "Have the girls all gone?" she asked, referring to the young Amish women who cleaned for her.

Mary Aaron nodded. "Ada told them they could go."

"That's fine. I just . . . I think I'll call upstairs and check on Mrs. Morris. I haven't seen her since yesterday morning. I hope she's not ill."

"I'm sure she's fine. You probably just missed her."

Rachel returned to the office and used the office phone to call upstairs. There was no way she wanted to give Mrs. Morris or any other guest access to her personal cell number. Certainly not with the amount of squirrels on the property.

Mrs. Morris answered on the third ring, her tone low and subdued.

Rachel pictured the tall, elegantly dressed woman with the steel-gray hair, pale gray eyes, and carefully applied, thick makeup. She was all angles and sharp elbows, a woman that it was impossible to imagine ever being a rosy-cheeked child.

"This is Rachel, your host. I was just checking on you. I

didn't see you this morning. I wanted to be sure you were okay."

"A little under the weather, is all."

"I'm sorry to hear that. Did you have lunch?" When the reply was negative, Rachel offered to bring her up a tray. "I have some lovely chicken vegetable soup."

"Thank you. That would be kind of you. And would it be too much to ask for a cup of Earl Gray and some saltine crackers?"

"Certainly," Rachel responded, genuinely concerned. "Just give me a minute to heat everything. Would you like a sandwich? I have egg salad or ham."

"Don't make a fuss. It's enough that you're providing room service. Either is fine."

A short time later, Rachel had Mrs. Morris seated at the table in her guest room with a fresh table runner and the promised lunch. "Do you mind if I stay and visit a while?" Rachel asked.

"Please." The older woman indicated the chair opposite her at the table.

Rachel took the seat. A copy of the King James Bible lay on the nightstand, but otherwise, the room was immaculate. Not a lamp or pillow was out of place, though the blinds were all drawn. Despite the white plaster walls, deep windowsills, braided rug, and the colorful painting of a farm meadow in springtime, there was an atmosphere of sadness.

Rachel wondered how Mrs. Morris could see the offensive squirrels outside with the room shuttered and semidark. "I'm sorry you couldn't join us at church last night," Rachel said when the woman didn't ask her to leave. "The music was beautiful."

"I didn't feel up to it." She picked at her egg salad sandwich. "I've not been my best this last year." She looked up and her gaze locked with Rachel's. "I feel I need to apologize. My physician has ordered a rather strong medication, and I sometimes get disturbing thoughts." She faltered and then went on. "I sometimes say foolish things." She rubbed her hands together, and Rachel noticed how thin she was. "It sounds silly for me to admit it, but I . . . I'm afraid of squirrels. My brother had one as a pet when I was five and it bit me rather badly."

"That would frighten anyone," Rachel replied.

"My parents were out of town, and my nanny took me to the hospital to be stitched up." Mrs. Morris held out a trembling hand, showing a thick white scar that twisted one pale finger. "It bled, of course, and it was painful. But I think, most of all, it was the hospital and nurses who frightened me. I was a shy child, and I wanted my mother."

Mrs. Morris gripped her fingers and gave a half-smile. "It sounds silly, I know, but to this day, I have nightmares about squirrels, very large ones."

Rachel made a soothing reply. "Maybe you'd prefer a room at the back of the house. One without oak trees outside the window? There's a beautiful view of the Amish farm country."

"No. This is the room I always stay in. I feel comfortable here. I like things to stay the same." She sighed. "But they never do, do they?"

Rachel nodded sympathetically. As the woman rambled on, Rachel wondered if she was in poor health. Clearly, she was lonely and needed someone to listen to her, but Mrs. Morris was a long way from the grouch that she and Mary Aaron sometimes secretly poked fun at. Rachel couldn't help feeling a little ashamed of herself. As an innkeeper, it was her duty to see to the welfare of her guests. Why hadn't she noticed Mrs. Morris's frailty before?

"I come here for the peace and quiet. I have a lovely apartment in a nice complex in Philadelphia." She took a spoonful of the vegetable soup. "Delicious."

"Do you have family?" Rachel asked when silence stretched between them.

"A niece in Seattle, and one son. But we're . . . estranged."

Mrs. Morris glanced up again, and Rachel sensed that it took a great deal of effort to hold back tears. "We . . . we haven't spoken in years—my son and I. My niece is pleasant enough, but we aren't really close. Cards at Christmas, that sort of polite but distant relationship. A sweet girl, really, but quite involved in her own life, as she should be."

"I'm so sorry," Rachel murmured. "It must be awful for you being . . . separated from your son. Is he your only child?"

Mrs. Morris nodded. "Do you have children?"

Rachel shook her head. "My fiancé and I are going to be married in a couple of weeks."

"I hope you are happy together. And if you do have children, cherish them. And don't try to mold them into someone you think they should be."

Rachel sat quietly. Sometimes it was better not to speak but to let someone else do so. Usually, people felt the need to fill the silence, and it seemed that was true with Mrs. Morris because soon she began to talk again.

"My husband worked long hours. He was never home weekends or holidays; his law firm always came first. It was important to him to bring in a substantial income, but the price was that I raised my Bruce practically alone. Chicken pox, strep throat, broken arm, always I was the one who sat up all night with our son. We lost my husband when Bruce was fourteen, but I saw that he went to the best schools, received an Ivy League education."

"You must have been proud of him."

"I was. Am. Bruce was always at the top of his class. But as soon as he finished his residency, he left for India to work with the poorest of the poor." She closed her eyes and winced, then pressed her stomach.

"Are you in pain?" Rachel asked, getting to her feet.

"It will pass," she said. "I took my pills just before you came up." Mrs. Morris inhaled slowly. "Please, I must be keeping you from something important. I'm sure you have more to do than to listen to the rantings of an old woman."

Rachel sat down again, wondering what illness Mrs. Morris was suffering from. "Nothing more important than being here and sharing tea with you. But you don't look well. We have a good doctor here in Stone Mill. I could call—"

"No, thank you, but I have quite enough physicians already." Her chin firmed. "I'm dying, my dear. Rather sooner than I'd hoped."

Rachel was taken by surprise by the announcement. "Are . . . are you certain that there isn't something more that can be done? Specialists? Second opinion?"

"Long past that. Now drink your tea." She offered that half-smile again. "I've been to Sloan Kettering. I've done treatments, and we've exhausted all avenues. Don't look so stricken. Death comes to all of us. It's just my time."

"Oh, Mrs. Morris, I'm so sorry," Rachel said. She could feel her throat constrict. In a moment, she'd be crying. "If there's anything I can do—"

"You are doing something. You're listening to me. No one wants to listen, especially when it concerns death. That's a taboo subject in America." She winced again and bit her lower lip. "I don't know why I'm pouring out my personal troubles to a perfect stranger, but it seems I am." She took another mouthful of the soup. "This is very good. It's difficult to find things that tempt my appetite. You can see that my clothes are falling off me. Nothing fits properly. The doctor wants me to drink protein shakes for athletes and formula for old people." She chuckled and took a little more soup.

"You were telling me about your son, Bruce," Rachel said gently.

Mrs. Morris nodded. "Yes, I was, wasn't I? Such foolishness that we argued. I thought he was rebelling against his upbringing, my decisions, me. I accused him of holding money in disdain because he'd never had to work for it. We argued bitterly. I told him that he'd been given everything." She shook her head again. "I was so certain that I was right, that I knew more of what he should do with his life than he did. I even told him that he owed me, his widowed mother, and that he was being selfish." She glanced away. "But he insisted God called him to devote his life to the needy."

"Some are called to serve," Rachel ventured. "I think if my child made such a sacrifice, I would miss him terribly, but I would be proud." And I'd make the effort to go wherever he was to see him, she thought, but wouldn't say out loud.

Mrs. Morris sniffed and tears began to run down her cheeks. "I don't know why I'm telling you this, except that maybe . . . tomorrow is my birthday. That's why I came to Stone Mill. I couldn't face being alone there in that apartment thinking of how my own selfishness ruined my life and kept me from the one person I loved more than anyone in the world."

Rachel couldn't imagine a woman her age being alone. Among the traditional Amish, families were huge and they were always together on the Sabbath, birthdays, and holidays. No one would leave an elderly relative to live without support and care, especially at the end of life.

Rachel rose and put her arms around her guest.

For a few moments, Mrs. Morris's body quivered with sobs and she wept against Rachel's shoulder, and then finally she regained control. "What you must think of me," she said. "But I'm terrified. I've made such a mess of my life and now I have to go home and make . . . arrangements for my own funeral." Her chin quivered and tears welled up in her eyes again. "I'm tired and I'm sick and I want to see my son. And . . . I know it's too late to make up for all those lost years."

Rachel patted her shoulder. "It's never too late to ask for forgiveness and to be forgiven." She glanced at the Bible on the nightstand. "Have you prayed about it?"

"I've tried, but . . ." She drew in a deep breath. "Why would God help me when I caused this grief myself? I returned my son's letters unopened; I refused to attend his wedding when he married a foreign woman of another religion, and I've never seen my two grandchildren. All these years, all these hurt feelings and bitter words, it's too late to make things right."

"With God, all things are possible. And I know that your son and daughter-in-law would love to hear from you."

"You sound like my minister." Mrs. Morris sniffed. "You may be right. I will pray on it." She stiffened. "But now, if you don't mind, I'd like the opportunity to regain my dignity and sample that pie you brought up with my sandwich."

Rachel handed her a tissue and the woman blew her nose. "Would you like me to stay for a while?" Rachel asked.

"Don't you have something worthwhile to do? This place can't run itself."

Rachel smiled. "If you want me here, there's nothing I'd rather do than stay with you."

"No, you've done enough. And I've cried enough." She made a shooing motion with her hand. "Go along and leave a silly old woman to finish her pie in peace."

Chapter 9

The following day, Rachel turned onto the gravel road that led to Charles Baker's property. A mixture of sleet and rain peppered off her windshield. She'd already been to the Hertzler farm, hoping to talk with Rosh. She wanted to know how he found out about Daniel and whether or not he decided to tell Mary Rose or if someone sent him to tell. Mary Aaron had been checking around and no one knew anyone other than Moses, Lemuel, and Joe who had been hunting on that side of Blue Mountain. But word had passed quickly through the woods when Daniel was found, and several Amish men had gathered around his body before someone called the police.

Rachel was still wondering about the discrepancy concerning the day Moses was arrested and how Rosh knew the police were at the farm. She knew it was probably a pointless detail, but it was still nagging her. Her questions went unanswered, though, because no one came to the door at the Hertzler farm, and there was no sign of a family buggy.

Rachel had also wanted to speak with Alma and Mary Rose to tell them that she had received the news that Irene Glidden had agreed to represent Moses and he would at least allow her to be present for his hearing. There was no one at home there, either. She hoped that her attempt to find Charles

Baker would be a little more fruitful. Otherwise, she would have wasted an entire morning.

As concerned as she was about Moses and the ordeal he faced, Rachel couldn't get Mrs. Morris off her mind. As an innkeeper, she had to draw a line between caring and interfering, but she wished there were some way she could contact the woman's son. Surely, if he knew the truth about his mother's health, he would let go of the years of contention and call her before it was too late. Rachel had prayed about Mrs. Morris last night, and she'd even spoken with Evan about her by phone.

He'd suggested she try to convince Mrs. Morris to talk with Reverend Hawkins, the new minister at their church. She might not be a Methodist, but the young cleric had a gift of providing comfort to those at the end of their lives. Although she'd only known Reverend Hawkins a few months, he was going to officiate at her wedding. As sorry as she was to see their old minister leave, Rachel had liked Reverend Hawkins from the day of his first sermon. Not only was he a compassionate and intelligent person, he was an excellent listener. She was sure that Leroy, as he'd asked his community to call him, had a true calling for the church, and best of all, he did it with a gentle handshake and warm laughter.

That morning, Mrs. Morris had come down for breakfast and said she was feeling a little better. There had been no reference to the conversation she and Rachel had shared in her room. Other guests had been present, so Rachel hadn't brought up the possibility of her talking with Reverend Hawkins at breakfast. However, she'd checked in on Mrs. Morris later and offered to set up a meeting with the minister. Since Leroy's wife taught preschool, he often had their six-month-old baby daughter with him, and little Sophie Marie's sweet face and adorable antics were wonderful for making friends out of strangers. Mrs. Morris said she would think on the meeting.

Rachel was pulling into Baker's dirt lane when her cell phone vibrated in her pocket. She braked to a stop and checked the caller ID before answering. "Hey."

"Hey. Where are you?" Mary Aaron asked.

"Almost to Charles Baker's."

"Why didn't you wait for me? I don't like you going out there by yourself. What if he's dangerous? I've been asking around. Most of the Amish think he's crazy, or at least crazier than most of the English."

"You had to pick up that new pottery consignment to list on the website, and I wanted to get this interview over with. I really need to do what I told Alma I would do . . . and Evan," she added. "Which is look into this mess and then be done with it. I'm getting married in a little more than two weeks, Mary Aaron."

"I know you are. And it's good of you to do this for Alma. For the whole community."

Rachel sighed, hoping she hadn't been too short with her cousin. "I also wanted to speak with the Studers and Rosh Hertzler, but no one was at either farm, so I thought while I was in this neck of the woods, I'd take care of talking to Baker. I spoke with Evan about him. I'll be fine."

"You told Evan you were going to Baker's place to talk to him?"

"Of course not," Rachel answered, her brow furrowing. "He'd tell me not to go and then I'd either have to go against the wishes of the man I'm about to marry or I couldn't go. Then I'd be breaking my promise to Alma. Anyway, Evan said that despite the complaints of his neighbors, Baker hasn't hurt anyone. He doesn't even have a criminal record."

Evan had also told her that Charles Baker had been a soldier who'd served in Afghanistan, possessed an arsenal of weapons, and should be approached with caution. But none of those facts were likely to put her cousin at ease, so Rachel didn't tell her.

"Maybe he hasn't hurt anyone yet," Mary Aaron replied. "But I don't trust him. It isn't natural, living all alone and boarded up like that. Don't take any chances."

"I won't. When have you ever known me not to—"

"Be safe? All the time," Mary Aaron interrupted. "Remember New Orleans?"

Rachel grimaced. "If I remember correctly, it wasn't just me. You were there. Who jumped out of the car and took off down Bourbon Street in the middle of the night? You could have been seriously hurt."

"Or you could have. That's why I'm telling you to be careful. Better yet, wait there until I can drive out and go with you. I'm sure I can borrow Hulda's car."

"I'm already here. I'll be fine. Take care of the gift shop and the guests," Rachel replied. "I should be back within the hour."

"If you're not, I'm coming after you. And I might be bringing the police with me," Mary Aaron said. "Or at least two of your brothers. And leave your phone on. At least then we'll be able to use it to find your body."

Rachel chuckled, amused as much by Mary Aaron's tech savvy as she was by the joke. "Don't worry," she said. "I'll be fine. And I'll make certain that Charles Baker knows that if he makes me uneasy in any way, my cop fiancé will be there in a matter of minutes."

"But Evan doesn't know you're there."

Rachel pursed her lips. "Mary Aaron, you aren't my mother. Stop worrying. I've got to go. I'm at the gate. I'll call you when I'm headed home." She hung up and put her Jeep in drive again.

At the fence, the three strands of barbed wire, and *Keep Out* signs, she stopped again. The actual fence wasn't much, an old pasture split-rail-and-stock-wire mix that was mostly rotten and rusted away. She could have easily taken down the barbed wire and driven through, but off to the right, she could see a gap in the fence line. Fortunately, Jeeps were made for off-road jaunts. It only took her a minute to make the decision.

She drove through the pasture, through the opening in the fence, and then back onto the dirt lane. It was overgrown, and although she could see where a vehicle had driven down it recently, it certainly wasn't used much. A hundred yards later, the rutted path ended in a substantial metal gate, reinforced with thick iron bars and flanked by a twelve-foot-high wire fence and several surveillance cameras. This fence was huge and stretched in two directions with no breaks in it to be seen. More signs were posted to deter visitors: *No Trespassing! Private Property*, and *No Visitors!* Her favorite was *Intruders Will Be Shot!*

Not wanting to be identified as an intruder, but determined to speak to the man behind the fence, Rachel blew her horn.

When there was no response, she got out and walked to the gate. Noticing a small square control panel that looked like an intercom, she pushed the button. "Hello!" she called into what had to be the speaker. "I'm here to see Mr. Charles Baker on an urgent matter."

A red light flashed on the gate, immediately followed by a siren. "*No admittance!*" a computer recording blared. "This is a poisonous reptile facility. You may be in imminent danger. For your own safety, turn around and drive away from the property at once." Dogs barking viciously, also part of the recording, completed the welcoming message.

Rachel pushed the button a second time. "This is Rachel Mast, from town," she said into the intercom. "Mr. Baker. I need to speak to you. Please."

The recording started again and the robotic voice continued until it reached the word *poisonous,* at which time it went silent. A deep male voice came out of the speaker. "Rachel? Which Rachel? Is this the young woman who sells hand-dipped candles at the farmers' market?"

"No, that's Rachel Yoder. I'm the Rachel Mast who runs the B&B."

"Rupert Rust's friend Rachel?"

"Yes," she answered, somewhat surprised that Baker would know Rupert. Rupert was an ex-marine who'd suffered from post-traumatic stress disorder and had recently left the English world to return to the peace of his Amish roots. "Yes," she repeated. "Rupert's a friend of mine."

There was a click and then nothing. Rachel waited a moment, then hit the intercom button again. "Hello? Mr. Baker?" She paused. "Hello."

She got no response. She waited, then tried the intercom again. Nothing. She couldn't see anything through the gate; there were metal plates bolted to the bars. Just when she was beginning to think Baker had no intention of letting her in, his authoritative voice came over the intercom again. "Get back in your vehicle. Wait there. I'm coming down. It will be a few minutes."

What have I gotten myself into? she wondered as she returned to her Jeep and closed the door. She waited.

And waited.

And then, just when she was seriously considering giving up, at least for the day, she heard the dogs. But these weren't recordings of dogs barking; they were live dogs, a pack of them. And they didn't sound particularly friendly.

A few moments later, a small panel slid open on the gate. "Stay in your vehicle," came Charles's voice. "The dogs aren't used to strangers and they will bite."

Lovely, she thought. *I'm going to be dog lunch.*

Soundlessly, the gate slid open, and she got her first glimpse of Charles Baker. What she saw was a big, stocky man in a military-style olive-drab field coat. He had long hair worn in a single graying braid, a thick beard, and yellow-lens sunglasses. It was impossible to guess his age behind the beard and the glasses, but his olive skin was tanned, his cheekbones as chiseled as skate blades, and his big hands were covered with black leather gloves. Over one shoulder hung what appeared to be some sort of semiautomatic assault rifle, and around his waist was a leather belt that held an assortment of weapons, including a holstered handgun and a bone-handled bowie knife with at least a fourteen-inch blade.

She rolled down the window. "Expecting a war?" she asked. She knew that it wasn't a professional way to begin her interview, but she couldn't help herself. "I can assure you, I'm not armed."

Charles Baker surveyed the lane behind her and then scanned the woods and field in all directions. Satisfied, he tugged off his fur hat and motioned to her. "You'd better come in. I don't like to leave the gate open for long."

"Do you want me to leave my vehicle here?" she asked, stalling for time. All of a sudden, she wasn't sure she wanted to go through that gate. Charles Baker looked as though he'd stepped out of some end-of-the-world movie. And then there were the dogs.

He shook his head. "No, best drive up to the house. It's not safe for you to walk. Snakes." He glanced back over his shoulder. "And the dogs." He motioned her through.

"Into the valley," she murmured under her breath as a tingling sensation crept up the back of her neck. And for the first time she began to seriously doubt the sanity of what she was doing. This man could truly be unhinged. She was glad she'd told Mary Aaron she was coming.

As Rachel eased her vehicle through the opening, she saw the dogs that had been doing all the barking. But they weren't barking now. They were as still as statues, crouched in the pine needles, watching her. Pit bulls. More than a half dozen. There was an assortment of other dogs as well, but it was the scarred pit bulls that caught her attention. They were definitely not used to strangers, and they looked hungry. She wished she had waited for Mary Aaron.

She stopped the Jeep and rolled down the window. "Mr. Baker, there's no need for me to drive to your home. We could talk here. I came because I have a few questions about the death of your neighbor Daniel Fisher."

"You want to talk to me, you come up to the house, sit down, and we talk proper. Otherwise, turn your little vehicle around and go home. Choice is yours."

She nodded and forced a smile. "I'll come, of course. I just don't want to take up too much of your time. I don't want to be a bother."

He came close to the window. "You're already taking up my time," he said. "And it is a bother. I have chores that need tending. But Rupert likes you. And he said he owes you big-time." He shrugged his broad shoulders. "So I'll see if I can answer your questions. Out of respect for him."

"Rupert is your friend?" she asked.

"He's a boy who's seen too much. He needs all the friends he can get."

A dog growled, deep in his throat, and started to get up. Baker fixed the animal with a gaze. "Enough," he said. The dog immediately dropped back onto his stomach. "Don't mind him," Baker said. "He's young. Not the best mannered yet." He turned and strode to the gate, pushed a button, and the big door slid shut behind her.

"You're welcome to ride with me, Mr. Baker," she suggested, leaning out the window.

"I'll walk. Need the exercise. And you can call me Chuck. If I invite you to my home, we're on a first-name basis. All right with you?"

"Perfect," she agreed. He nodded and waved her to move on up the road.

It veered left and climbed a steep incline that required her to downshift her Jeep. She crossed a small bridge that led, not over a stream as she guessed, but over a rocky ravine. Snaking back and forth, the lane climbed the mountain. Sometimes the way led through an overgrown tunnel of trees and other times along an outcrop of crumbly shale that made her wish for a guardrail along the exposed side. She wondered how long

Chuck Baker had lived up here, and how long it had taken him to construct his fortress retreat. Most of all, she wondered what she thought she was doing here and why she thought that she might discover something that the police detectives hadn't.

The lane finally ended at a smaller gate in a palisade wall of logs buried upright in the ground. She stopped the Jeep and glanced in the rearview mirror. She saw no sign of Chuck or the dogs and wondered how long ago he'd abandoned her and where he'd gone. She'd been so intent on not rolling down the side of the mountain that she'd never seen him go.

She waited again. The gate opened, and Chuck stood there smiling. Somewhere, he'd shed the rifle and taken a shortcut to get here ahead of her. He was still wearing the scary belt with the knife and handgun. "I've shut the nervous dogs up," he said. "Leave your vehicle there, please, and come into the house."

Reluctantly, Rachel left the comparative safety of her Jeep and walked through the gate. Inside, she stopped and stared. Ahead was a neat log cabin with stone chimneys at either end. To her left, running downhill, spread an old orchard, overgrown, but still showing vestiges of late apples and walnuts. On the hillside, beyond the picturesque cabin, stood a log barn and several smaller outbuildings, also built of logs. Beyond the structures were the remains of a garden, and a pasture with goats, horses, and a half dozen long-haired, shaggy, reddish Highland cattle. The open fields stretched several acres, a miniature high valley tucked into the folds of the ancient mountain.

Her astonishment must have been evident because Baker laughed, a deep, soft belly rumble. "Did you think I lived in a cave?" he asked.

"*Ne.*" Actually, she hadn't thought that far. After the fencing and bridges that were rigged to be dropped or raised up and the cameras and dogs, she wouldn't have been surprised by a WWII-type concrete bunker. What she *hadn't* expected was a quaint dwelling and homestead that looked as if it had been created two hundred years ago. Except for the wind turbine and the solar panels. "It's beautiful," she pronounced. "Do you live here alone?"

He shook his head. "I have my dogs, and there are twenty of them at last count. No, make that twenty-two. One was pregnant when I got her from the shelter in State College. Thoughtless kids. They buy a puppy, neglect her training, and then are surprised when she's not housebroken or takes a bite out of the neighbor's poodle."

"I see that you like pit bulls."

"They're the ones most likely to be left chained to a box when the owner moves or, if they're lucky, dropped off at the shelter. They need care and discipline. Nothing wrong with a pit. People say they're dangerous. It's the owners that are dangerous. You have no business owning something if you can't take care of it."

She looked up at Chuck and reconsidered her first impression of him. He sounded like a man who cared about the welfare of animals. In her mind, that didn't mesh with the paramilitary security and the guns. A complex man, she thought. *Nothing is ever what you expect on first sight.* "I don't want to keep you from your chores," she began. "If you could just answer a few questions about Daniel and your trouble with him—" She cut herself short, looking at him looking at her.

Baker's hooded eyes narrowed. They were so dark brown as to appear black, and for the first time, she wondered if he might have Native American blood. "I'm not answering any questions out here," he said. "You've come this far, and I only let you in for Rupert's sake. We'll talk inside. This wind is cold, and you could probably use something warm to drink." He slid a bolt into place on the gate and led the way down a path to the cabin. "You're safe enough in here," he said. "I don't make war on women, at least not those who aren't trying to blow me to smithereens."

"I can assure you that I'm not armed and I have no intentions of harming you or anyone else."

He chuckled. "Good. That makes me feel better." He gave her a long look, taking in her clothing. "You aren't Amish, but you dress like it."

"Born Amish; not anymore, though. I intended on talking with some of your Amish neighbors. They're more open if I don't wear jeans and a T-shirt."

He smiled. "You're smart. And determined. Most women would never have gone around that first wire gate. And few men, either." He pushed open the door and pointed to pegs against one wall. "You can hang your coat up there." He unbuckled his weapons belt and shrugged out of his heavy coat. "Just give me a moment and I'll make us a pot of tea. You do drink tea, don't you? My blackberry is excellent, but I have Irish breakfast or peppermint, if you'd prefer that."

"Peppermint, please," she said. Her stomach was a little queasy from the drive up the mountain. She glanced around. Inside, the cabin was as lovely as out. The walls were decorated, not with mounted deer heads as she'd expected but with Indian baskets, beadwork, and what appeared to be a very old bow and fringed leather quiver. Over the doorway she'd just stepped through hung a green stone Indian peace pipe with a wooden stem. An eagle feather dangled from it. "Are you Native American?" she asked.

"Enough to claim a tribal card. My dad's parents were part Shawnee. Mom was Oneida out of upper New York State."

"The Oneida are one of the five tribes of Iroquois," Rachel said.

"Good," he remarked. "You aren't completely ignorant about my heritage."

He waved her to a leather chair by the stone fireplace. This spacious room contained a galley kitchen and living area. There was a door leading off the kitchen and another at the far end of the room. A large ginger-striped cat was curled in a basket beside the hearth. "Oh, I forgot." She turned back to him before reaching the chair. "I brought you homemade cinnamon-raisin sticky buns. They're in the Jeep. I'll just go out and get them."

Baker frowned. "No, miss, you stay put. The dogs . . ."

"I thought you locked up the dangerous ones."

"None of them are too friendly." He raised a hand. "I'll get them." And before she could protest, he'd exited through the door.

She looked around at the interior of the cabin great room as she sat down. She'd been expecting to see weapons, high-powered guns, ammunition, knives, but instead, she saw rows of canned goods on every shelf. Strings of onions and dried herbs hung from the massive beams overhead. Everywhere she looked were jars and jars of preserved peaches, apples, string beans, corn, berries, and what looked like fish. Other shelves held hardbound books, dozens of them, not survival manuals but classics such as Dickens, Shakespeare, Walt Whitman, and Faulkner.

The cat raised its head and stared at her, then hissed. She jumped back. It wasn't a cat but a half-grown raccoon. The hair on the animal's back stiffened and it bared its teeth before darting past her and diving into a stack of wood near the door. Rachel stared after it, not certain if she should be frightened or amused. Who had a raccoon for a pet?

Abruptly, the kettle whistled. Rachel got up and went into the kitchen area and turned off the gas flame beneath it. From the stove, she could see that open shelves of the cabinets and island held containers of flour, sugar, and cornmeal as well as more mason jars filled to the brim with food. Her gaze lingered on two framed objects on the wall beside the window, a window framed with yellow cotton curtains. She took a step closer and stared. The frames held medals. One was the Silver Star, the second the Medal of Honor awarded by the American government for the most courageous acts under fire.

"Mugs are in that cabinet over the sink," Baker said as he entered the cabin.

Startled, Rachel jumped. She felt her cheeks grow warm. She turned to face him, not wanting to seem to be invading his privacy. "The kettle . . ." she began.

"Sorry, didn't mean to frighten you." In his hands was the basket containing the sticky buns Rachel had taken from the sweets laid out for her guests' pleasure. Ada baked them fresh at least twice a week. "How did you know that I have a passion for cinnamon buns? And these look as though they have nuts on top."

She nodded. "Are these yours, Mr. Baker? The Medal of Honor and the Silver Star?"

He looked down at the pastries. "I do fancy sticky buns. Never had the nerve to try to make them myself. I appreciate the gift more than you can know."

"The medals?" she repeated softly.

"Foolish of me to hang them up like that. Showing off, your Amish relatives would say, but I didn't know what else to do with them. It seemed cowardly to toss them out, at least disrespectful." He raised his head and met her look, and for a brief instant she saw a man carrying more than his share of mental pain. "You mind getting those cups out of the cupboard?"

Rachel turned to the cabinet and took down two vintage-style white coffee mugs that might have been used in any diner in the 1920s. The glimpse of the interior of the cabinet had shown her dishes and glassware neatly lined up and ready for use.

"Loose tea's in that canister on the counter. Teapot's under the sink." Baker took the plate of sticky buns out of the basket and set them on the round table. It was wood and appeared to Rachel to be handcrafted, like most of the furniture in the cabin. "Scoop's in the can. You need two scoops of the peppermint."

"You have no reason to be ashamed of those medals," she said. "You must have been very brave."

"Brave or stupid, probably a little of both, but I saw a lot of men who deserved them more than I did." His voice dropped to a raspy grating. "Men who mostly didn't come home or came home short of arms and legs or maybe eyes or half a brain." A visible shudder passed through him. "Bad memories," he said. "Stupid war, waste of lives. Not something I care to talk about."

"But you talk about it with Rupert," she suggested gently.

"Only when I need to, when it can ease his soul. For myself . . . It's why I live like this. Why I'm happier on my own . . . why I've had enough of orders from politicians who never wade through the blood they cause." He stiffened and his features smoothed out, hiding the anger behind a disarming smile. "When you've seen as much of mankind as I have, a raccoon makes good company. Now, let's have our tea, and I'll try to tell you what you came to find out."

Soon Rachel was seated at the table across from the man sipping peppermint tea and nibbling at a cinnamon bun. Her thoughts were racing, but she was determined not to leave there without answers. Baker was an enigma, but that didn't mean that he couldn't be capable of shooting his neighbor. "I came here to talk to you about your neighbor, Daniel."

"Right. You said."

"Did you know that Moses Studer confessed to killing his brother-in-law?" she asked, watching him for his response.

"Moses?" Baker shook his head. Clearly, it was news to him. "No way he killed a man. Any man, even Daniel."

"He told the police he did it. They arrested him."

"I don't care what he told the police. You ask me my opinion, I'm giving it to you. Moses didn't kill anyone. Accidentally, maybe, but not on purpose. He doesn't have it in him to put a bullet in a man deliberately."

"You aren't the first one to tell me that," Rachel said, "but I'd appreciate anything you can tell me about Moses and Daniel. And the family," she added. "How well did you know the deceased?"

He shrugged. "Not well. Like I said, I keep to myself."

"I understand that there was some kind of disagreement between you."

"You're danged—you're right there was. Pardon my rough talk. I don't get guests often, and never ladies. Daniel Fisher was a miserable, mean-hearted excuse for a man. I wouldn't waste powder or shot on him. If I wanted him dead, I know a lot of ways to make it look like an accident."

Rachel felt an unease come over her again, but she forged ahead, unwilling to let Chuck know that he unsettled her. "Actually, initially, the police thought it was an accident. Then determined it wasn't."

"What changed their mind?" he asked.

"I don't know." She looked up at him. "So . . . you disliked Daniel."

"Hated his guts. Always sneaking onto my land and shooting my deer. Told him to stay out. Always pressing for what wasn't his. Greedy scum. Amish clothes don't make a decent man, begging your pardon." He bit into the homemade pastry and closed his eyes. "Best cinnamon bun I think I've ever tasted," he pronounced. "A man could die happy after two or three of these."

Rachel watched him enjoy the treat. "I believe that Daniel Fisher thought the land was his."

"None of that he lived on was his. Come to them by his wife's dead father. Not an acre in Daniel's name."

"I mean that the Studer family believed that the old orchard where Daniel died was part of their farm."

Chuck spooned a measure of honey into his tea. His voice, when he spoke, was easy, but his narrowed dark eyes were hard. "You want to talk about land trouble? My people have had land trouble for the last couple hundred years. When the

English and the Germans came, they thought this land was theirs for the taking. But Shawnee and Lenape and other tribes have lived and died here for thousands of years."

Rachel listened, drinking her tea.

"I have solid title to this section of the mountain, granted by old charter from Billy Penn's son, a deed to more than six hundred acres. Legal enough to win a half dozen courtroom challenges. My great-great-grandmother had sense enough to marry a Scotsman so the land technically went to a white man."

"Then why does Daniel's family think the land is theirs?"

He shrugged. "Greedy, like I said. Trouble with the Studers didn't start until Daniel married the daughter. Before that, Alma's husband and some of his family hunted the orchard, but they knew it wasn't theirs. That tree stand where Daniel died was well inside my property line. Had he been where he was supposed to be, maybe he'd be alive today."

"Isn't your property fenced in?"

Baker scoffed. "That twelve-foot fence? Around six hundred acres? Not likely. I may be crazy, but I'm not a fool. That's just for show. I never caught Daniel at the gate. He always sneaked in. I tried talking to him. Made it clear I didn't want him or anyone else hunting on my property. But he wasn't much for reasoning. Had a temper, that one."

She thought about all the nice things people had had to say about Daniel at the funeral and the initial impression of him they had given. Then she thought about the things she had learned since and she wondered if you could ever really know someone. She cleared her throat. "Did you see Daniel the day he died? Maybe you were out hunting, it being opening day of deer season, and ran into him?" She tried to make it sound casual. "On your property, maybe?"

"I know what you're asking." He shook his head. "But I didn't see him that day when he was out hunting. Had I seen him, I'd have run him off. But I couldn't have seen him while I was out hunting because I'm no hunter."

She looked at him across the table. "You aren't?"

"Was before Afghanistan. No more. Seen enough shooting. Killing. More than enough. I keep the guns to guard this land against intruders. I've got no use for hunting. I don't eat meat."

The man was full of surprises. "You're a *vegetarian?*" she asked.

That half-smile softened his rough face. "You could say that. I like my eggs of a morning, and I do love an occasional fish fillet. But the deer and bear and smaller creatures, they're safe on my land. At least they are if I can keep men like Fisher out." He cupped his hands around his mug and inhaled the scent of his tea. "Hunting is pretty fierce in this part of the state. I look after my deer, put out salt blocks, see they have fresh water when the temperature drops. The world can be a dangerous place, Rachel, but this . . ." He waved a hand. "This is my sanctuary and maybe theirs, too."

Chapter 10

As Rachel pushed a shopping cart through the automatic doors of Wagler's Grocery, she mulled over her meeting the previous day with Chuck Baker. Despite his oddity, she couldn't help liking the man. But she knew she couldn't allow personal feelings to interfere with finding the truth about what happened to Daniel. She also knew something she'd had to learn the hard way: that not everyone told the truth.

She'd been annoyed with herself that she hadn't asked the one question she *should* have asked Chuck, and that was who *he* thought shot Daniel. He told her she was welcome to come back again to talk, and she intended to do so. She could ask him then. Before she talked to him again, though, she knew she needed the facts behind the land dispute. That had involved a trip to the county office to see who actually owned the land in question.

Like most old property deeds, ownership had been contested multiple times, but once it had temporarily passed out of Baker hands. The very helpful clerk there had found a break in ownership in the 1930s, which was later restored to the Baker family.

Apparently, the Bakers had fallen behind in taxes on an orchard and hay meadow during the Great Depression, and one Lemuel Studer, neighbor, had purchased the property at the sheriff's auction. The head of the Baker family, listed as

John, alias Munsee John, Baker, had come up with the required amount within the stipulated time of leeway and had reclaimed his land by paying the tax plus a penalty. The county, as per the agreement at the time of the auction, would have returned the money Lemuel Studer had paid out to him. The clerk said it happened all the time during the Depression. Lands were confiscated and auctioned off, but if the owner could pay up within a certain amount of time, the land reverted back to the owner. Which meant that the old orchard where Daniel died was legally owned by Charles Munsee Baker, and had been unencumbered since 1938.

That meant that either Mary Rose was mistaken about the land or she'd deliberately lied about it being part of their property. Who owned the land didn't really matter all that much. Just because Daniel died in Chuck's orchard, that didn't mean Chuck killed him. But if Mary Rose told an untruth about owning the land when she didn't, had she told others?

Now Rachel wanted to go to the orchard and see for herself where Daniel had died. But she had chores for the B&B that couldn't wait. First on her list was a little shopping. Ada had asked her to pick up half-and-half, cake flour, brown sugar, and pickling spice. What Ada intended to pickle in late November, Rachel wasn't sure, but whatever her housekeeper wanted, she was happy to supply. It wasn't sensible to question the grocery list when there were new guests arriving for the weekend. Actually, it was never wise to question Ada about anything having to do with the kitchen.

The store was busy with mostly women, both Amish and English, picking up something for supper. Outsiders often seemed surprised to see the Amish with a grocery cart filled with toilet paper, boxed cereal, and baking ingredients like flour and baking powder, but Amish families needed to purchase things they couldn't make at home. It always made her smile to see an entire family trailing behind mother and father, all dressed in their best go-to-church clothing. Knowing that most came by horse and buggy, Wagler's had always provided a shaded spot to tie the animals sheltered from the elements, a courtesy the new management had preserved.

Most of the shoppers were friends or neighbors, but Rachel didn't really have time to chat so she wheeled the cart quickly through the produce aisle, stopping only to pick up lemons and romaine lettuce. On second thought, the navel oranges looked nice and she loved oranges. Oddly, Bishop, who rarely would touch table scraps, loved the peel. The cat was constantly stashing pieces of orange peel under Rachel's bed and under her bathroom sink. She picked out a half dozen oranges, bagged them, and dropped them into her cart.

As she rounded the aisle she almost bumped into Margaret O'Meara and her husband, Fred. He was pushing the overflowing grocery cart and she was scolding him about the two bags of potato chips that he'd just added to their order.

"We have pretzels. We don't need those, and if I did want chips, it wouldn't be those."

"But I like them and they're on sale." Red-faced Fred, a tall, balding man with a potbelly, pointed to the display. "Buy one, get the second one free."

"And have you checked the date on the bottom?" Margaret demanded. Her shrill voice always reminded Rachel of nails on a blackboard. "They might be out-of-date, something the company wants to get rid of. Honestly, Fred, you're as bad as a child. I—" Margaret finally noticed Rachel and immediately donned her church face. "Rachel, how lovely to see you," she said, her voice as sweet as honey. "We simply can't wait for your wedding. You make such a sweet couple."

"Hello, Margaret. Fred. How are you?" Rachel smiled. Margaret was president of the Stone Mill Library Ladies, a women's organization that supported the town library and offered cultural opportunities to members and the public. She and her husband both sang in the Methodist church choir with Rachel, but truthfully, Rachel had never been able to take Margaret in large doses because she always seemed unhappy about something.

"Let me give you some advice, dear. When you and Evan are husband and wife, shop alone. Otherwise . . ." Margaret sighed heavily and rolled her eyes. "I declare, this man will be the death of me." She scooped up Fred's two bags of chips and shoved them back on the shelf. "The male of the species can't resist snacks. Honestly, bringing him along costs us a fortune in grocery bills." She leaned closer. "I find Wagler's on the expensive side, don't you? I can do much better at the discount grocery in State College."

Rachel, who'd been considering picking up the chips at the sale price, thought the better of it. She smiled politely, made a remark about the weather, and made her escape down the pet food aisle. Halfway along the aisle, she found her way blocked by the substantial bulk of Lois McCloud, wife of the town funeral director and best friend of Margaret. Rachel knew Lois well and liked her. Lois was a cheerful woman, also from church choir, who knew and told far too much about her neighbors and their doings.

"We're practicing Sunday, right after church," Lois reminded her. "Not six as usual. Don't forget. To make up for last week's Wednesday that had to be cancelled. You will be there, won't you?"

"If I can," Rachel said. She picked up a bag of cat food for Bishop and smiled politely. "I'd love to stay and chat, but . . ."

Lois took the hint and made her decision between dog chow and kibbles quickly. "I'm sure you must be busy with all your wedding plans and the inn. See you in church Sunday."

"I'll do my best to be there," Rachel promised, then hurried off in search of the next item on the list. She had just reached the far end of the pet treats when she heard Margaret's loud voice from the next aisle over.

"Lois, lovely to see you," Margaret squealed. "How is your husband's cold? We missed him in church last week."

Rachel moved on; it took her two aisles to find the pickling spices, which were with the canning jars. Then she backtracked to the baking aisle. There, to her pleasant surprise, she found Coyote Finch tossing bags of chocolate chips into her cart. With her, belted securely into the child seat, was an adorable little girl, her hair in tiny pigtails tied with red bows, wearing a sparkly red cowboy hat, a fluorescent red scarf, and furry boots.

Rachel smiled at the toddler. "Hi, Raysheene. Hey, Coyote. Where are the other kids? Helping Papa?" As usual, Coyote, a genuine ex-California free spirit, was dressed like no one else in Stone Mill and possibly like no one else anywhere. Her trim form was wrapped in an oversized Peruvian alpaca poncho; purple, skin-tight, faux-leather slacks; and macramé gladiator sandals that laced halfway to her knees.

"Yes, thankfully, the tribe is all with Blade." Her friend opened a bag of animal crackers and handed the child one. "Don't gobble, we don't want you to choke again," she admonished gently. "Raysheene is just coming to terms with solids. Her last foster mother still had her on a bottle and baby formula. Can you believe it? And she's such a big girl."

The child beamed and threw up her arms. "Big!"

Raysheene was the couple's newest foster child, a child born with Down syndrome whom they were in the process of adopting. Rachel was continually surprised by the Finches' ability to welcome mentally and physically challenged children into their large family, all the while growing their family business, homeschooling their brood, and maintaining a sense of humor.

"Love the new organic section," Coyote said. "I don't care how much chemical-free products cost, I'm buying them. I always liked Wagler's, but I'm over the moon since they started carrying organic wheat and rye flour. Raysheene has a delicate digestive system, and I have to be so careful with her diet."

Rachel nodded. "I like the changes here, too."

Wagler's had been an institution here in Stone Mill for decades. It had been difficult to imagine it without Ed and Polly at the helm, but the new owners seemed friendly and totally dedicated to keeping Wagner's a place where the community preferred to shop rather than drive over the mountain to State College. Everything here was practically the same as before, including the store name and staff, but they had updated and enlarged the deli and the produce section and added an aisle of organic foods.

Coyote leaned close. "You're quite the subject of a discussion over in aisle one. Margaret and Lois." She raised an eyebrow teasingly. "If people in this town were into gambling, I think there would be a running bet on whether or not your wedding will go off as scheduled."

Rachel grimaced. "Which one of them thinks that one of us will back out?"

Coyote chuckled. "Both of them."

Rachel shook her head. "You're a troublemaker."

Her friend laughed. "I know." She took a tissue out of her beaded purse and wiped the crumbs off Raysheene's mouth. The child giggled and Coyote hugged her. She glanced at Rachel. "Got to run. Hungry kids, hungry husband. You're welcome to join us for supper. Blade's making his famous vegan chili."

"Thanks, but I'll take a rain check," Rachel answered. "Lots to do at home."

Coyote nodded. "I can imagine, but you know you're always welcome. Anytime. You and Evan, if you can ever catch up with him."

"Cops' hours."

"And yours are just as bad." Coyote gave her a quick kiss on the cheek and headed off in the direction of the registers. Then she stopped abruptly and reversed the cart back to where Rachel stood. Her friend came close and asked quietly, "I have to ask you, how is Moses? Have you seen him again?"

Rachel shook her head. "I found a lawyer to represent him, but so far, he's not recanting his confession." She looked into Coyote's compassionate eyes. "I don't think he did it."

Coyote frowned. "Why would he say he had done such a thing? Do you have any proof?"

"Not yet, but I'm still asking questions."

Coyote squeezed her hand. "Follow your intuition. It's led you to answers before. Doing this, it's the right thing to do. No matter how it ends."

Rachel sighed. "You and Mary Aaron are the only ones who think so."

Her friend nodded. "I'll keep you in my prayers."

"And Moses. He needs them most."

Coyote smiled. "Both of you."

"Thanks," Rachel said. "We can use all the help we can get."

"Okay, I'm just going to put this out there. When you suggested a date, this wasn't what I had in mind. Not exactly my idea of a romantic afternoon with my girl," Evan protested. He walked ahead of her through the tall grass, carrying the wicker basket stuffed with the lunch Ada had made for them. "You know there could be rattlesnakes up here."

Rachel smiled and let him fuss. It was a beautiful fall afternoon, sunny with hardly a breeze. When she'd learned that he actually had a Saturday off, she'd begged him to take her on a picnic. And Evan had fallen into her trap by agreeing and offering to let her pick the spot, even though he thought a picnic in November was a crazy idea.

"You know, any other woman would choose a waterfall or maybe a quiet woods clearing beside a creek. But, no, my girl wants to picnic at the site of a homicide."

"It's important that I see where Daniel Fisher died. You describing it to me isn't enough. I'm trying to picture the whole thing in my mind," she said, hurrying to keep up with his long strides. This afternoon, he was wearing civvies: blue jeans, Dr. Martens, a medium-weight jacket, and a corduroy ball cap that read *Stone Mill Bears*. She thought he looked even more handsome than he did in his police uniform, more approachable, sweeter.

"Fine, we can check it out, but I put my foot down at actually eating under the tree stand where they found his body," Evan told her. "It's been a long week. I'm hungry and I want to relax with the woman I intend to marry. So we have a look and then we sit down and we enjoy our lunch. I don't want to think about or talk about Daniel Fisher or the Studers or any part of the investigation. Understood?"

"Perfectly. Let's talk about something else." She smiled slyly. "You know, we're the object of the town gossip. You and I."

He glanced over his shoulder at her. "And that's something new? Since when haven't you been? Or me for letting you wrap me around your little finger."

"I don't wrap you around my finger. I adore you, Evan Parks. And I can't wait to be your wife. In spite of what everybody says."

He stopped and waited for her. "And what is it that everybody says?"

It was the opening she needed to tell him about what had happened at Wagler's the previous afternoon. Because she kept telling herself she didn't care, but she did. "Coyote says the town is divided on whether or not I'll get cold feet and not show up at the church. She says everyone is talking about it."

"I've heard it, too. I met some of the guys after work at the pub."

"You were at the pub?" she asked, not minding, just surprised.

He shrugged. "My last days being single, I thought I should act like it."

She nodded. "Okay."

"Anyway, some of them were razzing me about you skipping out with an Amish guy at the last minute and leaving me at the altar."

She laughed. "You don't believe that, do you?"

"No, I don't." He caught her hand with his free one. "*Should* I be worried?"

"About what?" She looked up at him.

"About you getting cold feet."

"Evan, I told you. I want to marry you." She squeezed his hand. "I'll be there. Okay?"

"Okay," he agreed.

Rachel grimaced. "I think Margaret O'Meara, from church, may be behind this whole town twittering about the state of our relationship. Apparently, she found out where I was getting my dress and kept track of how many bridal gown fittings I missed. Then added a few."

He stopped and smiled at her, his face creasing in a boyish grin. "And the caterer. You missed that one, too."

"I had a good reason," she defended, making a face at him. "And, as I recall, you couldn't make it, either. That's why we had to reconsider the whole food thing."

"I was working. And I don't care what we eat at the wedding. Chicken. Steak, blueberry pie, bread and water."

"Which is why just letting my mother and Ada take care of the food was the best solution."

"I agree," Evan said. "I'm only interested in hearing the minister say, 'Do you take this man to be your husband, to love and to cherish . . .'"

"Me, too." She groaned. "Sometimes, I wish we'd eloped. Just gone off to Las Vegas and had Elvis marry us. It would have been less hectic."

"We still can," he offered, cutting his eyes at her.

"No, we can't. We have to make our vows before God and our families. My mother has finally come around and I'm not going to threaten that with a Nevada marriage."

"A courthouse ceremony would be legal."

"Yes," she agreed. "It would be, and that's fine for some, but not for me. And I don't think it would be for you, either."

Evan put the basket on the ground in the middle of the path and opened his arms. "Come here."

She stepped into them and he lowered his head and pressed his warm lips to hers. For a tender moment, they kissed, and a tingling joy spread through her. She pushed away. "That was . . . lovely," she murmured and stepped back.

He smiled down at her. "Have I told you that I love you?"

She nodded, smiling. "Once or twice."

He cupped a hand around his ear. "Come again?"

"I love you, too," she said.

"That's better." He caught her fingers and tugged. "I don't suppose I could have one more of those?"

"No more kissing. Eating our lunch. Talking. The kissing waits until after the wedding."

Evan clasped a fist to his heart dramatically. "She spurns me."

Rachel laughed. "She doesn't spurn you often, and that's the trouble."

They laughed together and he pointed ahead. She hadn't noticed the row of new fence posts and the four strands of barbed wire on the next rise. Behind the fence line was a relatively flat section of ground and the remains of an old orchard stretching to the left and back to blend into the wooded hillside of the mountain ridge.

"No one's tended the orchard in years, but there's enough fruit to bring the deer here every fall. Apparently, Daniel, or someone, regularly cut the barbed wire to get in. They take portable deer stands in. You'll be able to see the tree that Daniel's tree stand is in from where we're going to have lunch, but you can't see much of the actual stand. And I'm not letting you go over there. The crime scene is still taped off." He picked up the picnic basket. "Not much farther, but I'm not pointing out the deer stand until we have our lunch. First eating, then we satisfy your curiosity."

She nodded. "All right."

Evan kept walking. It was rocky ground and uphill. Rachel

could manage well enough, but it was more difficult than walking across a flat pasture, the footing uneven. "I'm serious," he warned. "You're not going to set foot on Baker's property. I'm not certain the man's mentally stable."

"He wouldn't hurt me, but I won't go in there if you don't want me to." She considered the information. "Mary Rose Studer seems to think the old orchard was part of their farm, and her mother didn't correct her when she said it. But it isn't. It belongs to Chuck . . . Charles Baker."

"That's why we questioned Baker. The detectives, not me. Because the death happened on his land."

"Why do you think that Alma and Mary Rose would say it was their farm?" Rachel asked.

"Maybe they didn't know. I doubt if they came up here. It's quite a hike, and steeper coming from the direction of the farmhouse. People say all kinds of things, especially during times of stress. It doesn't necessarily mean she was intending to lie to you."

Rachel followed him a few hundred feet farther up the slope to the spot he chose for their picnic. "This is lovely," she said, turning around to take it all in. A trickle of spring water bubbled through a crack in the remains of an old stone wall, creating an enchanting spot under a grove of oak and hemlock trees. Instead of weeds and dried grass, the ground was carpeted in thick, velvety moss that cushioned their steps. "Beautiful," she murmured.

Evan spread the blanket on the moss. Rachel knelt on it and opened the top of the wicker basket. The smells that drifted up were wonderful. "Fried chicken and peach hand pies," she said, closing her eyes and sniffing the delicious aromas. "Deviled eggs and pickles and—I don't remember what else."

"Cheese," Evan supplied, holding it up. "Sharp cheddar. Made in Belleville."

Rachel chuckled, opened her eyes, and began to remove

dishes, forks, and spoons. Ada had even tucked in a small jug of sweet cider. "She thinks of everything."

"Ada is a treasure, but she's twice as fussy as my mother."

"Maybe not *twice* as fussy," Rachel teased. "But she can be difficult."

"You're telling me. I'm a little scared about moving in with you after the wedding," Evan admitted.

She laughed. "It's going to be fine."

He glanced uphill and pointed again. "Up there. See the tree with the crows sitting in the top branch? That's the deer stand where Daniel Fisher was murdered."

"I thought you said you wouldn't show me until after we finished eating," she teased.

"I know you. You won't be able to enjoy your lunch unless I give in a little."

"You're really very sweet, Evan Parks."

"And you are a woman who always manages to get your own way."

Rachel shook her head. "Not always." She hesitated. "I do have a question."

"Why doesn't that surprise me?"

"Be serious, Evan. Daniel's death, first thought to be an accident, is now a murder. But you've never told me why."

"Why what?"

"Why the police are so certain that Daniel was murdered. If he was hunting from a deer stand, isn't it possible that he accidentally dropped his shotgun and it went off?"

"Two bullet wounds."

"Right. He was probably hunting with a double-barreled shotgun like most Amish in this valley. He fell and both barrels went off."

"Nope," Evan said firmly. "That's definitely not what happened. Mr. Fisher was struck twice with twelve-gauge deer slugs, both wounds being potentially fatal, but those shots didn't come from his weapon. Ballistics proved that. Secondly, the two shots were fired from different angles. Whoever killed him shot him once, probably knocked him out of the stand, and then put a second slug into him."

The enormity of that information took a few seconds to sink in. Rachel took a deep breath. "Why didn't you tell me that before?" she asked softly.

"Because it was confidential, information not meant for the general public. At least not at the time."

"And you feel comfortable sharing it with me?" she asked. Evan usually talked to her about his job, but he'd never given her inside information before without her really, really pressing him. And then he never broke the law, just walked very close to the line.

"May as well. Some idiot leaked the medical examiner's report to a reporter. It'll be on the local nightly news and probably in the papers by Monday." He held up his finger. "You're not to breathe a word until it comes out."

"I won't." She shivered, despite the warmth of her fleece-lined ski jacket. She couldn't believe someone had been callous enough to shoot Daniel, and then, as he lay bleeding, shoot him a second time. "What kind of person would do such a thing?" Rachel murmured, trying to imagine Moses Studer aiming a shotgun at his dying brother-in-law and pulling the trigger again. It wasn't possible. Asperger's or not, Moses wasn't a murderer.

"Let's not think about all that now." Evan offered her a saltshaker to season her chicken leg. "We don't get that much time alone. Let's talk about something fun. I booked a kayak eco tour. Lunch on a deserted beach is included."

"I just keep thinking that there's something I haven't found out about yet," Rachel said, barely hearing him. She gestured toward him with her drumstick. "Something the detectives haven't discovered yet, something that will make them realize Moses couldn't have done it."

"Not much chance of that."

"Why not?"

"Because the investigation is over. The district attorney has a confession. As far as he's concerned, Moses Studer confessed, and that makes him guilty. The case is closed."

"But why?" Rachel asked. "What if later down the road they find out that Moses didn't do it? Where will their case be then?"

Evan sighed. "It's about money, hon. The state has only so many resources and a lot of cases to bring to trial. Cases where the answers aren't clear-cut. It's not the best scenario, because you're right, years down the road, we sometimes find out we've put the wrong man or woman in jail. But it's how our system works. Unless DNA turns up or someone else confesses, your Moses Studer is going to be convicted for this crime. And there's little you can do about this."

"I can't accept that."

"Rachel, you can't solve the world's problems. Can't you let this go?"

She met his gaze. "Maybe . . . I think so . . . just not quite yet."

Chapter 11

Alma was standing at the stable door when Rachel drove up the Studer driveway, and immediately came out into the yard. Rachel had taken the chance that the Studers might be home at chore time, so she'd changed into her near-Amish garb and driven out to the farm again. After their wonderful afternoon together, Evan had left Stone Mill to escort his mother to a formal mother-son affair at her country club. The only child of a widow, he had obligations to his own family.

"Did you go to see Moses again?" Alma asked in *Deitsch* when Rachel got out of the Jeep. "Are they feeding my boy enough? Is he well?" she worried aloud, not really seeming to expect an answer. "I talked with the bishop. He says he will go to the prison to pray with Moses if they will let him in." She looked up at Rachel earnestly through eyeglasses that needed a good cleaning. "Do you think they will? I don't see why not. My son should have that right." The older woman was again dressed for outside work. She wore a man's heavy coat, muck boots, and a navy wool scarf.

"I've stopped a couple of times, but you haven't been home," Rachel told her, tugging on an old denim jacket she'd borrowed from her parents' laundry room months ago. "To tell you what's going on with Moses. Did Mary Rose mention it?"

"Come in." Alma motioned toward the barn. "We were just milking the cows when I heard your motorcar."

Rachel spotted Mary Rose at the clothesline across the yard, taking down a load of wash. She waved to her before she followed Alma into the old stone barn. Although it was still light outside, the stable had only a few narrow slits for windows, and it took a moment for Rachel's eyes to adjust to the semidarkness.

"The wind is sharp," Alma said. "No need for you to catch an ague."

Rachel offered a tight-lipped smile, taking in the sights and sounds of the barn. A person could learn a lot about someone else from the way they kept their animals.

There were five tie stalls and a larger box stall with several half-grown calves. She counted three cows and a driving horse, all munching hay and grain from their individual mangers. The stable was as clean and orderly as Alma's kitchen. There was an underlying scent of animals and dung, but the primary smells were sweet clover hay, molasses, and grain. Above her head, a low wide-plank ceiling told her that there was a substantial loft.

"I wanted to tell you that the attorney I spoke with will take Moses's case. He's still saying he did it, but at least he's agreed to let the lawyer help him. She'll make sure that Moses's rights are upheld." Rachel spotted Lemuel in a corner stall, seated on a low stool, milking a black-and-white cow. A lantern hung from an overhead beam, casting a pale light and even more shadows.

"I don't care what it costs," Alma said, breaking open a bale of hay. "We'll sell land if we have to." She walked down a passageway in front of the stalls and dropped sections of hay into each cow's manger. "That crazy Englisher on the mountain is always offering to buy our pastures. They're just growing up in brush anyway. More rock than soil." She took a breath. "My Moses didn't do this terrible thing, and they have to let him go. I don't understand why they would put him in prison. You only put bad people in prison. People who do the bad things."

Alma's words reminded Rachel of how naïve the Amish in Stone Mill could be. They really did hold themselves apart from the world. "Let's wait and see how much her fees will be before you start thinking about selling land. It's too soon for that."

Rachel glanced at the waiting cows. She could tell that there were still two to be milked by their full bags. She had been raised on a farm much like this one, and she'd always found well-tended barns to be comforting places. "Would you like help?" she asked. "I've been milking since I was six years old. At home, I mean. When I lived with my *mam* and *dat*."

"Would you?" Alma asked. "The three are a lot for Lemuel and he still has the sheep and hogs to feed. My hands are near crippled from arthritis." She raised her hands, covered in knit half-gloves. "My fingers are so stiff, I can barely pull a teat anymore."

"I'm sorry to hear that." Rachel started rolling up the sleeves on her coat. It was warm enough in the barn that she might end up having to take it off. "Have you talked to your doctor about it?"

Alma scoffed. "I don't hold with doctors and their drug-store medicines. I drink ginseng tea and I can a lot of cherries. Salome says cherries and tea help with the pain. She knows a lot about the old cures."

"Salome? *Ya,* the midwife." Rachel nodded. "I know her."

Salome Plank was an Amish lay-midwife who many of her people consulted for simple ailments. Salome was up in years, but she'd delivered many of the babies in this valley for generations and she knew a great deal about the properties of herbs and folk medicine such as using cobwebs to stop a wound from bleeding.

"She's a wise woman," Alma said. "She brought all three of my children into the world and one who never drew breath, God rest his soul. Born too soon, he was. Just a scrap of a baby. Not as big as a man's hand."

"Is there another milking bucket?" Rachel asked, looking around.

"I'll fetch it for you." Alma headed out of the barn and Rachel followed her.

In the barnyard, Alma walked a few feet away to where several milk buckets stood stacked. Rachel remained near the barn door. She watched Mary Rose take down one of the last sheets from the line, struggling with it in the wind. "Need help?" Rachel called.

"*Ne*. I've got it!"

Beyond Mary Rose, there was an open, grassy area and then, on the rocky slope, a hedgerow of Osage orange, often planted to keep livestock out of gardens. Movement caught Rachel's eye and she stared hard at the line of shrub trees. There was something there . . . no, not something—*someone*. For just an instant, she made out the form of a man. Then he saw Rachel and ducked down out of sight.

"Someone's out there," Rachel said, trying to decide if she should walk in that direction. "A man. Who could—"

"Pay no attention to him," Alma responded, clearly unconcerned. "That's Rosh from next door."

Rachel turned to the older woman. "But he hid when he realized I'd seen him. Why would he just stand there looking?"

"*Ya*, Rosh creeps around all the time. Likes to keep an eye on Mary Rose." She waved a gloved hand and picked up a bucket. "He's harmless."

"What do you mean, he *keeps an eye on Mary Rose?*" Rachel stared at the place where she'd seen him, but he didn't reappear. "It seems like odd behavior."

Alma shrugged. "Odd for some. Not for others. He's a

sweet boy, but shy. Hard worker. All the time he hunts and traps, fishes for trout in the creek, digs ginseng on the mountain to sell. Picks mushrooms. He and Mary Rose used to play together when they were young. Rosh is a Hertzler. You must know his parents. They belong to our church and are our nearest neighbors to the south."

"Actually, Rosh is someone I've been trying to catch up with," Rachel said, still keeping an eye on the hedgerow. "Mary Rose said he's the one who came to tell you what had happened to Daniel. Maybe he saw something in the woods that day while he was hunting. He might be able to help Moses." She turned to Alma. "Do you mind if I try to speak to him now?"

"Of course, if you think he could help my son. But you may not catch him. We tease him; he's like a ghost. One minute you see him, the next he's gone."

"I'd like to try," Rachel answered, watching Mary Rose, who had gathered up her clothes basket and was walking toward the house. "It will just take a minute, and then I'll come right back and help with the milking. I promise." She started across the yard toward her Jeep. "Which way is Rosh's house from here?"

The older woman pointed south.

Rachel nodded. "I won't be long."

Rachel got into the Jeep, started the engine, and drove down the long lane. When she reached the road, she turned in the direction of the Hertzler farm, drove a short way, and pulled off on the shoulder. There, she got out and hurried back along the road. She found a fallen log and sat down to wait in the shelter of a big oak tree.

No vehicles passed on the road. The only sound was the wind in the trees and the chattering of squirrels as twilight descended on the mountain road. Again, Rachel was swept back in time to her childhood. She could remember trekking through the woods with her father, picking edible mushrooms. Theirs was a big family, as most Amish families were. But her father had always taken care to spend time with each of his children, and she cherished those hours when he was hers alone.

He would point out the different types of mushrooms, warning her not to touch the poisonous destroying angel or the yellow stainer. Instead, she helped him to gather basketfuls of turkey tail, giant puffballs, and white chicken of the woods mushrooms that her mother would prepare for dinner and share at church. Her *dat* had also taught her to be wary of rock piles where timber rattlesnakes might hide and not to confuse the dangerous copperhead with the harmless hognose, milk snake, or black racer. It paid to keep your head about you when you went into the deep woods, especially alone, but her father never wanted any of his children to fear the mountains because the land provided so much for them.

In less time than Rachel thought possible, a crow squawked a warning cry, and a blue jay scolded an intruder. Rachel didn't move. She remained hidden behind the oak as a slim figure in a black watch cap, camo pants, and camo jacket moved silently out of the woods onto the road. She didn't call out to him until he'd almost reached her hiding place.

"Rosh Hertzler?"

The slim figure froze and his pale blue eyes searched the trees. "Who's there?"

"Rachel Mast. I've been wanting to speak with you, but you're hard to find." She stepped out from behind the tree. "I'm sorry. I didn't mean to startle you. I wanted to thank you for calling Mary Aaron that day to let us know that the police were questioning Moses." She studied Rosh. She must have seen him in town or at one of the church affairs, but she couldn't place his face. He stood no taller than her, perhaps not as tall, and his tanned features were almost delicate. Acorn-brown hair brushed the collar of his jacket and not the slightest shadow of a beard darkened his cheeks. In a dress and *kapp,* he could have passed as a girl, Rachel thought, but despite his size, there was nothing weak-looking about him. His gaze was guarded, and she had the feeling that he couldn't decide whether to talk to her or dart back into the woods.

One lean hand dropped to the bulging bag tied to his belt.

"You've been digging ginseng," she ventured. The season lasted only until the end of November.

"*Ya.*"

"On Studer land?"

He shrugged. "Different places."

"I saw you there, a few minutes ago. And you saw me. Why were you spying on Mary Rose?"

He shook his head. "Wasn't."

"Weren't you? It looked like that to me," Rachel said. "Alma says you like to watch her."

He shrugged.

She hesitated, considering what she should say next. She got the impression that if she wasn't careful, she'd spook him and he'd just take off into the woods again. "That day you saw the police going to the Studers'. You told Mary Aaron that one police car was there and another was driving up the lane. You said you were driving past. But you can't see the house from the road. How did you know the police were questioning Moses? Were you there on the property? Watching Mary Rose?"

He shrugged again.

"Rosh, you had to have been on the property. You must have been close to the house to know that the detective was asking questions."

He avoided her gaze. "Maybe I was."

She considered his answers or lack thereof. "Alma says you spend a lot of time in the woods, hunting and such. Mary Rose said you were the one who came to tell them about Daniel. So, I guess you were in the woods the day Daniel was shot?"

Rosh shifted from one worn hunting boot to the other. The tip of his tongue licked a chapped lower lip. "*Ya.*"

"Lots of people were hunting deer that day," Rachel said. "Were you?"

"*Ya,* I was."

She took two steps toward him. "Rosh, I need to ask you," she said softly. "Did you shoot him? Maybe . . . accidentally?"

Rosh rubbed at his chin with the back of a gloved hand. "Did you know him? Daniel. You know what kind of man he was?" He surprised her by meeting her gaze.

"Only what people say about him. I didn't know him personally. But a lot of people in the community thought he was a good person: a hard worker, faithful to the church, and kind to the less fortunate."

The young man's mouth twisted in disdain. "That was what he wanted folks to think. But . . ." One slim hand knotted into a fist, released, and then tightened again. His voice dropped. "Daniel had a mean streak."

Rachel thought back to what Moses's employer had said about seeing Daniel hit Lemuel. "How do you know he had a mean streak?" When he didn't respond, she went on. "Did you see Daniel strike Lemuel the day Daniel died? Before the hunt? Did that make you angry?"

The boy shook his head. "Don't know anything about that. Wasn't with them. I hunt alone."

"Sooo . . . did you know Daniel hit Lemuel?" she repeated.

"Heard about it. Don't doubt it was true. Like I said, he could be mean. He caught me in his barn one time. Beat the—" He looked down, his shoulders quivering. "Hit me, kicked me. Near broke my wrist. I wasn't doing nothing wrong. I'm not a thief. I'd never steal from nobody. You go to hell for stealing."

Rachel took a step forward, shocked by the idea that an Amish person would commit such violence. "He *beat you up?*"

Rosh's voice was muffled, almost as though he was trying not to cry. He wiped his nose with his sleeve. "*Ya.* He beat me up. Told me to run and never come back, else my *dat* would be laying me to rest in the cemetery."

His words shocked Rachel. Surely he couldn't have been talking about the man the elders in the community were talking about. The man who went out of his way to help a neighbor. "Did you tell anybody?"

He turned back to face her. His eyes were red and moisture pooled in the lower lids. His Adam's apple bobbed.

How old was he? she wondered. At first, she'd guessed sixteen, but something in his eyes . . . "How old are you, Rosh?"

"Nineteen."

Nineteen. Almost a man in the Amish way of thinking, though he looked younger. There was an unworldly, almost fey quality about Rosh Hertzler . . . but there was something more. Her gaze dropped to the hunting knife strapped to his waist just as a gust of chill wind found its way down the back of her neck. She shivered and, involuntarily, she took a step back.

Faintly, almost as if in a dream, her father's voice sounded in the recesses of her memory. "Look closely, Rachel, because the young ones are deceptive. Never trust the young ones. A good mushroom and a poisonous one are too much alike before they reach full maturity. What you're thinking is an oyster mushroom could be a death cap that hasn't quite reached its full growth."

"I gotta go," Rosh said. "I got chores at home. My father will be mad if I'm late for milking."

"What did your father say about Daniel beating you?"

"Didn't tell him. Said I took a tumble down the mountain." He turned away.

"Rosh, wait. Can you tell me how you knew . . . why you were the one who went to tell Mary Rose that Daniel had been shot?"

He stopped where he was and for a long second he said nothing, then he turned back to her. "Heard the commotion when he was found."

"Do you remember who was there? Who told you to run and tell his wife?"

"A lot of people there by the time I got there. Paramedics were there." Rosh met Rachel's gaze. "Nobody told me to. I wanted to. I thought . . ." He looked at the ground. "I thought someone who cared about her ought to be the one to tell." He turned again and walked away.

"Rosh!" Rachel called after him. "Why would you lie to your *dat* to protect Daniel Fisher? After he beat you."

"Why?" Rosh said. "Simple. 'Cause my father would have beat me again for causing trouble with the neighbor."

"Be careful," Rachel's mother cautioned. "Don't fall."

"I'm not going to topple off a peach basket." Rachel stifled a giggle. Her mother was afraid of heights and had been warning her of the dangers of breaking her neck since she was a baby. "And if I do fall, it's not that far to the ground." She stretched her arm to remove the cord that held up a hefty side of smoked bacon.

They were in the smokehouse at her parents' farm. She'd always loved the smokehouse with its rich smells of smoked shad, salted and sugar-cured hams, and, of course, the smoked hams that hung in rows from the dark beams overhead. Feeding a large family necessitated forethought and planning. And despite the two propane-powered freezers in her parents' cellar, the smokehouse provided a good deal of the meat served on the table year-round.

Rachel was helping her mother get ready for the midday Sunday meal that the Mast family would be hosting that day. Worship service was held every other Sunday in the homes of those who belonged to the church community. Services would start at nine sharp, and continue until noon or when-ever the preacher finished his sermon. Then everyone would take a two-hour break to share a light dinner before after-noon services resumed. Technically, no work and no cooking was done on the Sabbath, but no one would begrudge a woman adding a little bacon to the beans that had been sim-mering all night on the back of the woodstove.

Normally, Rachel wouldn't attend the Amish church, but her mother wasn't that far from her chemo treatments. She'd not regained her full health, and Rachel, who knew her *mam* wanted everything to be right for her friends and neighbors, needed to help this morning. Rachel had sisters, and Aunt Hannah could always be counted on, but Rachel wanted to do her part.

Rachel and her mother had gone for many years without talking to each other because of Rachel's life choices, and now that they were close again, Rachel wanted to spend as much time with her as possible. She felt that they'd dodged a bullet with the cancer. Her mother's doctors said that every-thing looked good, but they'd come too close to losing Esther for Rachel not to appreciate every opportunity she had to be with her mother.

And, if there was cooking to be finished off this morning, it was better that Rachel do it. Not being baptized, she wasn't required to live by the *ordnung,* the rules that each Amish church community followed.

"You remember the ingredients for my sugar cure?" her mother asked as Rachel used a butcher knife to slice off pieces of bacon from the larger section of meat she'd placed atop a barrel kept in the smokehouse for just this purpose. "Watch your fingers, child. That knife's sharp."

"You can cut yourself just as easy with a dull knife as a sharp one," Rachel replied. "Isn't that what you always told me? And, *ya,* I remember the recipe for your rub." She recited back what she'd been taught since she was ten years of age.

"It came to me from my grandmother and her mother before her. Don't forget it, and don't share it with your guests. It's our special family recipe."

Rachel carefully rewrapped the side of bacon in clean cheesecloth and got back on the basket to hang it from the overhead hook again. There the precious meat would be safe from vermin and from the cats that her *dat* sometimes let sleep in the smokehouse to discourage mice from nesting in here.

The sound of buggy wheels on the frozen ground made Rachel glance out the one small, barred window. The blue-tinted and bubbly glass was old with a swirling bull's-eye pattern, but she could still see through it well enough to recognize the young man getting out of Mary Rose's buggy. He helped her down with the baby, and then led the horse to the open shed that had been prepared for the horses. The previous day's beautiful fall weather had given way to gray skies and the threat of rain, and possibly a light snowfall, and her father didn't want to see any horses tied outside in the cold on such a day.

"That's Rosh Hertzler helping Mary Rose," Rachel mused aloud. She turned to her mother. "How well do you know him?"

"Well enough to know that he's sweet on Mary Rose," her mother answered tartly. Rachel's surprise must have been evident because her mother laughed. "What? You don't think that a young woman as pretty as Mary Rose might have admirers?"

"*Ya*, of course," Rachel answered. "But . . . her husband only died a week ago."

"Two weeks, or near as. And Rosh was smitten well before that. I think he's always liked her, and now there's opportunity." She shrugged her thin shoulders. "Life goes on, daughter. She's a woman alone with a child to look after. Mark my words. She'll be married within the year."

"But to someone like Rosh? He's . . . he's younger than she is, too young to be married."

"He's of legal age. Nineteen, two months ago. We were invited to his birthday supper. He's a nice boy; he'll make a good match for someone. He's good to his mother, and you can always tell a man's character by how he treats his mother."

Rachel watched through the little window as Rosh tied up Mary Rose's horse and removed its bridle. He had a gentle way with the animal. "He doesn't strike you as a little odd?"

Her mother seemed to think about it for a moment. "You mean the way he's always roaming the woods? They say he's a bee charmer. His mother says he robs wild bee colonies of their honey and never gets stung. Not once in his life, to her knowledge. I suppose you could call that odd." She laid the slices of bacon out on a platter and examined them. She leaned close and sniffed the meat, then smiled and used the butcher knife to cut the strips into smaller pieces. "And Rosh is the only boy in the family. He'll probably inherit his father's farm in time. Runs right alongside the Studer acres."

"He just seems so . . . young," Rachel repeated.

"He's not got his full growth. Time will fix all that." She chuckled. "Sometimes, you still seem very young to me."

When her mother drew the knife over the bacon, her sleeve slid up and Rachel noticed a bruise on her wrist. Rachel swallowed as apprehension washed over her and she pulled up her mother's coat sleeve to get a better look. "That's a nasty bruise," she said. "How'd you get it?"

Her mother smiled. "I know what you're thinking; it's not the cancer. You worry too much. I wasn't paying attention. Struck it on the corner of the cabinet. Old skin. I bruise easy since the cancer. It'll go away in a few days."

"If it doesn't, be sure and mention it to your doctor when I take you for your checkup next month. It's on the twentieth, isn't it?"

"*Ya,* the twentieth." She picked up the platter. "We'd best get back to the house. I need to get this bacon into the beans before services begin."

"Right." But Rachel wasn't thinking about the bacon. She was thinking about a bruise. A bruise she'd seen elsewhere. On Mary Rose's wrist that first day she'd gone to visit the Studers after Daniel's funeral. Mary Rose was young and wouldn't bruise easily.

Which made Rachel wonder . . .

What if . . . Joe had said that Daniel had hit Lemuel. And Rosh had told her the previous day that Daniel had beat him up. She hated to jump to such an awful conclusion, but what if there was truth to it? She looked to her mother.

"*Mam,* have you ever heard anything about Daniel Fisher having a bad side?"

"What do you mean?"

"That he might have been . . . *harsh* with Mary Rose? Harsh . . . handed?"

Her mother shook her head slowly. "*Ne,* nothing like that. I have heard he had a temper, but a lot of men do, especially young ones. Your Uncle Aaron has the worst temper of anyone I've ever met, but he'd cut off his own hand before he'd strike your Aunt Hannah." She started for the door. "Of course, you never know what goes on between a man and his wife."

"So, what you're saying is that there's a *possibility* that Daniel could have abused his wife?"

Her mother turned back, her features growing solemn. "I suppose it's possible."

"But . . . wouldn't she have told someone?" Rachel asked incredulously.

Her mother thought on that a moment. "*Ne.* Most women would hide such a thing out of shame . . . or fear of the man and what he might do. Not a thing a man would want known. Our bishop wouldn't stand for it. You remember, he put Andy Peachy on warning of being shunned for yanking on Elsie. A man and woman are equal under God, and it is wrong for any man to use his strength to harm his wife."

Rachel studied her mother's face. "So, Mary Rose might have been afraid of Daniel."

"A lot of *mights* in your thinking, Rachel." She raised a finger. "*Cast not the first stone,* daughter."

"But he *could* have been abusing her, and she and her family could have kept it a secret," Rachel said.

Her mother nodded. "Possible, but you could be wrong. And saying something like that aloud, you don't want to be wrong."

"Well, I'm going to ask Mary Rose straight out." Rachel folded her arms over her chest. "Of course, what are the chances she'll tell the truth? Especially since Daniel's dead. But what if . . . what if he did beat her and she killed him for it?"

Her mother scoffed. "That's a step too far. Mary Rose doesn't have the gumption to swat a fly. Don't make accusations you can't prove. It's wrong to blacken a dead man's name without proof."

"So how could I go about finding out? There has to be more to this. It doesn't make sense that a good man without enemies would be killed without a good reason. He wasn't robbed and . . ." She almost told her mother that Daniel had been shot a second time, but she bit back her words. It wasn't her message to deliver. "Why? Why was he killed?" she said. "There has to be a motive."

"Well, if it was me asking such questions," her mother said thoughtfully, "I'd talk to the midwife. She delivered Mary Rose's baby, and she tended her through a rough pregnancy. No matter how tight-lipped a woman is, she's vulnerable when she's with child. And Salome is a woman other women naturally get close to. If anyone knows if such things went on, it might be her."

"You think Salome will talk to me?" Rachel pushed open the smokehouse door.

"Doubt it," her *mam* pronounced. "Salome probably knows more secrets than that old mountain out there, and so far as I know, she's never let slip a one." She walked out into the cold gray morning. "But you'll never know until you ask."

Chapter 12

I'd talk to the midwife. Rachel's mother's words echoed in her head as she downshifted to make the final ascent to the small, gray stone house tucked into the side of a wooded hill. The road seemed almost too steep for a horse and buggy and Rachel wondered how the midwife's clients reached her. A low stone wall surrounded the house and a tidy herb garden. Smoke puffed from the chimney on one end, giving Rachel hope that this time, after two other attempts, she'd found Salome Plank at home.

Rachel parked her vehicle outside the fence. An arched frame held what must be climbing roses over the gate. Down the hill and to her left lay a vegetable garden with raised beds and a small stone stable. There was also a pasture with a three-rail wooden fence containing sheep and goats and one mule. The midwife, Rachel remembered, drove a mule rather than a horse when she called on her clients or made the trip to town or church services. A string of antique sleigh bells dangled from the gate, and when Rachel pushed it open, they rang loudly in the still air.

Almost immediately, the door swung open and Salome Plank called a cheery greeting in *Deitsch*. "Come in, come in out of the cold, Rachel Mast. How nice to see you."

The tiny midwife was all in black: black dress, black stockings, black elder's *kapp,* and black shoes. Only the hair curl-

ing around her surprisingly unlined, heart-shaped face broke
the pattern; Salome's hair was snowy white. Her laced, high
leather shoes were much like the ones Rachel remembered
her Grandmother Mast wearing. And, as was always, Salome
was smiling. "Not a one has been by all day and I was just
boiling up a cough syrup. None down sick yet, praise His
mercy, but winter is coming and the little ones will have their
mothers up walking the floor with them." She came out on
the step to welcome Rachel with a hug, and Rachel caught
the swirling scents of Ivory soap, peppermint, and cinnamon.

"You're hard to find at home," Rachel said. "You really
need a cell phone. How do your mothers find you when
they're ready to deliver?"

Salome laughed, a merry, tinkling sound. "When did you
come? Yesterday morning? Mary and Zack Hostetler welcomed another little son into their family, Mary's fourth in
six years. Both doing splendidly." She waved Rachel into a
tiny sitting room where darkened beams stretched overhead
and a corner fireplace crackled.

Stretched on the hearth was a yearling-calf-sized, shaggy
gray dog of no certain breed. Two bright blackberry eyes
peeked out from under a fringe of hair to inspect the visitor.
Apparently, Rachel passed muster, because the dog's eyes
closed and the lazy animal's head dropped back onto oversized paws, the hairy tail flopped once, and the sound of
snoring rang through the little house.

"Pay no mind to Uzzi," Salome said. "He's big, but a
friendly sort." Using a long-handled wooden spoon, the midwife stirred the bubbling mixture that hung over the fire in a
copper kettle. "No spiders in my cough syrup," she teased.
"And not a single toad. Nothing but my good apple cider
vinegar, lemons, and clover honey from my bees."

She motioned Rachel to a coatrack. "Take off your coat.
It's warm in here and you don't want to take a chill when you
go out."

As she removed her outer things, Rachel glimpsed the

kitchen through a narrow doorway. She could remember being there with her mother once before she was old enough to go to school. She'd been fascinated by the herbs hanging from the kitchen ceiling and the long table with its jars of unfamiliar objects and dried berries. "I was here Monday afternoon, too," she said, eager to get into the reason for her coming.

"Monday, hmm, two days ago. Abraham Sweitzer's daughter Sylvia. Visiting from Ohio. Seven months along with her second. The first was a breech, but Sylvia carried full term. A long labor, according to her mother. But, fortunately, a healthy baby girl at the end of it. Anyway, the young mother's back was aching, and she'd started with a few regular contractions. Better safe than sorry. I stayed with her most of the day until they passed. Stopped on the way to tend a burn on Jethro Peachy's thumb. Foolish man to let it go untended so long. But Sylvia's right as rain," the midwife chattered on. "By my calculations, she'll carry safely another six to eight weeks. And hopefully, this one will know which way to turn to find the door."

"I see," Rachel said, wondering how Salome managed to talk so much without drawing a breath. She had more energy than two five-year-olds.

The midwife chuckled. "So, you're getting married in two weeks to that handsome Englisher policeman. We'll be sorry to lose you from the faith, Rachel, but not all are called. *Ne,* they are not. God, in His mercy, has plans for all of us and none can judge another's."

"*Ne,* I mean *ya.* He does." Rachel wasn't quite sure what part of the midwife's statements to reply to or if any reply was necessary. She smiled and nodded. "He does," she added. "I'm sure He does."

Salome drew her stool a little closer. "Your mother tells me that she's come to accept your decision. It troubled her a great deal, but she recognizes your right to choose. And she sees the good heart of your young man."

A log fell and sparks sprayed up. Rachel inhaled the sweet

smell of apple wood. "Evan is a good man," she agreed. "The best."

Another chuckle bubbled up through the midwife's rosy lips. "There are quite a few who expect you to leave him empty handed at the last moment. But I see by the glow on your face that you are content to join him in honest wedlock." She nodded. "And time enough, too. You should not wait too long to bring little ones into the world. You're not old, but neither are you twenty-one. English women sometimes wait too late to start thinking of children and then it can be more difficult." She smiled and patted Rachel's arm. "Has your mother spoken to you?"

Rachel nodded. "*Ya,* we talk all the time, now that the . . . misunderstanding has been smoothed over."

"*Ne,* dear. That's not what I mean. I'm asking if she explained God's plan for a man and woman. Has she explained the wonders of procreation? Told you the things a young woman should know before . . . before she becomes a wife?"

Rachel's eyes widened and she felt her cheeks grow hot. "You . . . I . . . " she said, flustered, suddenly realizing that the midwife thought she'd come for a discussion on the birds and bees. "I . . . I didn't come for personal reasons."

Salome Plank wasn't the least offended. She smiled and patted Rachel's hand. "Ah. Well, naturally, I assumed . . . many young brides-to-be are more comfortable talking with me than with their mothers or sisters. Of course, the girls today have access to the clinic and books which . . . Never mind." She smoothed her apron with both hands. "If not for your intimate life, then what? Salves? Creams? Tinctures?" The midwife's sharp eyes inspected Rachel's hair. "You're clearly not in need of a medicated rinse to rid you of lice or mites." The intense gaze dropped to Rachel's face. "And you have a lovely complexion, so it isn't a cure for breakouts. . . ."

"It's not me," Rachel protested weakly. "I'm here to talk about a patient of yours. Mary Rose Fisher? I believe you cared for her during her pregnancy and delivery."

Salome nodded. "I did. That's no secret. She is a natural. Her labor went on for several days, but she faced it bravely, and she is blessed with a beautiful infant, healthy and strong."

"It's not the baby I need to know about," Rachel continued. "It's Mary Rose. I'm sure you know this; I know how our community talks." She shook her head, still flustered. "I'm attempting to help her brother Moses. He's confessed to shooting Mary Rose's husband, but I don't believe he's telling the truth. I've been talking to a lot of people trying to get to what really happened."

The dog rose and came to lie beside Salome on the colorful rag rug, resting a hairy canine chin on her shoe. Absently, the midwife leaned down to pat the dog on the head. "I don't know anything about Daniel's death, Rachel," she said. "I was sitting with Cyrus Verkler all that day and night. He hasn't long for this world, poor man. His heart has long worn out. Only his spirit keeps him alive. He hates to leave his wife. She's not in the best of health, either, but fortunately, she has her daughters to lean on."

"What I was wondering was if . . . you treat people for more than childbirth, right?"

"I'm not a licensed medical professional," Salome said as if she had memorized the statement. "I use nothing but the old remedies that have come down to us for generations. Common sense, my girl. Garden herbs, honey, willow bark, witch hazel, aloe, and ginseng. You'd be surprised how many ailments can be eased with patience and ginseng tea or salve. I'm no doctor and I don't deal in love potions or hexes. I do no more than pass on the wisdom I learned at the knee of my mother."

"But . . . what about injuries?" Rachel pressed. "Didn't you set a broken arm for my Uncle Aaron when he was a boy? He speaks of it often. Says you gave him a maple sugar sweet to take away the pain of moving the bone into place. Surely you must have taken care of more serious injuries. Sewn up cuts? Cleaned infections?"

"Little of that now. Most folks are away to the clinic and rightly so. But when your uncle was a lad, there were few doctors of any worth within driving distance and none of the cell phones that the young take for granted. A mother comes to me with a weeping child with a twisted arm, what was I to do but try to help as best I could? They'd send me to jail for that today, I suppose. Even my catching of babies is frowned upon by the Englishers, although I suspect that I've brought more into the world than most of those fancy hospital doctors. And few mothers have I ever lost. Some babes, I'll admit, but that is always in God's hands. Fifty years and two I've been helping mothers. I'd have to be a fool not to have learned a thing or two about my craft."

Rachel shook her head. "You misunderstand. I'm not here to judge you. And I don't doubt that you know more about delivering healthy babies and helping mothers than I could imagine, but it's Mary Rose in particular I need to ask about. Have you ever treated her for an injury?"

"An injury?" Salome rose and went to the kettle. She stirred the contents with the spoon and pushed the swinging iron arm back over the fire. "I'm not sure I'm comfortable with your questions. My patients don't expect that I will gossip over their conditions. A midwife . . . even a granny woman, must keep personal things private."

Rachel answered the first question, ignoring the rest. "I'm asking about bruises, broken bones, lacerations . . . anything that would cause you to suspect someone hurt her."

Salome concentrated on the fire, stooping to add another log and adjusting the iron arm so that the kettle was not suspended over the hottest section.

"Please," Rachel said. "This is important. Did you treat Mary Rose Fisher for any injury that might have come from an altercation with someone? With her husband?"

"Now you are prying into matters that belong between husband and wife," Salome answered tartly. "I'm not saying I ever saw such a thing. I'm not saying I didn't. What woman would come to me if she thought that her private matters such as that were to be talked about by someone she trusted? You ask too much, Rachel. Why would you ask me such a thing?"

"I told you," she replied earnestly. "I'm trying to find out who had reason to kill Daniel. If he was abusive to Mary Rose, then . . ."

Salome turned to Rachel. "You're suspecting her of shooting her husband? That sweet child who never exchanged a cross word with anyone? You need to look further and rethink your questions. I believe you have good intentions, but Daniel is dead. What he may have done or may not have done on this earth is out of our hands. It is God alone who will judge him now and either reward him or cast him down into the pit."

Rachel stood up. "I didn't mean to offend you, Salome. I only came to you out of desperation. I need to find Daniel's killer, and I need to find him or her soon before a judge sentences Moses to prison for the rest of his life for a crime he didn't commit. If you know anything that will help, please reconsider and tell me."

"Maybe you're talking to the wrong person." She hesitated. "I hear talk. Maybe you should ask Mary Rose's neighbor Rosh who he thinks shot Daniel."

Rachel frowned. "You suspect Rosh may be involved in Daniel's death?"

"I suspect no one, but . . ." The old woman lowered her voice. "I did hear someone say that Rosh's mother feared for her son's life."

"From who? Who was Rosh afraid of?"

"I cannot tell you whether the story is true or false, but it was repeated in my hearing—not to me directly, you understand. You should probably talk to the man with the fences and the dogs. I overheard this person say that the crazy English er who lives on the mountain caught Rosh digging ginseng and threatened to nail his ear to a tree and leave him for the black bears if he ever caught him trespassing on his property again." The midwife pursed her lips and frowned. "Who would say such a terrible thing to a boy only trying to make a living in hard times? A man so heartless might be cruel enough to take the life of a neighbor he didn't like."

The woman went to the outer door and opened it. Clearly, the interview was at an end. "You must come again whenever you are in the neighborhood or when you are in need. You are a dear girl with a loving heart. But ask me no more questions about my patients, for I have no more to tell you."

That night, in her bedroom, Rachel stood beside her whiteboard with a red marker in her hand. "I just feel as though we're going in circles," she said to Mary Aaron. "And we're getting nowhere."

Mary Aaron sat cross-legged on the bed. She was wearing blue jeans and a tie-dye tee. Her feet were bare, and Rachel noticed that her cousin's toenails were painted a pale pink, a color that looked identical to the new nail polish that Rachel purchased at the boutique next to the wedding shop when she'd gone for her last fitting.

"Don't look at me," Mary Aaron said. "I've talked to my brothers and your brothers and half the men in the valley. Most of them were hunting that day, but no one knows of anyone hunting near Daniel. I got the same story Joe gave you about how he and Moses were supposed to hunt with Daniel, but then went on their way. Of course everyone had heard it from Joe."

"Did you ask your father?"

Mary Aaron nodded. "I spent the afternoon helping cook at *Mam*'s and he came in for the noon meal. He had heard that a couple of men walked up to have a look after Daniel was found, but they were all hunting a ways away. The conversation got a little uncomfortable after that. He told me I'd been *rumspringa* long enough and it was time I took my baptism classes and married Timothy or someone else he approved of."

"Does your mother agree with him?"

Mary Aaron nodded again. "If anything, she's worse than he is." She sighed. "It was not a good day, lots of arguing. Sometimes I wish . . ." She trailed off.

"It's hard, I know." Rachel sighed. "It was awful for me, trying to decide. Stay or go."

"I love my mother and father, and home is home. I love it in the kitchen when *Mam* and my sisters are there, but right now, it's easier when I stay away."

Rachel rolled the marker between her fingers. "Aunt Hannah blames me, doesn't she? She probably thinks I'm a bad influence on you. Tempting you into the world's false vanities."

Her cousin rolled her eyes. "Actually, that sounds more like *Dat*. It's depressing. Everyone keeps telling me to make up my mind, and the more they try to force me, the less I'm sure of what I want."

Rachel came over to the bed. "What about Timothy? He's already baptized. If you leave the Amish faith, you can't be married. Do you care for him?"

"Of course I do, but I'm not sure it's what you feel for Evan. Does that make sense?" She shrugged. "Timothy is such a good person. But, in spite of his goofing around, he's devout. You're right. There's no way he would ever leave the faith. His mother is trying to convince him to court one of the Miller twins."

Rachel sat on the edge of the bed and rubbed Bishop's head. The big Siamese closed his eyes and began to purr loudly. "How do you feel about that? Would you be hurt if he did start courting someone else?"

Mary Aaron worried at the corner of a thumbnail. "That's the thing. I'm not sure how I feel about that. I want Timothy to be happy, and the Miller twins are both sweet. Either of them would make a good wife for him. You know them,

Emma and Annie. They live right next door to Timothy's parents, and the two families have always been friendly. It would be a good match."

"For you as a way of getting away from him, or for one of the twins?"

Mary Aaron grimaced. "I thought we came up here to try and figure out who killed Daniel Fisher, not dissect my private life."

"Sorry. But I worry about you," Rachel said, patting her cousin. "You know I just want you to be happy. I'll support you, no matter what you choose."

Mary Aaron exhaled. "I know that. I'm just . . ." She shrugged again. "Let's not talk about this anymore tonight."

Rachel opened her mouth to speak again, but Mary Aaron whispered, "Please?"

With a quick smile, Rachel returned to the whiteboard. "So, no information from any hunters, except Joe and Lemuel and Rosh. Can you think of anything we haven't looked at? Anyone who would have a reason to kill Daniel?" She erased the column that said *Hunters* and replaced it with *Persons of Interest*. Without further comment, she listed *Moses, Mary Rose, Rosh,* and *Charles Baker.*

"Why Mary Rose?" Mary Aaron knitted her brows. "She'd have the most to lose, wouldn't she?"

"I don't really think she's a suspect, but I'm getting desperate here. If Moses didn't do it, *someone* did."

"And Rosh?"

"I think he has a serious crush on Mary Rose. He watches her all the time. That's how he knew the police were there that day that they arrested Moses. Who knows what he thought? He's a strange kid." She shrugged. "Maybe he thought if Daniel was out of the way, he could marry her."

"Sounds far-fetched."

"You think I should take his name off the board?" Rachel picked up the black felt eraser.

"No, leave him there. We know from the past that nothing is as far-fetched as the truth." Mary Aaron, still seated on the bed, nodded at the board. "And the Englisher? You said he was nice. You still think he might have shot Daniel?"

Rachel stared at the board. "Truthfully? No. It's beginning to look more and more as though Moses really did do it. But why? An accidental shooting is one thing. But Evan said he was shot twice, consecutive shots. Why shoot Daniel a second time? That doesn't fit with Moses's personality. I just can't see him committing a violent act like that. The whole confession is just so . . . dramatic . . . like something you'd see in a movie. What if he's trying to protect his sister?" She pointed to Mary Rose's name.

"If what you suspect is true," Mary Aaron pointed out, "that Daniel may have been beating her, that's motive."

Rachel set the eraser back on the table. "I don't want that to be the answer. Maybe it's easier to think that Chuck could have killed him. He was a soldier. And we know he's taken human lives before. That would make solving this easier, don't you think?"

"Do you want easy or do you want to find out what really happened? Maybe you should add Lemuel to that list. Joe said that Daniel hurt him that day. Maybe he was angry and confronted Daniel. Maybe—"

Rachel shook her head. "Lemuel is hardly more than a child."

Mary Aaron sighed. "So we're back where we started. We don't really have anything, either to help Moses or to hurt him."

"I don't know; I might be onto something with the idea that Daniel was abusive. I had the feeling that Salome knew more than she was willing to tell me."

Mary Aaron retrieved Bishop's favorite cat toy from the bed and tossed it in front of the cat. The big Siamese yawned and stretched out his front paws, disdaining to chase the feathered mouse. "You got the message I left for you on the bulletin board by the computer, didn't you? Bella said you were supposed to come down and make your final choices for flowers for the wedding, but you didn't come in."

Rachel grimaced and pressed the heel of her hand to her forehead. "That was when I was at the midwife's place. I completely forgot my appointment with Bella. It would be a lot simpler if this were an Amish wedding. Why do they make it so complicated? I just want to get married."

"Simple?" Mary Aaron chuckled. "Your mother would invite two hundred of her closest friends and relatives and we'd be making bushels of creamed celery."

Rachel's smile was wry. "We'll probably have close to that many guests. And, thankfully, *Mam* and your mother are in charge of the food. That's another thing. Evan's mother expects canapés and she's still complaining that there will be no champagne. She wanted us to have one of those multitiered cakes with a little bride and groom on the top. I tried to explain to her that we have a table full of cakes baked by our guests, but she doesn't get it."

"Will you have to have Thanksgiving dinner with her tomorrow?"

Rachel nodded. "We're taking her out to a restaurant. Apparently, it's a family tradition. It's been the two of them since his father died, and she's not much of a cook."

"A restaurant?" Mary Aaron looked dubious. "Will they have turkey?"

"Of course. With all the trimmings."

"But it will be a store-bought turkey, not one his mother raised and cooked."

Rachel laughed. "I cannot picture my future mother-in-law ever plucking and cooking a turkey. Next year, I'll do the cooking, and I'm sure Ada will find me one raised by one of her daughters or granddaughters." She crossed to the small refrigerator. "Hungry? I've got sandwiches and a big salad."

"Mmm, sounds good."

"Is your family fasting again on Thanksgiving?" Rachel asked. Her own parents and most of the Old Order Amish she knew would spend the day in quiet prayer. There wouldn't be worship services, but instead of roast turkey and all the side dishes there would be bread and cheese and some simple fruit such as apples. Thanksgiving was not to be a day of celebrating but one of contemplation, Bible reading, and personal communion with God.

"*Ya*," Mary Aaron replied. "I told *Mam* that I'd be there, so long as you don't need me here at Stone Mill House."

"You go. We have only two rooms occupied, and I've invited Mrs. Morris to join us for dinner. The Wiggens family is going to a friend's house in Belleville. I'm not sure if Mrs. Morris will feel up to it, but if she does come, Evan's mother will be on her best behavior and the afternoon will go a lot smoother."

"I hope she's easier after you and Evan are married," Mary Aaron said as she unwrapped a roast beef sandwich. "This smells delicious."

"I put that spicy mustard on it that you like," Rachel said. "I think she will be. She has been a really good mother to Evan. I think she's just afraid that she'll be alone after we're married . . . that he won't be there for her. I told her that will never happen. We may have to rub off a few burrs on both of us, but we'll adjust. I'd never treat his mother with less respect than my own."

"I know you wouldn't." Mary Aaron paused between bites of her sandwich. "I just can't imagine spending Thanksgiving in a restaurant eating turkey raised in some tiny cage. Will you and Evan and his mother spend time in prayer?"

Rachel considered how to answer. "Just grace. No extended time of prayer." She picked at the crust of her sandwich. "If you become English, you can still be strong in your faith in God, but in the world God becomes a smaller part of your life. Most English people don't think of Him first as the Amish do."

"I wouldn't be like that," Mary Aaron said thoughtfully. "I couldn't be. If I become an Englisher, my faith will still come first." She looked up at Rachel, her pretty face earnest. "That's possible, isn't it? To live a godly life and also drive a car?"

Chapter 13

"Of course it's possible. It's something I've had to struggle with," Rachel admitted. "I haven't always been successful, but I keep trying."

"And Evan, does he feel the same way?" Mary Aaron's face was earnest. "Will your home be centered around God?"

"I hope so. But living as an Englisher is harder in some ways than living Amish. Nothing is as simple as it was when I lived at home. The bishop and the elders told us how to live and we did it as best we could. I don't think we worried as much about staying on the right path because it was laid out for us."

Mary Aaron winced. "It sounds complicated."

"It is. My mother told me that the *ordnung* isn't a rope to bind us but a cradle to rock us. Does that make sense to you?"

"*Ya,* it does. Sometimes I get impatient with the rules. They seem silly, like the straight pins instead of buttons and that it's all right to ride in a car but you can't own one. But when you get down to it, I can see that buttons are a symbol of something bad in the past."

"Soldiers who came to kill and imprison us for our faith," Rachel said.

"Exactly. So, by not using buttons today, we remember those who died rather than deny God's message. And not having an automobile keeps you closer to family and neighbors." Mary Aaron smiled. "I'm glad I can talk about it with you. Timothy doesn't understand. He just accepts the *ordnung.*"

"But he still sneaks out to see movies and I know he has a cell phone," Rachel teased.

"*Ne,* actually he doesn't. He gave up both. Next thing you know, he'll be wearing a hat with a wider brim to tell everyone how conservative he is."

"You think he's showing off?"

Mary Aaron shook her head. "*Ne,* it's just his newfound enthusiasm for the sermons the young preacher gives. Not so much God smiting this one and that and more New Testament and the teachings of Jesus. *Mam* says give Timothy time and he'll find his balance. He was a good person before he got so religious and he'll be a good person after. But she does warn me not to wait too long or I might lose him. She says half the mothers in the valley will be pointing him out to their eligible daughters, and she might be right."

"She might be. But don't use that reason to marry. Marry him only if you love him and you know you want to live out your life as he does."

The two finished their sandwiches in silence and then Rachel returned to the whiteboard. She circled the words *Persons of Interest.* "I think we need to add Lemuel here as well."

"Lemuel? Really?"

Rachel stared at the board. "According to Joe Troyer, he and Moses went off together after the fight in the woods between Joe and Daniel. Joe didn't hunt with him, though. He didn't hunt with Moses or Lemuel."

"You think Lemuel did it and Moses covered for him? Or they both did it together?"

"I don't know. But something was going on in that household."

"Something bad enough for a fourteen-year-old to kill his brother-in-law?" Mary Aaron asked, her eyes round with surprise.

"My gut tells me that isn't what happened." Rachel sighed. "He's just a kid, but . . ."

"Put him on the list. One of us can talk to him. See if he was with Moses. Maybe you can ask Moses."

"I don't know if I can get in to see him in prison again until he's allowed to have regular visitors." Rachel added Lemuel's name on the board under *Persons of Interest.* "Evan had to call in a favor to get me in the first time."

"How about Joe? He didn't seem too fond of Daniel, either," Mary Aaron suggested. "Maybe he was angry or even embarrassed by what happened that morning. He told you himself he was alone after that. Maybe he came back around and shot Daniel out of that tree stand."

"Sounds a little far-fetched. Remember, we're talking about the Amish here."

"All these scenarios are far-fetched," Mary Aaron pointed out. "Add him to the list."

Rachel wrote in Joe beneath Rosh and Lemuel, then turned to her cousin. "I need to talk to Salome again."

"The midwife?" Mary Aaron looked perplexed. "I thought she wouldn't say anything about Daniel."

"It wasn't what she said. It was what she *didn't* say. She got upset and asked me to leave after I brought it up. She knows something that she's not telling. And my guess is that it has to do with how Daniel treated Mary Rose."

"Which would mean what? Mary Rose might have killed him?"

"No . . . maybe. I don't know," Rachel said. "She could have, I suppose. But it doesn't seem in her nature."

"Which brings us back to the idea that someone close to her, someone who loved her and saw her being mistreated, may have decided to do something about it. Someone like her brother."

"A brother or a friend."

"You mean Rosh."

Rachel stood back and stared at the names on the board. "I'm not ready to accuse anyone. I'm just trying to look at the big picture. Who would want Daniel dead and why?"

"So, you do suspect Rosh?"

"He's always hanging around the Studer farm. And he's known Mary Rose all his life. My mother said he had a crush on Mary Rose and Alma said pretty much the same thing." She lifted her shoulders and let them fall. "Maybe he wanted to protect her from Daniel?"

"Or maybe he wanted to get rid of Daniel so he'd have a chance with Mary Rose?"

"Right," Rachel agreed. "I told you I saw him get out of Mary Rose's buggy Sunday morning."

Mary Aaron got up off the bed. "Everyone I know thinks Rosh is harmless. Sweet and a little odd, but a boy with a good heart. Even I think he's a good kid. I hate to say it, Rae-Rae, but Moses is still the one who looks the guiltiest. And I know you're tired of people saying this, but he *did* say he did it."

Rachel turned to her. "I'm not ready to accept that. Are you sure you can't think of anything we've missed?"

"Not really," Mary Aaron said. She sliced a section of apple Rachel had put out on the table and dipped it in her mother's special caramel sauce. "What's happening with the lawyer? Have you talked to her since she agreed to represent Moses?"

"Tried to. Got nowhere. She took my phone call, but told me in no uncertain terms that anything that passed between her and her client was strictly confidential. She said she appreciated my interest in the boy's case, but that she couldn't tell me anything other than that she asked for and got the hearing delayed. She's hoping that a little time in prison will make Moses reconsider."

"If he does," Mary Aaron said, "if he admits he lied, will they let him go?"

"I doubt it. Not unless they get another confession. Unfortunately, the justice system isn't open to recanting. I've been reading up on the subject on the Internet. Apparently, a large percentage of those imprisoned for a crime but later released because of DNA evidence were jailed on false confessions."

"I'd never confess to anything I didn't do." Her cousin munched on her apple.

"Neither would I, but a lot of people do. I have to believe that Moses is one of them. The lawyer did say that she didn't think it would be helpful for me to visit him again. If I say the wrong thing to Moses, she thinks I might do more harm than good."

"Which means you can't ask him if Lemuel hunted with him all day."

"No. But I can go back and talk to Lemuel again. Maybe he'll feel a little less intimidated by me and I can find out if he was with Moses."

Mary Aaron passed Rachel a slice of apple. "This all seems so crazy. Do you really think Moses is innocent and knows who killed Daniel and is trying to protect them?"

"It's the only thing that makes sense with this case." Rachel set down the marker. "I want to go back and talk to Chuck Baker again, too. I didn't ask him if he saw anything in the woods that day. Maybe I'll do that first thing in the morning."

"I'll go with you," Mary Aaron volunteered. "I don't like the idea of you up there in the woods with him by yourself."

"I thought you promised your parents you'd be there with them for Thanksgiving."

"I will be. Right after we talk to the crazy English prepper, you can drop me off at the farm. Then you can meet Evan and his mother for your delicious Thanksgiving feast." Mary

Aaron wrinkled her nose. "I think I'd rather be eating bread and butter and praying with the family than going out to a restaurant. Who does that on Thanksgiving?"

"Apparently, I do." Rachel smiled sheepishly and then they both laughed.

"Chuck, it's Rachel. Rachel Mast. Could you let us in?" Rachel said into the intercom at the main gate. She and Mary Aaron had done the over-the-river-and-through-the-woods thing to get around his first defense of barbed wire. "I need to talk to you again. I've brought my cousin with me, and I have a sweet potato pie for you. We won't take up much of your time, I promise."

She glanced back at the Jeep, where Mary Aaron waited. Her cousin was properly dressed in full Amish attire, complete with white *kapp,* for an afternoon of prayer and Bible reading with her family. Rachel was in jeans, hiking boots, a sweatshirt, and her barn coat. There was no way she was going up on the mountain in her dress clothes. She'd have to make certain that she left enough time to dash back to the house and make herself presentable before Evan arrived to take her to the restaurant.

When there was no response from Chuck, Rachel repeated her request. She returned to the Jeep, got out of the cold, and waited. After ten minutes, she tried again. Still nothing. "I can't imagine why—" she started to say to Mary Aaron, but then she broke off abruptly as the prepper's voice sounded through the speaker.

"Go away, Rachel! I can't see you today. I'd rather not see anyone. It's . . . it was a bad night. Having a bad day. I'm sorry . . . really sorry."

"Chuck! What's wrong? Can I help in some way?" she asked.

"Yes, just go away and leave me alone. I can't be around people today. You. It isn't safe."

"Chuck, please. I promise it will just be a couple of minutes." In the background, she heard the whining and barking of the dog pack and then there was a click and everything went silent. "Chuck?" She waited again, but there was no further communication. Perplexed and disappointed, she went back to the Jeep. "He won't let me in. Said he'd had a bad night, whatever that means. But worse, he said it wasn't safe for me. What do you suppose—"

"No idea." Mary Aaron shook her head.

"So, we just give up and leave?"

"What else can we do?" Her cousin grimaced. "I'm not dressed for mountain climbing, and no way am I letting you try to force your way in there. If the man says it's not safe, you take his word on it."

Rachel started the engine and turned the Jeep around. "He didn't say who or what I'd be in danger from."

"Maybe it's for the best that he wouldn't let you in," Mary Aaron said, glancing over her shoulder at the forbidding gate. "Chuck Baker is one of your suspects."

"Persons of interest," Rachel corrected.

"*Whatever.*" Mary Aaron turned toward Rachel. "If there's the slightest possibility that he's a killer, does it make sense that you—that we go up there? I know you want to prove that Moses is innocent of Daniel's murder, but it can't be at the risk of your own life."

"Chuck wouldn't hurt me. He might have killed Daniel, but I know I'm safe with him."

"You know that?" Mary Aaron frowned. "How do you know?"

"It's just a feeling. He likes me."

Mary Aaron threw up her hands. "Okay, so maybe he won't kill you. Instead, he'll tie you up and hide you in a cave. Rachel, if the man isn't right in the head, you don't know what he'll do."

"Chuck has his problems and he might be capable of doing physical violence to someone, but not to me. Somewhere

PLAIN CONFESSION   179

under that scary shell is a gentle soul who is desperately trying
to find peace."

"So maybe you should pray for him."

Rachel sighed. "I have."

"I will, too. In the meantime, what are you going to do
with the pie?" She pointed to the backseat.

Rachel smiled. "I'll leave it for Mary Rose and her family.
After what I went through to sneak it out of Ada's pantry,
I'm not going to try and put it back."

"She'll never know. She made at least a dozen pies for the
B&B. Chocolate, peach, apple, pumpkin, and sweet potato.
What's she going to do? Count them? Ada's gone for the day
with her family. She won't know whether your guests ate it
or you did."

"She'll know," Rachel insisted glumly. "Ada knows everything."

"Why not give it to Evan's mother?"

"She wouldn't eat it. She once asked me if Ada's home
kitchen is inspected by the state. She has the idea that the
Amish are living back in the nineteenth century and don't
have her standards. Evan's mom likes her pies wrapped in
shrink-wrap and baked at a factory. She's always telling sto-
ries about an Amish girl they hired to help in the kitchen who
brought them homemade butter that tasted sour and eggs
that hadn't been properly washed."

"Ew. *Mam* wouldn't stand for us bringing in eggs from the
chicken house without washing them before we put them in
the egg cartons."

"My mother, either," Rachel agreed. "It's going to be interesting, having her for a mother-in-law."

Mary Aaron laughed. "Just take her out to Aunt Esther's
kitchen. You could eat off her floors. She'll soon set her
straight."

"Maybe I will," Rachel said. "But in any case, she's not
getting this sweet potato pie and neither is Chuck Baker."

A short time later Mary Aaron instructed Rachel to let her out at the end of her father's lane. "No sense in taking the chance that *Dat* will see you in those jeans. Especially on Thanksgiving Day. He wouldn't be pleased."

"No, he wouldn't," Rachel agreed.

They'd stopped at the Studer place to leave the pie, and Alma had kept them talking longer than she'd wanted. Alma had been upset, her eyes red and swollen from weeping. The older woman looked as if she hadn't slept at all. As Rachel and Mary Aaron drove out of the driveway, the midwife was just approaching in her open two-wheel cart. Either Salome was coming to spend the day of prayer and fasting with the family or she was coming to see a patient. Rachel couldn't help wondering which it was.

As Mary Aaron walked away from the Jeep at her parents' house, Rachel pulled her phone out of her pocket and checked the time. She grimaced, seeing that it was later than she'd thought. She'd have to hurry if she was going to be ready.

She was a mile from the house when she blew the right front tire. It wasn't a total disaster because she had a good spare and she knew how to change a tire. But it did delay her enough so that when she pulled into her drive, Evan was there waiting.

Rachel inhaled sharply. "Sorry," she said as he opened her driver's side door. "I had a flat."

He was in his best suit. Sometime since she'd seen him last, he'd gotten a haircut, and his shoes were shined so that she could see her reflection in them. "I told Mom that we'd pick her up in thirty minutes." His expression was grim.

"I'm sorry," she said.

"Mrs. Morris joining us?"

"No." Rachel pressed her lips together. "Evan, I'm sorry. The time just got away from me."

"Do whatever you have to do and do it as quickly as you can. You know how she hates to be kept waiting."

And so did he. Rachel swallowed. She felt terrible. If only

she hadn't driven over that nail, she would have been home safe. She'd perfected the art of dressing in a hurry years ago. She'd twist up her hair and add just a hint of lipstick. "I'll be down in ten minutes," she promised.

He sighed. "Rachel, you knew this was important to me," he said. "And to Mom. What was so imperative that you had to leave the house instead of getting ready?"

At this point, she didn't want to get into a discussion about Moses. "Grab a bottle of water or a cup of coffee," she told him. "I won't be long."

"I'll wait in the car."

She kissed him on the cheek. "Let's not argue," she said. "It's my fault. I'm running late, and I take the responsibility. Can you just let it go at that?"

He glanced away, then back at her. "It's just . . ." His mouth tightened. "I think I should come first once in a while. Just once in a while, Rachel. And I can't help thinking . . ."

"Thinking what?"

"That you're having second thoughts about marrying me."

"We talked about this." She grasped his hand, looking up at him. "No, Evan. I'm not having second thoughts. I can't wait for our wedding. I want to marry you."

"Then why . . ." He pulled away from her. "Just do whatever you do to make yourself beautiful. I'll call Mom and tell her that we'll be there soon."

"I'll make it up to you," she said. "And to her. But let's put this aside. I don't want to argue with you, today of all days."

"Me, either," he said gruffly. "So get a move on."

"Yes, sir, Officer," she said teasingly. But Evan didn't laugh, and Rachel groaned inwardly. It was going to be a long day and she had no one to blame but herself.

"Yes, I had a nice Thanksgiving. How about you, Bella? With your family?" Rachel leaned her pitchfork against the wall of her garage/goat barn and spoke into her phone. It was Friday evening, and she was late getting the animals fed and cared for. It had been one thing after another all day, and she'd never gotten around to calling the florist back. And now Bella had caught up with her. Sometimes Rachel wished she didn't have a phone, at least not a cell phone. Her mother's life was so much more peaceful without one.

"Yes, Bella," Rachel said. "The wedding is still on and we still want the flowers. No, I understand. I'm not particular. Whatever you think best. Nothing over-the-top. No, no orchids. I'm not really even a roses girl. Can't you get something simple from your supplier? Daisies maybe?" She sighed, listening to Bella chew her out. Rachel knew she was at fault here, but she really wasn't in the mood to be called on the carpet.

"I know, and I apologize. Everything has been hectic. I know I promised to come in, but really, I trust your judgment. Just a nice bride's bouquet, flowers for the church, and a few arrangements for the house. I'm not having attendants."

Rachel paused. Listened. "Yes, his mother will want a corsage. My mother will be there, but she wouldn't want one."

Bella's voice buzzed in her ear. "Yes, I'm absolutely certain. You can send her a bouquet to her house on the Monday after the wedding, but nothing at the wedding."

Rachel tucked the phone under her chin and used both hands to toss in a fresh block of hay. The goats crowded around, bleating and shouldering one another, trying to snatch choice pieces of the hay. She leaned against the stall rails and smiled at the goats' antics. One had gotten down on her knees and was crawling in underneath her mother, while a young kid reared up on his hind legs and bleated pitifully.

Bella went on for another minute, and then Rachel said sweetly, "Talk to you soon. I'm sure the flowers will be beautiful. Good night." She ended the call and slipped the phone into her coat pocket with a sigh of relief.

It rang immediately, and this time Rachel didn't hesitate. It was Evan. "Hey, you," she said warmly.

"Hey yourself. What are you up to?"

"Feeding the goats. Hay." She laughed at her own silly joke and he chuckled. "You?" she asked.

"Highway patrol."

"You're calling your girlfriend while you're on duty?"

"No, I'm not. I'm on my officially approved break. Stopped at the Starlight Diner for a quick burger."

"With cheese, I suppose. And fries."

"You know me too well," he admitted.

"I wouldn't think you could eat anything after all you ate at the restaurant yesterday."

"I hope it wasn't too bad for you," he said. "Mom can be overbearing at times. But she'll love you. I promise."

"No," Rachel said. "It was half as bad as I was afraid it was going to be."

"I couldn't leave her alone on Thanksgiving."

"Of course you couldn't. But next year, I'm cooking. She's invited to our house."

"You're cooking or Ada's cooking?"

Rachel smiled. "Maybe a little of both?"

They were both quiet for a moment, but it wasn't a bad quiet. It was the comfortable kind that two people who love each other can share.

"I called because . . . Rachel, I just wanted to say I'm sorry for being a jerk yesterday."

"You weren't a jerk. I was late, and I'm late a lot. It was my fault."

"And you said you were sorry. I should have accepted your apology and moved on, but I didn't. I need to get better about that."

"We both have a lot of adjusting to do."

"Yeah, I suppose we do. Friends?"

"You bet."

"Good. Got to go now," he said. "Time to put on my cape and defend the world against the forces of evil."

"Be safe out there," she murmured, suddenly serious. "I love you."

"And I love you. More than you'll ever know."

A few more sweet words, and they ended the call. "God keep him safe," she prayed under her breath.

The bleating goats dragged her back into the moment.

Rachel laughed. "You'd think you didn't get fed twice a day," she said. "You are so spoiled." But she broke off another section of hay bale and tossed that into the stall.

As she reached for another, she heard the squeak of the door hinges and felt a gust of cold wind on the back of her neck. She turned to see the outline of a man in black, looming in the shadows. Then, he twisted, pulling the door shut, and slammed the wooden bar into place.

Rachel let out a small gasp as the ghostly figure stepped into the light, revealing a craggy, bearded face camouflaged with streaks of black paint.

It was Chuck Baker.

Chapter 14

Rachel stared at the hulk of a man, her thoughts racing. Her mouth went dry as prickles of fear raised goose bumps across the nape of her neck. "Charles?" She sounded breathless and frightened. She didn't want to sound like that . . . to sound so helpless. *Think*, she told herself. She took a step backward, and her gaze darted toward the pitchfork leaning against the wall.

The prepper's expression sagged from fierce to sorrowful and he drew back. "Rachel, what's wrong? Are you scared of me? You aren't scared of me, are you?"

She caught her breath. "You . . . you startled me," she said. Not just his sudden appearance but the fact that he'd barred the door. Why had he barred the door if he didn't mean her any harm?

"You needn't be afraid of me," he said. "I'd never hurt you. I'd never hurt anyone. At least . . . I hope I wouldn't." He looked down and then up again.

"Okay," she said, still a little uneasy. "Why did you bar the door?"

He looked at her quizzically, then hitched his thumb in the direction of the door. "Because it's windy out?"

She almost laughed out loud when she realized how silly her response to him had been. "I'm sorry. You just startled me," she repeated.

"I came to apologize for yesterday . . . for turning you away yesterday."

Rachel shook her head. "Don't worry about it."

"I mean it, Rachel," he said. "You're the last person I'd ever hurt. You've been so kind to me. I was hoping . . . I was thinking maybe we could be . . . friends. It's been a long time since I've had a friend."

Relief washed over her, and her knees felt suddenly weak. She glanced at the bale of hay, wondering if what was left of it would hold her or she'd end up looking like a total fool by sliding onto the concrete floor.

Chuck took another step forward and touched the smudge of camouflage on his cheek. "I don't like people to see me at night," he said. "So, I guess I am a little crazy. That place where they sent me would make anyone crazy. Four tours, four too many. You can't trust anyone, you know. An interpreter we had, someone we'd eaten with and laughed with and slept beside, he shot two of the guys in my patrol. Shot them in the back. Killed them without blinking an eye. And I've seen cute little kids rigged with suicide vests. I shouldn't be telling you this stuff, but I can't get it out of my mind. Still, it's wrong to talk about it. No need to keep you awake nights."

Rachel remembered with a rush of compassion that he'd said he'd had a bad night. "Do you have nightmares?" she asked him. "Maybe you should talk about it. Have you considered—"

"Seeing a shrink?" He gave a grunt of disdain. "Saw my share of them in recovery. They think they've got it all figured out, but they don't. It makes no sense. We kill them. They kill us. You can't tell friends from enemies, and friends today may be enemies tomorrow." He paused. "Not you, I mean."

"It must have been terrible for you," she said, taking a

step toward him. "But I was thinking about God. I find comfort in prayer."

He scowled. "I've tried praying. My mother raised me to believe, but . . . it's hard, you know. You keep wondering if there is a God, how can He allow such pain? The psychiatrists say I'm depressed. That I've got brain damage and PTSD. Maybe I do, but who wouldn't? There aren't any rules over there. There should be rules. Good guys, bad guys, civilians. Little kids shouldn't be sent out to blow up people, and they should be able to sleep in their beds without bombs dropping on them. Don't you think?"

Rachel nodded.

"I was afraid to let you in yesterday. Sometimes I get worrying about nuclear war, about the end of what we have in this country. I'm better off alone then. I jump at shadows, you know. And Patton, my raccoon, didn't come home. I thought . . ." He shook his head. "I don't know what I thought. One of the dogs tangled with a black bear. Not much of a contest. I had to bury him, and I was afraid that Patton might have . . ." Chuck slapped his forehead with the palm of an open hand. "A lot of steel up there, you know. I get headaches, but don't worry, I'm good tonight. I wouldn't have come if I didn't think I could hold it together."

"Is your raccoon all right? Did you find him?"

"Yeah. Patton's fine. Came trailing in early this morning looking like he'd had himself a good old time. Probably got himself a lady raccoon he—" Chuck's face reddened. "Pardon me. No call for such talk to a lady. I guess I do spend too much time alone. I forget my manners."

"Won't you come into the house? Have some coffee and a piece of pie? I've got at least three kinds of pie."

"No, thank you. I'm not much for making social calls. I feel easier on the mountain. I don't usually leave it except to take on supplies or pick up a pit bull that needs a place to call home." He glanced around as if to confirm that they were alone. "I felt bad about turning you away yesterday, real bad. You must have come back for a reason."

"Just a few more questions," Rachel said. "I had my cousin with me. Mary Aaron. You'd like her. She's Amish."

Chuck nodded. "You still think I might have been the one to kill Daniel, don't you?" The corners of his mouth twisted into a wry smile. "But that doesn't make any sense. If I'd wanted him dead, it wouldn't have taken two shots to do the job. I could have taken him out just as easily with a section of wire or my bare hands. I may be crazy, Rachel, but I'm not stupid. And I've got ears and cops talk. Two shots tells the police that it was murder. A quick blow to the back of the neck kills him just as fast and doesn't leave evidence." He thought for a moment. "And I'd have disposed of the body. Hard to convict for murder when there's no body."

Rachel shivered despite her coat. "That's supposed to make me feel better?"

He exhaled, sounding frustrated. "I'm telling you that I didn't do it. I wouldn't kill a man over a deer or over a piece of land. I've got enough blood on my hands."

Rachel inhaled softly. "Is it true that you caught Rosh Hertzler digging ginseng on your land and threatened to nail his ear to a tree and leave him for the bears?"

Chuck laughed, a deep, rumbling explosion of mirth. "I did. Do you know how rare ginseng is today? How much they sell it for? The state keeps making the season shorter and shorter to try and protect it, but Rosh doesn't always follow the rules. And he doesn't respect property lines. I've warned him to stay off my mountain. Do you know how long it takes a ginseng patch to get established? I didn't set the dogs on him. I didn't lay a finger on him, but I did try to scare the sh—scare the *dickens* out of him. And since he has two whole ears left, I don't appear to have done him much damage."

Rachel tried not to let her amusement show. "So, you didn't hurt him?"

"Ask him yourself. Boy plays loose with deer and trout season, but I've never known him to lie."

She met his gaze and held it. "Okay, Chuck, so tell me something. And this is what I really want to know because I think you might be one of those people who's a good judge of character. Who do *you* think killed Daniel Fisher?"

Chuck shrugged. "Can't say. I'd be less than truthful if I told you that I was sorry to be rid of him, but I'm not the murderer you're hunting for."

"You must have an opinion. You have strong opinions on most subjects."

He tugged at his beard thoughtfully. "I haven't given it much thought."

"If you have any thoughts on it, I'd appreciate it." She returned the pitchfork to the place where it belonged against the wall. "I'm trying to keep Daniel's brother-in-law from spending the rest of his life in prison. I don't believe he's the guilty one and neither does his family. Don't you have any ideas of who might have done the shooting? Any thoughts on who I should talk to?"

Chuck sighed. "All I can tell you is that, statistically, when something like this happens, it's rarely a stranger. Usually, you'll find that the killer is someone who knew the victim well. Maybe even the person who claimed to discover the body. I'd say you need to look closer to home."

Who did discover the body? She didn't know the answer to that. Rosh said it wasn't him, but what if he had proved Chuck wrong? What if he was a liar? "How do you know that?"

Chuck grinned. "I read a lot. Mostly mysteries." Then, he turned back to the door and raised the wooden bar. "I brought you something. A present. For your wedding."

She was genuinely touched. "You brought me a wedding gift?"

"Sort of a cross between an apology and a wedding gift." He opened the barn door. "I left it on your porch step."

"Thank you, Chuck," she said as she followed him out of the barn.

"I hope you like it." He closed the door. "You might think it's foolish. It was passed to me from my granny, but I've no use for it. If you don't want it, do with it what you please."

"I don't know what to say," Rachel admitted. Charles Baker might be a long way from normal, but she believed him when he said he didn't kill Daniel Fisher. Chuck's might be a wounded heart and mind, but she was convinced that they were good ones. "I hope that you will let me come back and visit you someday. I like the idea that maybe we could become friends. And I'd like you to meet the man I'm going to marry."

"Evan Parks? We've crossed paths already. He may not be aware of it, but I know him and I approve. You bring him up to the mountain. If it's a good day, I'll let you in."

Rachel looked around. There were no unfamiliar vehicles in the yard. "Did you come on foot?"

Chuck laughed. "No. My truck is parked not far from here. You take care of yourself, Rachel. Don't be too trusting. The world isn't as friendly as you think." He took a few steps into the darkness and then turned back. "And if the zombies come or the bad guys drop nukes on us, you and Evan come find me. I've got a shelter built into the heart of the mountain, protected by living rock. I've got an endless supply of fresh water and enough provisions to last us until Gabriel blows his horn. You and your husband . . . you're welcome to join me in my shelter. I can't promise how, but we'll survive."

Tears sprang into Rachel's eyes, her heart touched by his offer. She didn't believe in end-of-the-world scenarios, but she knew he did. Which made his offer all the sweeter. "Thank you." She walked to him and stood on her tiptoes to kiss him on the cheek. "I like you, too, Chuck Baker."

She stood there, then, and watched until his big form melted into the darkness. Not a twig snapped or a leaf rustled. She might have been watching a ghost vanish in the mist.

On the porch step, she found a ten-inch-high pine-needle basket, fashioned in the old Indian style and decorated with dyed porcupine quills. Carefully, she carried the beautiful object inside and placed it on the kitchen table. She lifted the lid and took out a length of soft buckskin. The wrapping contained an exquisite pair of Shawnee beaded and fringed moccasins small enough to fit a toddler. Rachel lifted the tiny shoes and sniffed the soft leather. They'd obviously been sewn with love and had never been worn.

Cradling the little moccasins in her hands, Rachel closed her eyes and whispered a silent prayer for the person who'd made them and for the man who'd given them to her. Tears clouded her vision. "No," she whispered. "No, you didn't kill Daniel."

Which led her to what Chuck had said. *"It's rarely a stranger. Look closer to home."*

Shortly after eleven the following day, Rachel parked her Jeep in the cobblestone drive behind George O'Day's early-nineteenth-century stone house. When it was built, the O'Day Mansion had been the home of a wealthy merchant. Furnished with period German and Pennsylvania Dutch antiques, the house had always slightly intimidated Rachel. The wide plank floors were cushioned with Turkish and Iranian carpets, and some of the doorknobs were silver. Shelves of first-edition books lined the walls, and a staff had always kept the rooms dusted and the chandeliers polished.

Now, unfortunately, the staff included around-the-clock nurses. Her friend George was fast approaching the final days of his life. Rachel went to the kitchen entrance, crossed the screened porch with its lovely wicker furniture, and knocked at the back door. When there was no answer, she turned the knob and stepped into the dark kitchen. Spacious and equipped with every modern convenience, a stone fireplace, and massive overhead beams, the space was everything that a cook could possibly want without losing the charm and patina of an historical house.

"Ell!" Rachel called. "George! It's Rachel!"

There was an explosion of high-pitched barking, the squeak of tiny claws on hardwood, and a small white bichon launched herself at Rachel. She bent over and the dog leaped into her arms and began to lick her face. "Yes, hello, Sophie," Rachel said. She deposited Sophie firmly on the floor and the little dog proceeded to spin in circles and hop on her hind legs.

"Rachel." Ell appeared in the doorway that led to the dining room.

"I hope you don't mind. I just let myself in," she said.

Ell smiled and hugged her. "You know there's an open-door policy for you here. George will be thrilled. It's been one of his good days."

"Is he in a lot of pain?" Rachel asked quietly.

Ell shrugged. "He's very brave. His nurse gave him his meds about a half an hour ago. She just left to pick up a new prescription."

Ell was all in black, as usual, but instead of a long black dress, she wore black jeans and a black sweater set. Her long crow-black hair was pulled back in a ponytail, and she'd limited herself to a single nose and eyebrow ring, both in silver. Each delicate ear boasted an array of tiny silver fishhooks and cobwebs, and her only nod to her customary Goth makeup was black eye shadow and liner.

Ell was George's niece by blood and his daughter of the

heart. She may have said that George was having a good day, but Rachel could read the truth in the anguished expression in the young woman's gaze.

"I haven't seen you in the bookstore lately," Rachel said.

Ell nodded. "I decided to take a few weeks off and be with him. We don't have much time, and . . ." She swallowed as her large, expressive eyes teared up. "I guess we were in denial. The doctors didn't think his remission would last as long as it did. We had a lot of good time together we hadn't expected. But it's still hard."

Rachel hugged her friend again. "At least he has you." As Ell stepped back, Rachel noticed the heavy antique ruby ring on her left hand. "Did I miss something?"

Ell's cheeks colored. "Yes. Will wouldn't take no for an answer and I finally said yes. George has given us his full approval and a prearranged honeymoon in Venice and Florence. I know that he was hoping he'd be here a few more years. He wanted to see Will and me settled and . . ."

"With a family of your own?" Rachel said. She knew Will Simpson, the town's new dentist, and liked him wholeheartedly. She couldn't have thought of a better match for Ell if she'd planned it herself.

"George has been trying to have us set a date for the wedding, but I . . ."

"You aren't ready yet." Rachel nodded. "I understand. Marriage is not anything to rush into."

"It's not. I want to be certain before I take my vows." She shrugged. "I mean, I know that Will is the right man. But is it wrong to just enjoy being engaged for a while?" She met Rachel's gaze. "You don't think I'm being selfish?"

"I think you're being sensible. If Will really loves you, he isn't going anywhere, and you're young yet. Marriage should be forever."

"That's what I think. You know Will was raised Mennonite." She smiled shyly. "We've been attending the reformed

Mennonite church in Belleville. That might be a good fit for us." Her eyes twinkled with mischief. "No one has even remarked on my black dresses."

"The important thing is whether you feel it's right for you." Rachel glanced into the dining room with its old Kirman carpet and the massive German furniture. "You set up a hospital bed for George downstairs?"

"Yes, in the big parlor. We made room by moving out the baby grand. You know George can't be far from his books. He's been hoping you'd stop by and wondering why you hadn't."

"I'm sorry." Rachel felt a wave of guilt that she hadn't been to see him in the last three weeks. "All of a sudden the wedding is almost here."

"A week from today." Ell clasped her hands.

"I've also been asking questions about the Fisher shooting."

"It's all anyone is talking about at the bookstore. You go on in to George. You know the way." Ell stepped back to let her pass. "I need to take Sophie out. She's not as young as she used to be and if you don't take her out . . ." She chuckled. "But I don't have to tell you. You've had her as a house guest."

Rachel moved through the dining room and wide center hall. She paused at the half-open parlor door. "George," she called softly. "Are you awake?"

"Awake? Of course I'm awake. Get in here, girl. I can't believe it took you this long."

Rachel took a deep breath and stepped into the grand parlor. It was much as she remembered it with the rows of leather-bound books, the marble fireplace, and silver candlesticks. The hospital bed dominated one corner of the room, complete with IV poles and a heart monitor. George was propped up into a semi-sitting position, a stack of books spilling across his lap and a laptop on the desk beside the bed.

"Get over here and give me a hug," George insisted.

"Love the hat," Rachel said. A knit seaman's cap covered

the scars on his bald head, but nothing could hide the ravages of the disease.

George, being George, was wearing colorful striped silk pajamas and a man's vintage silk smoking jacket in silvery gray. A small tube delivered oxygen to his nose, and an IV line ran directly into his left arm. He'd lost even more weight since she'd last been here, and the bones stood out on his face, wrists, and hands. Hugging him was like embracing a scarecrow.

"Not a pretty sight, am I?" he asked.

"Your color's good."

"Good for what? A ghost?" George laughed. "No need to pretend with me, my girl. I won't let Ell do it, and I'm not about to let you get away with it. I'm dying, plain and simple." He clasped her hand. "Now, that's out of the way. What can I do for you? How can I help? I know you're playing detective again." He patted the bed. "Here, sit here beside me. The nurse is out and I've given the staff the day off. Just me and Ell and Sophie."

"You know I've been praying for you," she said as she sat on the edge of the bed.

"You don't need to tell me that. And you know well enough that I need all the prayers I can get. But the Lord in His mercy gave me time with Ell, something I never thought to have. She'll do wonders with the bookstore and the other businesses, and she's found herself a capital young man. He'll keep those shiny teeth as white as snow." George chuckled at his own joke, coughed, and then brought a tissue to his mouth. "You know what I've done and you know I'll have to answer for it, but I still give thanks for His blessings. I've had far more happiness in these last years than I deserve."

"Ell is a wonderful young woman," Rachel agreed. "And she has your brains."

"And a bigger heart than mine." George coughed again and when he spoke again, his voice was strained. "We don't have much time before the cancer rears its head and bites."

He tapped his head. "Not up here. No pain here"—he touched his midsection—"but it's spread to my bones and that can be a bit much. So, ask what you came to ask and see if I can do something to help."

Rachel nodded and took his hand in hers. His skin was cool to the touch and his fingers so frail. Her heart sank. George had his faults, but he'd been a good friend to her and it wasn't her place to judge him. "You're not to worry about Sophie," she said. "I'd like to take her when the time comes. If you'll let me."

A tear spilled down George's sunken cheek. His complexion was the shade of cornstarch and his eyes were sunk back into his head. "I'd like that," he said. "Ell will protest, but you know she prefers her cats. Sophie will be happier with you at Stone Mill House. After all, she is a part owner there."

"Yes," Rachel agreed. "She is."

"Good." George's voice came back stronger. "I'll tell Ell that Sophie is to come with you and no arguments." He waved toward a pitcher of ice water. "Would you pour me a glass? I'll need a straw."

Rachel's hand trembled as she poured the water and held it for George to sip.

"That's enough," he said, coughing again. "That's my drink of choice now. Those nurses are always trying to get me to drink energy shakes and that nasty stuff in the cans, but I'm not hungry anymore and I'm putting my foot down. No feeding tubes. Now, what can I tell you that you haven't figured out for yourself about this murder?"

"Moses has confessed. Moses Studer is—"

"Yes, yes," George said impatiently. "I know who the Studers are, and I know about Moses's condition. Whatever gossip the housekeeper doesn't bring me, Ell or one of the nurses hears in town. You're thinking Moses is innocent?"

Rachel smiled. "Yes, that's about it."

"And you've tracked down that crazy Indian who lives on the mountain who Daniel was arguing with?"

"I have," she agreed. "But I don't think he shot Daniel Fisher, either." She looked down at him. "I feel as if I'm going around and around in circles and getting nowhere. I was wondering if you had any thoughts on the matter."

George gripped her hand with surprising strength. "To find the killer, you need to find the motive. Why do people kill? If they aren't insane, they need a good reason. It's not easy to kill another human, and I'd be in a position to tell you that. It goes against the grain. So what would be a good enough reason to do such a thing?"

"Some people kill for money," she ventured.

"True, but this isn't the case, is it? With Daniel Fisher dead, the farm stays with Alma Studer and her children, but it never really left their hands. And that's a poor hill farm, not really worth a lot of bother."

"So we can say Daniel wasn't murdered for gain."

George winked at her. "My thoughts exactly. Not for gain. So what's left? Passion? I do hear that that neighbor boy is very attentive to the young widow. I suspect that he'd set his heart on her a long time before Daniel came along and married her. Rosh could have killed Daniel to get rid of him and give him a chance with the girl."

"Possibly," she agreed. "And people sometimes kill to protect someone else."

"Someone or something," George said.

The sound of Sophie's barking echoed through the house. "Here comes trouble," George said. "But you haven't quite gotten to the heart of this mess yet. Have you thought much about the deceased? Why would somebody hate him enough to kill him?"

"Most of the Amish have nothing but good to say about Daniel. He was a faithful member of the church, a hard worker, a blessing to his wife's family."

"And you believe that?" George asked shrewdly.

"Not everybody said that, but enough to put the community opinion squarely in Daniel's corner. Daniel was, at least in public, exactly the type of man the church community praises. And Moses, unfortunately . . ."

"Isn't," George finished. "Moses is different, which makes him a good scapegoat."

"And he confessed to the crime. The authorities . . . most people in the community don't believe anyone would confess if they weren't guilty."

"Which we both know is a lot of hooey."

Ell came to the open doorway. "Rachel, would you like some tea? Coffee?"

"Did you feed Sophie her lunch?" George asked. "It's about that time." He glanced at Rachel. "And bring Rachel some of that pumpkin coffee you tried to tempt me with yesterday. She loves it."

Ell nodded and disappeared into the hall.

"That girl makes the best coffee," George told Rachel. "She's the only one in the house that can use that fancy coffee-maker."

Rachel folded her arms across her chest. "So, out with it, George. What do you know about Daniel Fisher that I don't know?"

"About time you asked." He pointed to the green leather-backed notebook on the desk. "In there. I don't sleep much at night, so I have a lot of time to look up stuff on the Internet. Not to mention that I pride myself on knowing more about every person in this county than their own mothers."

"Tell me," she said, reaching for the notebook.

"The short version or the long version?" Then he pressed a hand against his hip and gritted his teeth. "Short would probably be better for us both. Daniel Fisher moved here two years ago from an isolated community in Wisconsin. He came alone and quickly ingratiated himself into the valley. Mary Rose Fisher is his third wife."

"His third? But—"

George cut her off. "Now listen. Once the pain gets serious, I don't think so well. Here are the facts. Daniel Fisher was married at age twenty to Susan Gingerich, a Canadian citizen. Daniel moved to Ontario with his wife. Eleven months into the marriage, Susan suffered a fall and died from complications of childbirth. Daniel returned to his father's home, where he married Jane Stoltzfus the following year."

"Don't tell me that Jane died as well?"

George shook his head. "Divorce."

"Divorce? The Amish don't divorce," Rachel protested. "That can't be right."

"I think our Daniel proved to be a less-than-satisfactory husband. Claiming spousal abuse, Jane filed for an order of protection from the police six months after they were married. Three months later, she filed for divorce. There's a photo of her on the web showing her in a hospital bed. Someone had beaten her badly. It made the local news, but Jane later dropped the charges. Either she left the Amish after her divorce or moved to another part of the country. But we know where Daniel went."

"So it looks as though he might have been abusive to his spouses," Rachel said. "But how could he have moved here without anyone learning about his past? Usually, there's communication between your old bishop and your new."

"According to the news article, Daniel Fisher's father was the bishop of his local church." George shrugged. "I suppose they'd want to hush the whole thing up."

"Or Daniel confessed to beating his wife and said he was sorry. If he was convincing, the church community would have to forgive him," Rachel said. "It's part of the faith, and the crime would be as though it never happened."

"It's all I could find out," George admitted. "And it doesn't prove he was physically abusive to the Studer girl." He pressed the green notebook she had given him back into her hand. "It's all in here so you can double-check what I told you."

"Nothing you told me proves he beat Mary Rose or his other wives," Rachel said, thinking out loud. "But if Daniel was abusive, it would have given someone a good enough reason to kill him." She met George's gaze. "And I think I know who I need to talk to again."

Chapter 15

The midwife was just loading a large black suitcase into the back door of a gray-top buggy when Rachel pulled into her yard.

"Salome," Rachel called as she jumped out of the Jeep. "Could I talk to you for just a moment?"

The midwife was dressed in her customary black dress and stockings, but wore a black wool scarf instead of a bonnet or *kapp*. Her oversized coat was blue denim without buttons and lined with sheepskin. She shook her head. "I have to go," she answered in *Deitsch*. "Irma Coblentz's husband just came to tell me that she needs me. She's in her third trimester and is having contractions. I'm sorry you came all the way out here, but I don't have time to dally."

Rachel knew Irma from the farmers' market. She was a large woman with a large family. Irma didn't belong to Rachel's parents' church community, but her farm wasn't far away. "This will only take a moment," she pressed the midwife.

"I like you, Rachel, even if you have strayed from the flock. And I'd like to help you, but my patients come first." She climbed up into the buggy and reached for the reins.

"Wait," Rachel said. "I'll come with you." She dashed back to the Jeep, tossed her keys under the seat, and dug her navy scarf out of a basket on the floor. She'd come to the midwife's home in one of Mary Aaron's dresses and coats. If she remembered correctly, Irma and her husband, Shadrack, were very conservative, but had always been friendly toward her.

Salome turned the buggy around. "Come if you like," she called, pulling back on the reins to halt the mule. "But don't blame me if we get snowed in. Smell the air. Weather's coming in fast over the mountains. And even if it doesn't snow, there's no telling how long I'll need to stay with Irma."

Rachel glanced up at the dark clouds racing overhead as she hurried toward the buggy. Hulda, who'd come over to tend the office at Stone Mill House, had warned her of dropping temperatures and the possibility of four to six inches of snow. Rachel knew that the wisest course would be to return home, but she was determined to get some answers from Salome. "I'd be happy to drive you," she offered. "My Jeep is good in snow."

"I don't like motor vehicles. Too bouncy. And I trust my mule and this buggy a lot more than I do your car. I've been traveling these roads in snow, rain, and heat for a lot of years, and I'm not ready to give it up yet." She frowned. "You'd best not be in the way. My first duty is to the mother and the second to that babe. I've no time or patience for coddling you."

Rachel smiled. "I won't be in the way," she promised the midwife. "Remember, I was there when my younger brothers and sisters were born. And, if I recall, I was more help than hindrance."

"If you're coming, climb up," Salome said. "We're wasting time jabbering."

Rachel scrambled up into the buggy, not in the least offended by the midwife's fussing. Usually jolly, Salome grew serious and tart when it came time to deliver a baby or to help a mother. The woman's mouth tightened and she leaned forward, making clicking noises to the mule as she guided the animal out of the yard.

A short distance from the house, Salome turned the mule off the blacktopped road and onto a narrow wooded lane. "I don't suppose you've forgotten how to drive," she said.

"Don't suppose I have," Rachel said.

Salome passed the leathers to her. "You may as well do it then. My joints are aching today. Makes me certain this is snow coming. If I'd stayed home, I could have soaked them in warm apple cider vinegar. That helps, and of course, there are lots of other ways to reduce the pain. The best thing is to keep active." She draped a section of a feather tick over Rachel's lap and tucked her gloved hands into her wool-lined coat.

"Thank you," Rachel said.

"Rest your feet on that rock. I keep them on the hearth to heat. Toasty feet will keep the rest of you from taking a chill." Salome smiled at her. "Truth is, it's nice to have company on a cold day. Keeps me from worrying about what I'll find when I get to Irma's."

Rachel was surprised to hear the midwife express her fears. Salome was known from one end of the valley to the other for her steady hand and steadier character. They rode in silence for a while, and Rachel, who'd been on edge to question the older woman further about Mary Rose, was content to let the peace of the creak of harness and the rattle of buggy wheels over the frozen ground seep through her. She sensed that this wasn't the time to ask. Instead, she rested her feet on the heated rock and snuggled inside the feather tick. Occasionally, birds flew up from the branches overhead, and once the mule and buggy disturbed a browsing doe that was nibbling on tree bark. All Rachel heard was the snort of the mule and the snap of branches as the deer bounded away into the forest. Snow and sleet began to spit and then to swirl on the gusts of air. Rachel was glad that Salome had thought to cover the mule's back with a quilted blanket so that the animal wouldn't suffer from the cold.

Soon, the wooded lane opened up into a rocky pasture. Ahead, Rachel saw the chimneys of the Coblentz house and the great gray stone barn. Barking dogs announced their arrival and two teenage boys came out to greet them and take the mule. "How's your mother faring?" Salome called.

"Good, good," answered the oldest of them. "*Dat* says to tell you to make haste, though, because the little one does."

The midwife slid down out of the buggy and made to pick up her black leather satchel from behind the seat. "One of you lads take the suitcase," she said. "Mind you don't drop it." She glanced at Rachel, who'd slipped the strap for the satchel over her own shoulder. "The suitcase has towels and linens and such. This small case is my blood pressure kit, my fetoscope, and my instruments. I've been meaning to get myself one of those suitcases on wheels, but so far, it's just thinking and not doing. This is early yet for Irma's time. It's probably just a false alarm."

A plump, red-cheeked teen daughter opened the kitchen door for them and waved them in. "*Mam* says she thinks this is for real," she said. "Let me take your coats. It's getting cold out there, isn't it?"

Other girls of various ages held smaller children, one a toddler. Rachel tried to remember how many children Irma Coblentz and her husband had.

The kitchen was spotless and smelled of apples and spice. A huge kettle of soup simmered on the stove. Shadrack, short, wiry, bald, and not much older in appearance than his teenage sons, waved them through a spacious living room. "She's in the parlor," he said. "I'll be outside in the barn with the boys if you have need of me. Thank you for coming so promptly." If he was surprised at seeing Rachel with the midwife, it didn't show. He smiled and nodded and hurried out, clearly preferring the cows to women's affairs.

Rachel smiled back, dodged children and a tabby cat, and followed Salome. A girl about thirteen in a starched apron and black scholar's *kapp* clapped her hands and called to her young siblings. "Come on, now. Leave Salome and Rachel to look after *Mam*."

"Does she have the new baby in that bag?" a pigtailed cherub about six asked.

"Maybe," the teen replied. "But maybe she's not brought a baby at all but a bag of dried turnips." The other kids giggled, and the big sister clapped her hands and shooed them out.

An old-fashioned white iron double bed had been set up in one corner of the parlor near the Papa Bear woodstove that stood in front of a sealed-off fireplace. Rachel thought she'd see the expectant mother in bed, but that was not the case. Irma, clad in an everyday housedress and apron, her hair covered with a blue scarf, stood on a low stool with a bottle of vinegar, vigorously scrubbing the panes of one of the parlor windows with a cloth.

"Irma Coblentz, get yourself down off that stool," Salome scolded. "Do you want to fall and bring on the child before its time?"

The mother laughed heartily. "It's coming soon, whether I clean these windows or not. And what with all the company I get once the *boppli* is here, I'd not have anyone think I keep a dirty house."

Rachel glanced around the room. Painted a soft shade of green, the chamber was far from ill kept. The hearthstones were scrubbed clean, the paint in the room had been freshly applied, and the propane lamps and older kerosene lamps gleamed with nary a fingerprint to be seen. Someone had recently blackened the woodstove, the basket of wood was neat, and the braided rug was bright and welcoming. By the bed stood a white table, a stack of fresh towels, and likewise of sheets. The bed had been stripped to the mattress and covered with plastic sheeting. A kettle and a pot of water boiled on top of the woodstove, and a cradle waited nearby, tiny sheets and blankets new and soft.

"Are you hungry?" Irma asked as she climbed down from the stool. To Rachel, the big woman didn't look near her time or even in distress. "My oldest baked an *apfelstrudel* and a hickory-nut *kuchen*. I can offer you coffee, tea, or hot cider. The cider's wonderful this year. Our Spitzenburgs produced a bumper crop, God be praised."

"Sit down, will you, Irma," Salome instructed. "We'll gladly take coffee and a sweet, but we'll sort you out first. Rachel, open that satchel and hand me the blood pressure kit."

The girl who'd opened the kitchen door for them came with a basin of soapy water and a towel. Rachel glanced at the midwife, then nodded, and proceeded to wash her hands and dry them before opening the case. Meanwhile, Salome followed suit, rolled up her sleeves to her elbows, and washed thoroughly. Irma took a seat on the edge of the bed and offered a meaty arm for the blood pressure cuff. But before Salome could take the reading, the woman's mouth tightened, her eyes widened, and she groaned.

"They're coming close together. I started with the backache about midnight, but I didn't want to trouble you before—" She sucked in a deep breath.

Salome laid a hand on the woman's midsection. Rachel didn't need to be a midwife to see that Irma was in labor.

"I'll need to take a look," Salome said, catching the expectant mother's ankles and easing her up onto the mattress.

"What can I do to help?" Rachel asked when Salome gave her a look that confirmed her suspicion.

"Get those instruments into that boiling water." And then to Irma, "You were right. Good thing you called me when you did."

"It was such a raw day I didn't want to call you out for

nothing," Irma explained. "If it's all the same to you, I don't want to lay down. I think I need to walk a little."

"You know how this works," Salome told her patient, offering her hand to help the woman to her feet. "However you're most comfortable."

Two of the older girls remained in the room, and another woman, a middle-aged neighbor woman who Rachel recognized as Annie Raber, soon joined them. She was obviously a good friend of Irma's because the two laughed and talked easily. Annie and one of the daughters walked several circuits of the room with Irma, and then everything speeded into high gear.

In a half hour, Salome handed Rachel a squirming baby boy, small but red-faced and screaming. Rachel wrapped the infant in a warm towel and carried him to the arms of an older sister. And then, to everyone's surprise, Irma gasped and began to weep tears of joy as a second baby, every bit as lively as his brother, slid into the midwife's capable hands.

"You're certain there's not a third one?" Annie demanded. "As fat as you are, Irma, you could be hiding three or four in there."

Irma laughed good-naturedly. "No more so far as I can see. But there's always next year."

"I don't know," the midwife teased. "I can wait around to see."

"Hush, the both of you," Irma exclaimed. "Are they healthy? Are they breathing right?"

"As right as rain," Salome pronounced. "And as alike as two peas in a pod. Identical twins, unless I miss my mark. And with as much hair between them as Shadrack has on his head."

Irma laughed and began to hiccup.

Salome passed baby number two to Rachel, and called for a mug of warmed cider for the new mother. "Have you thought of names?" she asked when Irma's face had been washed and she was propped on pillows.

"Shadrack's favorite brother is Jubal. We'd thought of Jubal for a boy, but two boys . . ."

"What about Jabel, *Mam?*" the eldest daughter asked. "Didn't we hear about him in church last Sabbath? Jabel would go with Jubal, don't you think?"

"*Ya,*" Irma agreed. "We'll ask your father what he thinks, but he's not so fast to come up with names. I'm sure that will suit him. Jubal for the first twin and Jabel for the second. What do you think, Salome?"

"I think those are fine names," the midwife declared. Then to Rachel, "Take a bit of yarn from my bag and tie it around the oldest's ankle. Otherwise, we'll never tell them apart."

"What nonsense," Irma said. "You give them to me. Let me hold them. I'll not mix them up, I promise you." She laughed again, a hearty laughter that spread to all of them and filled Rachel's heart with the wonder of what she'd just witnessed.

Three hours later, after both of the twins had taken nourishment and Irma was on her feet, Rachel and Salome piled into the buggy for the trip back to the midwife's home. To Rachel's astonishment, Irma followed them to the kitchen, a baby in each arm, and instructed her girls to wrap a generous slice of the *apfelstrudel* in wax paper for each of them to take with them.

"You're sure you're all right to go?" Irma asked. "You don't want Shadrack or some of my boys to drive you down the mountain?"

"My mule will do fine," Salome assured her. "You sit now and let those girls of yours tend to you. Annie, make certain she minds me. I'll be back in the morning, but if there's any change with you or the twins, you send someone to fetch me. I'll come no matter the hour."

Fortunately, buggies, with their high wheels and light construction, were well equipped for snow, and the mule's strong and steady disposition kept them from bogging down in the ever-increasing drifts or sliding off the wooded lane. The temperature was cold but not dangerously so, and the swirling snow frosted the trees and hollows with white.

"Those precious babies," Rachel said, breaking the silence as they rolled along. "It's such a miracle that they were born so perfect and Irma delivered them so easily."

"New life is always a miracle," the midwife said softly. "And Irma's body is doing exactly what God intended it to do. Childbirth is a natural thing, like breathing. It doesn't always go like that, but Irma is sensible and surrounded by the people and place she loves most. And the twins were not much above six pounds. Her last little boy was much bigger." Salome patted Rachel's arm with a gloved hand. "You did well. You have common sense and compassion. You would have made a halfway decent midwife if you'd started training younger in life."

"Instead of in my dotage as I am now?" Rachel laughed. And then, after a moment, she said, "You know why I came with you today. And it wasn't to start training as your assistant."

The older woman sighed. "I know, and I've been thinking over what you said to me when you came to my house before. But you must understand how important it is to me that I keep every woman's secrets."

"Every woman's, but not every man's, and not a man who hurts one of your patients." Rachel reined in the mule and turned to face Salome. "I've reason to believe that Daniel abused Mary Rose and that might have been the reason for his death. She wasn't his first wife. He was married twice before. The first marriage ended in his pregnant wife's death due to a tragic accident. His second wife brought criminal charges against him for abuse and left the Amish church to get a divorce."

"Are you suggesting that Mary Rose might have shot Daniel because he was hurting her?" Salome asked, the shock plain on her face.

"One of her family, but maybe Mary Rose. I don't know. That's what I'm trying to find out. Maybe Moses really did kill him. But maybe he didn't. And if Mary Rose did it, Daniel's behavior toward her would make all the difference to her defense. If she feared for her life or the safety of her baby—"

"Daniel's judgment is in God's hands now."

"But Moses or Mary Rose or even the neighbor Rosh might be judged by court of law."

"Drive on," Salome said. "He'll get stiff if he stands still in this wind. We aren't far from his stable and a warm oat mash for him and hot chocolate for us."

Rachel sat there, the reins in her hand. "Please, Salome. I told Alma I'd get to the bottom of this."

"Very well." The midwife sighed. "I will say this one time and only one time and if called to the police or court or whatever, I will not speak of it." She paused and then went on. "I cannot tell you anything for certain, but I had my suspicions. Bruises. Falls. Accidents, according to Mary Rose. And once, I treated her for a badly sprained wrist. She said she fell down the cellar stairs. Her husband always seemed caring. He drove her to her checkups with me and waited while I examined her. She seemed to me like any young bride who cared for her husband."

"But you suspected that Daniel was beating her?"

The midwife nodded. "There was something in the anxious way she looked at him, and once . . ." She puckered her mouth and grimaced. "This could be an old woman's idle mind, but someone was behaving badly in that household. More than once I saw Lemuel with black eyes or swollen lips. And he avoided his brother-in-law as much as possible." Salome threw up her hands. "There you have it. No proof. Simply suspicion. And suspicion never caught the cat that was stealing the cream."

"No," Rachel agreed, shifting her gaze to the snowy road. "But it would tell us that there was a good explanation for how the cream was vanishing."

Rachel dropped two bags of groceries on the kitchen counter. Ada paused in rolling out biscuit dough and looked at her. "Did you remember the stick cinnamon? And the nutmeg? We're almost out of nutmeg."

"*Ya*," Rachel replied in the same dialect. Ada always spoke to her in *Deitsch* although her English was perfect. Her housekeeper didn't even have the heavy accent that many of Rachel's Amish friends and relatives did. "I'll bring them right in."

Ada shook her head. "*Ne*. I'll send one of the girls. Mary Aaron needs you. She's in your office."

Delicious smells were seeping from the oven. Rachel wanted to peek and see what Ada was baking, but Ada said that opening the oven door spoiled the temperature and ruined the baked goods. Rachel spied a stuffed chicken sitting in a Dutch oven on top of the gas stove and guessed that would be tonight's supper. "Have I told you how much I love you, Ada?" she teased.

The housekeeper grunted and returned to her biscuit dough.

"Don't forget the groceries. The milk will freeze if it stays out there long," Rachel reminded her and made hasty retreat from Ada's domain.

"Lydie!" Ada called. "I need you in the kitchen." Lydie was a sixteen-year-old granddaughter who'd finished school in the spring and now was in training with Ada. Fortunately, her grandmother seemed to approve of her, and Lydie was quick and hardworking. Rachel was imminently glad that she wasn't one of Ada's charges, although, at times, she wasn't certain who was working for whom.

Rachel snatched up Bishop, who was stretched out in the hallway, hung her ski jacket in the hall closet, and stroked the big cat as she made her way to the office. "Ada said you wanted me," she said to her cousin.

Mary Aaron glanced up, hastily shut down Facebook, and spun around in the high-backed office chair. "Babs called twice this morning. From the dress shop in State College."

"I know where it is," Rachel reminded her gently.

"Apparently, you were supposed to pick up your wedding gown?"

Rachel made a face. "Forgot." Her inquiries into Daniel's death were going nowhere. And she had so much to do before the wedding and honeymoon. She'd be away more than a week, and . . . Rachel rolled her eyes. Why had she agreed to go away with Evan next week? Wouldn't it have been better to wait a few weeks or even a few months until this was settled with Moses and things had calmed down from the wedding? As much as she was looking forward to being Evan's wife, she just wished all this fuss could be over with.

Mary Aaron stood up, and Rachel got a good look at her. Her outfits lately had been interesting when she'd been experimenting with English clothing, but this was a bit much. Her cousin was wearing a short plaid wool skirt, almost a kilt, with a big kilt pin, blue-and-yellow-striped tights, and a pink, fuzzy, oversized sweater with a cartoon snowman on it. The pièce de résistance was the high, fake-leather army boots, also pink, which had seen better days. "Have you been shopping at Second Chance again?" Rachel asked. "Are you planning on getting your ears pierced next? I saw some cute rhinestone cat earrings in the window this morning."

"I'm not getting holes punched in my ears," Mary Aaron responded tartly.

"Good, that's one thing I don't have to worry about. But if

you change your mind, I can always do it for you with a needle and a potato. It's the way I pierced mine."

Mary Aaron looked hesitant, which was difficult to do with the upswept ponytail on the left side of her head. Unconsciously, she began to worry the corner of her thumbnail with her teeth, something she only did when she was under stress. "Actually, Rae-Rae, there's someone waiting in the little parlor."

"Guests?" She tried to think if she was expecting anyone. And why had Mary Aaron put them in the private parlor? They rarely used that for their guests.

"Not guests, exactly. But I suppose you could say guests of a guest."

Rachel put the cat down. "Why the mystery? Who is it?"

"Dr. Morris and his family."

"Who?"

"Ssshh," Mary Aaron cautioned. "Do you want them to hear you? It's Mrs. Morris's son and his family. They've come to see her."

"Why, that's wonderful."

Mary Aaron shook her head. "It is except that Mrs. Morris isn't down here. I think . . . that is . . . I thought you could talk to them . . . explain."

"Explain what? Why isn't Mrs. Morris here with them? Is she ill again?"

Mary Aaron tucked her hands behind her back.

"Maybe our minister was able to convince her to contact her son," Rachel mused. "She must have called him. Oh, I'm so relieved."

Mary Aaron shook her head. "*Ne,* she didn't call her son. I did."

Rachel stared at her. "You did?"

"I felt so bad because of what you said. That . . ." Her cousin lowered her voice to a whisper. "That she was dying and alone. So I tracked down her son and I called him."

"How did you find him?"

Mary Aaron shrugged. "I Googled him. You can find any-body, especially a doctor. They're both doctors. Did you know that? Bruce and his wife. They have a practice in Phoenix."

Rachel couldn't believe that Mary Aaron had the nerve to do what she hadn't. "And you told him that his mother was dying?"

Rachel's cousin shrugged. "Someone had to, didn't they?"

Chapter 16

Rachel was momentarily stunned. This was out of character for her cousin; this was more her own MO. "I'm sure you only wanted to help, but . . ." She hesitated and then went on. "Mary Aaron, Mrs. Morris told me about her cancer in confidence."

"And you told me," Mary Aaron countered. "You must have known that I might do something about it. We talked about what a shame it was."

"Mary Aaron," Rachel said gently. "We don't have the right to interfere in her life. It's not how . . . Englishers don't take well to interference from strangers."

Mary Aaron looked as though she was about to cry. "I don't understand. If one of our neighbors was fighting with her sister and not speaking to her and she became critically ill, my mother would call or write to the sister. Even the bishop would let the neighbor's relatives know she needed them. Everyone has disagreements, but family is always there for family."

"Maybe in the Amish world, but not in the English." Rachel dropped into the second chair and leaned forward, trying to figure out how to make her cousin understand the cultural differences. "Lots of English families are alienated from each other. People die and no one goes to their funerals."

"That's ridiculous," Mary Aaron protested. "How could they? We are all human. None of us is perfect, but who is so bad that they don't deserve loving arms around them when they pass out of this world? Doesn't the Bible teach us to forgive? Aren't we supposed to return harsh words with gentle ones?"

"*Ya.*" Unconsciously, Rachel slipped into *Deitsch.* "But not everyone lives by our faith."

Mary Aaron rose. "Well, what's done is done. I found Mrs. Morris's son and I called his office, and he called me back. He didn't even know where his mother was. Apparently, he has someone at her apartment building who watches over her for him even though she doesn't know it. She told him that his mother went away again, but he didn't know she was coming here. I told the son that she was ill and that she said she doesn't have very long to live. The son and his wife and their children got on a plane and came at once. They're here."

"Have you told *her* that they are here?" Rachel asked. She wondered what Mrs. Morris would think. She might be angry. And she, herself, was certainly to blame for sharing a confidence with Mary Aaron. But at the same time, she couldn't help admiring her cousin for doing what she believed was right, no matter the cost.

Mary Aaron hesitated. "*Ya,* I told her they were here."

"Then why hasn't Mrs. Morris come down to meet them?"

Mary Aaron rubbed her hands together and then bit at the ragged sliver of fingernail again. "That's why I need you. She won't come down."

Rachel looked at Mary Aaron. This was getting better by the moment. "She won't come down?"

"She's locked her door, and she told me to tell them to go away." Tears filled Mary Aaron's eyes. "It's so sad. That nice man and lady and those two little boys. They've come all this way to see her, and now she won't budge from her room."

"Do you know why she doesn't want to talk to them?"

Mary Aaron shook her head. "I suppose she's still angry with them."

Rachel sighed and glanced away, thinking. "How long have they been waiting?"

"An hour," Mary Aaron said, wiping her teary eyes. "I'm so sorry. I just wanted to help, and I think I've made everything worse."

Rachel nodded. "It's all right. I'll see what I can do. Go to Ada and ask her to make up a tray for Bruce and his wife and children. Go to them and see what you can do to make them comfortable: toys for the little boys, crayons, and coloring books. If the children are tired after their journey, show the family to the yellow room. It's empty and the Matthewses aren't expected for another day. Just try and keep them all happy until I can convince Mrs. Morris to see them."

"I can do that," Mary Aaron promised and she quickly made her escape.

Rachel looked at her cat, which had wandered into the room. "Any brilliant ideas of how I'm going to clean up this mess?"

The big Siamese closed his eyes and turned his head away, his trick whenever he wanted to ignore her. Apparently, Bishop thought that if he couldn't see her, she couldn't see him, either. And there were times when he preferred to be invisible.

Which, right about now, didn't seem like a bad idea. Invisible, or anywhere but here, would have been nice. She wished she were in State College picking up her wedding dress. Or even at the Studer farm having the hard conversation she needed to have with Mary Rose. Then Mary Aaron would have had to deal with the Morris family and their dysfunction.

As soon as those thoughts went through Rachel's head, she was overwhelmed by her own selfishness. How could she be thinking of her own inconvenience or embarrassment when her guest was upstairs dying alone? What was wrong with her that she had forgotten compassion? She might not be able to help Alma save her son from spending the rest of his life in prison, but she could take the time to try and help Mrs. Morris bridge the gap between her and her son. She'd opened this home to guests knowing full well that part of her job would be to welcome them and make their lives easier while they were with her. And if she didn't continue to do her best, regardless of her own inconvenience, then she'd chosen the wrong career.

Taking a deep breath, Rachel forced herself to go up to Mrs. Morris's room and knock on the door. "Mrs. Morris, it's Rachel. Could I come in?" she called. She knocked again when there was no response. "Mrs. Morris?"

"Go away. I told the hippie Amish girl. I don't want to talk to anyone," came a small voice.

Rachel hesitated, then checked the doorknob. It was locked. Common courtesy said that Mrs. Morris deserved her privacy. But Rachel's Amish upbringing wouldn't stand for that. Instead of walking away, Rachel slid aside a painting on the hall wall and removed a ring of keys. "Mrs. Morris," she called again. "I'm coming in." And, knowing that it was a terrible idea for multiple reasons, including probably breaking some law, she unlocked the door anyway.

Her guest was standing at a window with her back to Rachel, and it was clear from her body posture that she was in distress. Rachel went to her at once and put her arm around the older woman. Mrs. Morris's stoic posture crumbled and she turned and clung to her, weeping.

Rachel rocked her against her chest and patted her shoulder. "There, there, shhh. Don't cry. Please don't cry. Are you in pain?" She led her to the bed and patted the coverlet. "Why don't you sit down. Catch your breath."

Obediently, but still sobbing, Mrs. Morris eased onto the bed.

"Are you hurting?" Rachel asked again. "Should I call the doctor?"

Mrs. Morris shook her head. "No, no, it's just . . ."

"Just what?" Rachel urged, supporting the woman with an arm around her shoulders. "Can I get your pain medication for you?"

Mrs. Morris shook her head and raised tear-swollen eyes to meet Rachel's gaze.

Rachel walked to a dresser and plucked several tissues from a box and handed them to her guest. "Can you tell me why you won't come down and visit with your family? They've come so far to be with you."

Mrs. Morris accepted the tissues and wiped her eyes.

Rachel pressed her lips together, searching for the right words, and then went on. "Mrs. Morris, don't you think it's time to let go of old grievances? To forgive your son for the past?"

"No, no, that's not it. I just . . ."

A fresh wave of tears overcame Mrs. Morris and Rachel's heart ached for her. "I don't understand then. Why won't you come down and see your son?"

"Because . . . because I'm afraid," she murmured. "So afraid."

"Oh, Mrs. Morris." Rachel stroked her arm. "What are you afraid of?"

She wiped at her eyes with a tissue again. "To . . . to see him. My son . . . and his wife. I don't want their pity. I know they hate me and—"

"No, you don't know that. How could they hate you?"

"How?" She sniffed and looked up at Rachel. "Because I've been a wicked, selfish, bitter old woman. I wouldn't speak to my only son. I returned his letters unopened. And I've never seen his wife or my own grandchildren. What kind of mother does such a thing?"

Rachel had no response for that.

Mrs. Morris sniffed. "How could they have come for any reason other than pity?"

"No. No, that's not why we came." The soft, slightly accented voice was that of a stranger.

Rachel turned to look at the slender, small-statured woman standing in the doorway. She had long black hair and a dark complexion. Her face with its huge dark eyes was not beautiful but serene and very kind. Mrs. Morris's daughter-in-law stepped gracefully into the room and a round-faced baby with the same striking eyes and dark hair peered out from a fold of her multicolored sari. Close behind her came a little boy, fairer in complexion but possessing the same hair color and amazing eyes, his small hand clutching his mother's tightly.

"We've come," the woman said, "to take our mother home."

"Home with us," the child echoed sweetly.

And then, before either Rachel or Mrs. Morris could reply, the woman in the sari, the two children, and a tall, ungainly man with thick glasses and tears in his eyes rushed into the room and enveloped Mrs. Morris in a combined embrace. Endearments and apologies and introductions mingled with more hugs and not a few tears, and somewhere between the baby's squeals and the exclamations of joyous reunion, Rachel slipped out of the room and closed the door behind her.

A bewildered and distraught Mary Aaron stood at the top of the stairs, and at least one guest door was open and an inquisitive face stared out.

"I'm sorry. I couldn't stop her." Mary Aaron threw up her hands.

"It's all right," Rachel assured her cousin and then her curious guests. "It's fine. No, really, it's good. Family." She wiped away a few stray tears, almost too emotional to speak rationally herself.

"Are you sure?" Mary Aaron asked.

Rachel nodded. "*Ya*, I'm sure."

She followed Mary Aaron down the stairs and into the gift shop. At the moment, no one was shopping and the room was quiet. "Well, that, Mary Aaron, is what Englishers call making an error in reverse."

"What?"

Rachel laughed, still feeling a little emotional. "You may have done what appeared to be the wrong thing, contacting Mrs. Morris's family without her permission. But in the end, it worked out." She went behind the counter and began to open a box containing three faceless Amish dolls that had come in that morning.

The dolls were hand-sewn and about fifteen inches high with yarn hair and dresses, bonnets, capes, and shoes that could be removed. They were crafted by an elderly Amish woman who lived at the far end of the valley. The dolls were copies of one that the seamstress had received from her grandmother when she was a child, and they had no facial features because of the belief that it was wrong to make an image of a person. Each doll was an individual, and each had a name, stitched meticulously onto the bottom of a foot. These three were Emma, Laura, and Lena. So far, every doll that the artist had produced had sold quickly. Rachel couldn't keep them in the shop.

"Ah." Mary Aaron nodded. "The English world is pretty complicated."

"*Ya*, it is. But on a totally different subject," Rachel began, but then Mrs. Rivera came in and Mary Aaron rang up the baby quilt she'd asked to have gift wrapped earlier. Rachel finished putting out the three dolls in the children's corner and waited until she and her cousin were alone again before continuing with her private conversation. "What I wanted to ask you was . . ." She looked up at her cousin. "I can't remember anyone saying who discovered Daniel's body. Do you know who it was?"

Mary Aaron shook her head. "*Ne*, I don't. I don't think

anyone ever said. There was so much confusion when they found him." She considered the subject and then lifted her hands and let them fall. "I don't know who was the first person to find him. I guess I just assumed it was Moses. You know . . . because he . . . because he said he did it."

"I can't believe we didn't ask," Rachel said. "But it must be in the police report."

"Why do you want to know?"

"I think I'll ask Evan when we—" Rachel broke off as she heard footsteps descending the stairs. It was Mrs. Morris and her son's family. Rachel went to the doorway.

"Rachel!" Mrs. Morris's gaunt face was radiant. "I hope it won't be an inconvenience, but I'll be leaving today," she said. She glanced up into her son's face. He smiled down at her, and she wiped at her eyes with a tissue. "I'm going home . . . to . . ."

"Philadelphia first," the daughter-in-law explained. "And then, if she's well enough to travel—"

"We're taking her home with us," the son finished.

"To live with us forever!" the small boy declared. "Our own grandmom!"

Mrs. Morris clasped her hands together. "Can you believe it? Did you see these wonderful children? The oldest is the spitting image of Bruce when he was that age."

Rachel looked at the excited child and then back at his father. Whatever the resemblance, perhaps one had to be a doting grandmother to see it. The little boy was adorable but clearly took more of his looks from his South Asian mother than from his father's family. But it didn't matter so long as the notion brought joy to a woman who hadn't experienced much of it in the last years.

"You've been so good to me," Mrs. Morris insisted, taking Rachel's hands in hers. "I hate to leave Stone Mill House and all your wonderful staff, but I need to be with my family."

"Exactly so," Rachel agreed, leaning to brush a kiss against the older woman's cheek.

There was no telling how long the family would have together, or what the coming weeks would bring, but for now, looking at all the joyous faces surrounding her, Rachel was certain Eloise Morris couldn't be in better hands.

Tuesday morning was the last meeting that Rachel and Evan had with their minister before the wedding, and although Evan was working that day, he'd gotten permission to go on duty a little later than his normal shift required. They ended the session with a prayer and hugs all around before they left the church by way of a side door that led to the parking lot. In the doorway, Evan paused to put on his hat and then opened an umbrella for her before they stepped out into the mixed rain and sleet that had been falling since before the sun came up.

"Yuck," Rachel said. "Nasty weather. You be careful out on the road."

Evan had been pulling extra shifts for the past few weeks, and she worried about him when the temperature dropped and winter storms moved in. Actually, she worried about him all the time when he was working, but he loved what he did and he was good at it. Evan believed that he was a much better trooper than a detective, and maybe he was, she thought. He certainly looked handsome in his uniform.

"Last week of being single," he declared as they prepared to make a dash for their vehicles. "Getting nervous?"

"Nope," she said. "Excited, but not nervous." Once before, she'd accepted his offer of marriage but then backed out. This time, she felt none of the apprehension or doubts she'd had then. "I'm absolutely, positively certain that we're going to make the best couple."

"One hundred percent?" he teased.

She reached for his free hand. "A hundred percent."

Evan shook his head. "Sorry. Want to, but I'm in uniform. No public displays of affection."

"Of course not," she agreed, then seized his hand and darted out into the sleet.

He could have pulled free, but instead, he came with her, trying to keep the mixture of sleet and rain off her head and shoulders with the bobbing umbrella.

She ducked behind a church minibus and spun around, stopping short. Blocked from the view of the street by the vehicle, she raised on her toes to kiss him. For a brief second, their lips brushed and she felt a warm rush of sweet happiness. Looking directly into his eyes, she said, "I can't wait for Saturday to become Mrs. Parks."

"Me, too," he said huskily.

Rachel giggled. "We both can't be Mrs. Parks."

Evan groaned and kissed her again on the forehead. "Into the Jeep with you, woman, before someone sees us and I get into serious trouble for kissing a woman while in uniform."

She squeezed his hand, savoring the tender moment. Here they were, standing in the cold and rain, under gray skies and on an icy blacktop, and she felt as if they were the only people in the world. "I love you so much, Evan," she said, and uniform and all, he bent and kissed her tenderly once more.

"And I love you," he said. "And I thank God every day that He brought us together." He took her hand again, led her to her Jeep, and opened the door for her. "Stay out of trouble today," he warned. Rain was dripping off the brim of his hat and ice crystals piled on the shoulders of his coat.

"You, too." She slid into the front seat and slid her key into the ignition. "Hey, can I ask you a question before you go?"

"Sure." He started to fold up her umbrella.

"It's about Daniel," she admitted sheepishly.

Evan groaned and his eyes narrowed in a frown. "What about Daniel?"

He was obviously less than pleased. She knew he was going to be. But she couldn't let this go. She had to know. "Do you know who discovered his body?"

Evan shrugged. "Not offhand." His mouth tightened. "Rachel, it's time to give up on this. You're becoming obsessed. You've got to let it go. Moses probably confessed because he actually did it."

"Probably, but not positively. Evan, listen to me. I—"

"No, you listen to me for once." He shook his head and handed the wet umbrella to her. "For once, don't be so bullheaded. It's honorable that you tried to help Alma and Mary Rose and Moses and the boy, Levin or Levy or whatever his name is."

"Lemuel, his name is Lemuel."

"Whatever. You tried your best, but you aren't a detective. Once again, you've gotten involved in something you shouldn't have and I think you've let your emotions take over. You aren't being objective." He glanced away and then back at her. "You know, they say that justice is blind."

"That's what I'm worried about," she protested, gesturing with one hand.

"No, you don't get it," he insisted, getting wetter by the moment. "Justice relies on facts. It doesn't matter whether Moses has Asperger's syndrome or if he's Old Order Amish or . . . or Buddhist. The rules are the same for everybody. You found him a good lawyer, but if you hadn't, the system would have seen that he was provided with a legal defense. Every defendant is considered innocent until he or she—"

"Confesses?"

He exhaled. "Look, I don't have time to argue with you, and I've got a long and apparently damp shift ahead of me. We can discuss this later, but you know how I feel. You tried your best, but you haven't found anything that would dispute Moses's confession. It's time to end your amateur investigation and focus on us—on our wedding. On me. On our new life together. Can you do that? For us?"

She gripped the steering wheel, feeling defeated. "Yes, I can. I will."

"All right, then. Good. Talk to you tonight."

He turned abruptly and hurried to his police car. She could tell by the stiffness of his back and the way he held his head that he was still unhappy with her, but he'd get over it. Evan never held a grudge. That was one of the things she loved most about him.

"Love you," she called after him. He slammed his car door.

"Well, that could have gone better," she said aloud. Grimacing, she turned up the defrost on the dashboard. Evan pulled up beside her, beeped once, and pulled out of the parking lot and onto the street. Rachel watched him go. He was right. She had been putting so much energy into Moses's case that she hadn't been giving her impending marriage the attention it deserved.

She just had a few loose ends to tie up.

Taking out her cell phone, she pulled up the number for the police department and dialed. After a few minutes on hold and several repeated explanations, she was able to speak to someone who could tell her what she had to do to get a copy of the initial police report detailing Daniel's death.

A helpful woman told her that she could come in and pick it up. The case was closed and the information was available to the public for the asking. After she ended the call, Rachel sat there, her windshield wipers going and the slush on the window sliding back and forth. Bits and pieces of things various people had told her about Daniel went through her head.

Rosh had said he hadn't found Daniel's body. That he only ran to tell Mary Rose himself so that the terrible news would come from someone who cared about her rather than the English police.

But what if he hadn't been telling the truth? What if he'd lied to her?

Was it possible that Rosh had discovered the body and then gone to Mary Rose? The lie wouldn't be a big deal unless there was more to it . . . unless it was part of a cover-up.

Was it possible Mary Rose cared for him as he obviously cared for her? George had told her that statistics proved that the person who reported a murder was often connected to the crime. Had Rosh and Mary Rose planned this together?

Rachel started the engine. Now that she was sure that Daniel had abused his wife, there might be a reason for Daniel's death. Rosh loved Mary Rose. Was it possible that he'd killed for her?

Or had Mary Rose done the deed herself?

Chapter 17

Rachel picked up her wedding dress at the bridal gown shop, but instead of taking it home, she drove out to the Studer farm. After the near-argument she'd had with Evan, she had resolved to do as he asked and set aside her investigation of Daniel's death. He was right: It was time to move on. The tiff with Evan hadn't been serious and all was well between them now, but it was the wake-up call reminding her it was time to get her priorities straight. What mattered was her impending wedding, and the life she and Evan would build together.

That said, it still wasn't all that easy to stop thinking about Moses and his family. Rationally, she saw Evan's point. But every time she thought of an Amish boy like Moses locked in prison for the rest of his life, she wanted to cry.

There were still a few missing pieces of the puzzle that kept nagging at her. Once she'd put her mind at ease, she told herself, she could move on without regrets. After all, if she'd tried her best and come up with nothing to prove Moses's innocence, then maybe she'd been wrong all along. And that was certainly possible. Being Amish didn't mean a person wasn't capable of great evil. It simply wasn't something she'd seen often, because, as a whole, they really were gentle and God-fearing people.

Mary Rose's mother met her at the door of the farmhouse with the sleeping baby in her arms. "Come on in. I just got her off," Alma whispered, looking down at her granddaughter. "She's teething and was up for hours last night. Poor little fatherless mite."

Alma looked as though she hadn't had enough sleep, either, and Rachel's sympathy was for the adults in the house. With so many little brothers and sisters, she'd known what it was to be wakened by an unhappy baby, and she'd spent enough hours rocking or walking sick or teething children to appreciate the situation.

"*Mam* always diluted oil of cloves with water and rubbed Baby's gums when they hurt," Rachel suggested, keeping her voice down. "And she said that a clean, damp washcloth, chilled in the refrigerator, for Baby to bite down on helps, too."

"I forgot about the oil of cloves," Alma replied, motioning her inside. "It's been a long time since Lemuel was an infant. I'll mention that to Mary Rose."

"Is she at home?" Rachel intended to ask Mary Rose about Daniel's abuse, and if she didn't think the information she received would go anywhere, she would sit Alma down here, today, and admit that she could do nothing about her son's arrest.

"Upstairs, cleaning the attic. You can go up, if you like. I'm embarrassed to say that it's dusty up there. I shouldn't have let it go so long." She pointed toward the front of the house. "The steps lead up to the second floor and then to the attic."

Rachel pushed open the door and stepped into the shadowy space to find Mary Rose washing one of the windows at the far end. Like many of the attics in the valley, the floor was constructed of rough-cut boards. The structural beams overhead were hand-hewn and marked with Roman numerals, the numbers once used to assemble the house.

Mary Rose turned to face her with a spray bottle in her hand. "Nothing's happened to my brother, has it? I had the worst dream last night. Is Moses all right?"

"As far as I know," Rachel assured her. "I haven't seen

him since the one day." She drew closer. "I'm sorry. I didn't mean to startle you. I was on my way home from State College. I picked up my wedding gown and just thought I'd . . . stop by," she finished softly.

"You're getting married on Saturday, aren't you? To that English policeman."

"*Ya*," Rachel said. "I am. I just drove to State College to pick up my dress this morning." She resisted the impulse to describe her wedding gown to Mary Rose. Although it was a simple one, an Amish girl wouldn't be able to appreciate a white dress with lace and buttons down the back. It would seem proud.

"Was the baby still sleeping when you came in?" Mary Rose turned back to the window and began wiping it. "I have to keep cleaning. We do what we can when she's not wanting something." She glanced back over her shoulder at Rachel. "She's a good baby, but you know how babies are. It makes me wonder how mothers manage when they have a houseful of children." She smiled, and Rachel realized that Mary Rose had a lovely smile. "I'm surprised you found the time to come all the way out here when it's so close to your wedding. My own wasn't that long ago and I remember how exhausted I was in the days just before we were married."

Had she ever heard Mary Rose talk so much at one time? Rachel wondered if it was because Alma wasn't in the room. Or, was it possible that now that she was free of Daniel Fisher, her true personality was coming out? It was true that people mourned in different ways, but Mary Rose didn't seem like a woman who'd been widowed only weeks ago. She seemed almost lighthearted. Driving over, Rachel had convinced herself that Mary Rose couldn't have had anything to do with her husband's death; now she was suddenly suspicious again.

The girl finished the window to her satisfaction and picked up a broom and began to sweep the area beneath the window. "*Mam* has some flowers that we're going to move up here to catch the winter light. She likes her plants, but there's hardly room for them on the windowsills downstairs."

Maybe you should have swept the floor before washing the window, Rachel thought, but she didn't say so. Instead, she pushed forward, determined to get what she'd come for. "Mary Rose—" She heard what sounded like a squeaking board on the attic stairs and she turned to glance through the open door. The stairway she'd just climbed was dark, and she couldn't see anything but shadows. She thought she'd heard a footstep on the stairs, but maybe it was her imagination playing tricks on her?

As if answering her unspoken question, Mary Rose said, "This house has been here a long time. It creaks in the wind and the floors settle. Don't pay it any mind."

Rachel nodded, turning back to the young woman.

Mary Rose had swept dust into a heap and was brushing it into a dustpan. There appeared to be several old chests and a trunk against the wall, all covered with sheets. Hanging from the ceiling beams were old cords that might once have held curing hams or bacon, but now they merely dangled like so many spider legs. A row of old-fashioned chairs and a small round table waited for the day they might be needed or perhaps sold to some English antique dealers. Near the window was a wooden high chair that seemed sturdy enough but had served many babies.

Again, there was a creak coming from the direction of the staircase and Rachel glanced back a second time. She wondered if Alma was creeping up the steps to listen to what they were saying. If she was that kind of mother, maybe that was an explanation for why Mary Rose seemed somewhat timid. An overbearing mother could do that to a young woman.

"Mary Rose," Rachel said quietly. "I know Daniel wasn't the man many people thought he was." She hesitated. "And I know that he hit you hard enough to leave bruises. I saw it myself. After Daniel died. That day in the kitchen. Remember? You told me you ran into the pie safe."

"I'm going to clean up this high chair for the baby," Mary Rose said, picking up the old wooden high chair and moving it toward the door.

Silence stretched between them. Tiny bits of dust sparkled in the feeble rays of sunlight shining through the window. Rachel waited. Usually, people who were nervous would say something, anything, to fill the quiet. When Mary Rose didn't, she asked, "Why didn't you say anything about that when I asked you about him and your marriage?"

It took a long time for her to answer, but when she did, her voice was surprisingly strong. "He was my husband and the head of our household. I didn't always obey him as quickly or as willingly as I should. If Daniel had to reprimand me, it was my fault."

Rachel took her arm and looked into her face. "How can you say that? What kind of a man abuses his wife or those around him? He had no right to strike your brothers or to injure your arm so badly that you needed medical attention for it."

Mary Rose pulled away, her features defiant. She strode across the attic and began shifting some wooden crates of assorted household wares. "Daniel didn't hurt my arm that time. Did Salome tell you it was Daniel's fault? I told her that I fell down the cellar steps. She asked me outright and I told her I tripped and fell. That's what happened. I'm clumsy. Sometimes I don't pay attention to what I'm doing and I have accidents."

"That's how women explain injuries caused by their abusers. That's how they cover for them."

"I'm not covering for Daniel." She dropped a crate purposefully and it made a loud *bang*. "I told you. He did hit me a couple of times. Not that it's any of your business," she added.

A strong gust of wind rattled the windows and caused a shrill chord along the edge of the roofline and the end of the house. Rachel shivered, but she couldn't shake off the unpleasant feeling this attic gave her. It smelled of dust and something more, maybe sadness. She certainly felt sad for this young woman standing in front of her defending a bully and a tyrant.

Rachel sighed. "Mary Rose—" Something squeaked behind her and she spun around. She marched back to the attic door and closed it firmly. If Alma or Lemuel or anyone were on the stairs, they'd not hear so well through the thick door panels. "Doesn't this give you the creeps up here?" she asked, turning back to the younger woman.

Mary Rose shrugged. "*Ne.* Moses and I used to play up here when we were children. Once he was stung by a wasp, but other than that, nothing ever hurt us." She scowled. "Why are you asking all these questions about Daniel? He's dead. It doesn't matter now what he did to me."

Rachel thought for a moment. This wasn't how she was expecting Mary Rose to respond. She didn't sound like a woman frightened enough or angry enough to commit murder. "You're positive that it wasn't Daniel who hurt your arm the time you went to Salome?"

"I know whether or not I fell down the cellar steps. I broke three quart jars of peaches on the way down. I'd say that was a fall. Popped the lids on two more. We had to eat those peaches for supper. What a waste when we needed them for this winter and we'd already had peaches twice that week."

"So you aren't denying that Daniel was abusive? You're just saying he wasn't responsible that one time."

"That's what I'm saying. Mostly it was just a slap here or there, or maybe he would grab my wrist a little too hard, getting my attention. But he always said he was sorry afterwards. And he was so sweet. He did have a temper, but he was trying to get past that. He was getting so much better. And he never lost it without good reason."

"You mean with you?"

She shrugged. "Any of us, I suppose. We were a lot to take on." She paused, and seemed to be thinking.

Rachel waited.

"Moses and Daniel never got along because Moses never gave Daniel the respect he deserved," Mary Rose said. "And he was used to being the man of the house."

"Moses was."

"*Ya,*" Mary Rose agreed. "It was hard for him to accept that Daniel had the right to give the orders here after we were married. What Moses didn't understand was that without Daniel's sweat and his savings, we never would have been able to hold on to the farm. We needed livestock, roof repairs, and a new well dug. Daniel saved us," she finished softly.

Rachel pressed her hand to her forehead and drew it slowly over her head. "Did you love your husband?"

Mary Rose found her cleaning rag in one of the wooden crates and crossed the attic again to attack the dust on the high chair. "I respected him. I didn't know him that long before we came to an understanding. Concerning marriage. But I could see that it was best for me and for our family to accept his proposal."

"Then you didn't love him."

Mary Rose shook her head. "It's not so simple. Maybe for you, but I had my mother and my brothers to think of. Daniel was young and hardworking. He had money to buy seed and new equipment and he brought two teams of horses to work our land. Before he came, we struggled. Sometimes we barely had enough to eat. Things had to be done when he arrived. Hard work. Moses and Lemuel didn't like that. Moses especially."

"You're saying Daniel was a hard taskmaster?" Rachel suggested.

"You're putting words in my mouth. Why do you want Daniel to look like a bad man? He wasn't. Everyone liked Daniel."

"You said so yourself, not everyone," Rachel corrected. "Not Moses or Lemuel . . . or Rosh."

Mary Rose's lips tightened and she turned her head away. "Moses is not like other men. You've seen him. He's different. Peculiar, some say. He was born that way."

Rachel thought about explaining to the young woman that her brother probably should have been diagnosed years ago. Such a diagnosis might even have helped make things easier for him in prison. But what was the point now? Instead, she said, "His boss told me he works hard and that he's trustworthy."

Mary Rose scrubbed harder at the wooden tray on the high chair. "I'm not finding fault with Moses. He does work hard, but he doesn't always understand what needs to be done. It's better when someone tells him what to do."

"But not Daniel. He didn't like it when Daniel gave him orders."

Mary Rose removed the tray and started on the seat. She dipped her rag in the bucket of soapy water and wrung it out before she wiped the seat down. "Daniel didn't know anyone like Moses. He didn't understand that you couldn't yell at him. It's best if you explain what you want and then go away and leave Moses to work it out his way. Daniel thought he was slow, but he isn't. Moses is smart."

Rachel brushed away a hanging cobweb. "Did you and Moses get along well?"

"*Ya.*" Mary Rose's voice grew warmer as she spoke about her brother. "Moses and I were always close. I love him very much and he loves me. He loves all of us, but it's hard for him to show it. And after Daniel and I were wed, I didn't have so much time for Moses anymore." She paused again. "Truth be told, I don't think he would have liked any man I married. Our family changed, had to. And Moses likes things to stay the same."

"What about Lemuel? How did he feel about Daniel?"

Mary Rose threw her cleaning rag into the bucket with more force than necessary. "Why are you asking these questions?"

"I'm trying to help Moses," Rachel said patiently. "Don't you want to help him?"

"You know I do." Mary Rose grimaced. "Lemuel has always been the baby of the family. He was ill a lot when he was young, and it was natural that *Mam* fussed over him. Daniel thought she was spoiling him. Daniel thought it was time my little brother learned to be a man. It was for Lemuel's good to teach him discipline."

"You mean he disciplined him?"

Mary Rose sighed and pushed back hair that had fallen from her *kapp*. "Sometimes I thought Daniel was too hard on him and on Moses."

"Hard in what way? Physically?"

Another sigh. "*Ya,* maybe Daniel was quick with his hand."

A silence stretched between them. Rachel waited.

"But he never had brothers or sisters," Mary Rose continued. "He couldn't understand why we were so close. Some of the trouble between Daniel and me was my fault, because I tried to interfere between him and my brothers."

Mary Rose went back to scrubbing the high chair and Rachel debated how to ask her next question. She wondered if it was wrong to speak of Daniel now that he was gone. But wasn't it also wrong to leave Moses in jail if he didn't belong there? She studied an old stool that had one broken leg. In the end, she just came out with it. "Did you know that Daniel was married before?"

"Of course."

Rachel looked up in surprise. "You knew you weren't his first wife?" she asked, wondering if the young woman had misunderstood the question.

"There were no secrets between us." Methodically, Mary Rose lifted the wet cloth and wrung it out before getting down on her knees to wipe the legs of the high chair free of spiderwebs and dust. "His first wife fell from a ladder and injured herself so badly that she died. It was a terrible loss for him."

"But he married a second time not long after."

"*Ya,* but that, too, was a blow to Daniel. His second wife didn't want to remain Amish. Daniel's faith meant everything to him. When he refused to leave the church with her, it tore their marriage apart."

"And nearly took her life," Rachel said softly. "Daniel beat her badly enough to put her in the hospital. She had broken bones, internal bleeding, a fractured jaw, and—"

"All that I have heard," Mary Rose said sharply, "was what Daniel told me." She scrubbed at the oak high chair as if she could rub away the grain of the wood. "He said that she attacked him and he struck back to defend himself. He insisted that the English newspaper people made it seem worse than it was to sell papers. They never said that the woman threw things at him and hit him."

"Daniel didn't go to the hospital with injuries. His wife did."

Mary Rose avoided eye contact, but her voice was surprisingly strong. "True, but Daniel knew he had done wrong. He confessed and asked forgiveness on his knees in front of his church elders. He was truly repentant. And you know that means he was forgiven in God's eyes." She dropped the rag and looked up. "Daniel had a bad temper, but he promised to try and control it. I knew his faults, but I married him anyway. We were working things out with Preacher Paul's help."

Rachel mulled over that for a moment and moved on. "Why didn't Rosh like Daniel?"

"I'm sure you've heard the gossip. Rosh wanted me to be his wife. He'd been saying it since he was ten years old. And maybe, had the circumstances been different . . . I would have waited for him," she said softly. She looked up at Rachel. "But I needed a husband. *Mam* needed me to marry." She shrugged. "I told Daniel about Rosh because I was his wife and it was my duty. Daniel got angry and forbade Rosh to set foot on this farm. Rosh thought that was unfair."

"Did you kill Daniel?" Rachel asked abruptly.

"Kill my husband?" Mary Rose's face went sickly gray.

"*Ne!* I did not. How can you ask me such a thing? I could never kill another human being. And I could never have killed my husband. I am a sinner like all of us, but not so great a sinner as that."

"But now that he's dead, you feel free?"

Mary Rose groaned. "God help me, I do. It is peaceful in this house now with just the baby and us. Is that wrong?" Her eyes glistened with tears. "To be glad sometimes that my husband is dead? Will I go to hell for that?"

"I don't believe so. I think it proves you're human." Rachel lowered her voice. "Mary Rose, are you sure it wasn't Rosh who shot him?"

Mary Rose shook her head. "He couldn't. He's not like that. He's sweet. There isn't a mean bone in his body."

"But did Rosh know that Daniel hit you? That he abused you and your brothers?"

The expression on her face hardened. "Don't say that. Rosh couldn't have killed Daniel. He wouldn't have . . . and . . ."

"And what, Mary Rose?" Rachel closed the distance between them and looked directly into her eyes. "What were you going to say?"

Mary Rose gave a small cry and slumped onto the floor. Sitting with her legs under her, she clapped a hand over her mouth and rocked back and forth. "*Ne, ne,* it's not possible. Rosh is not a killer. Not even for me would he . . ." She groaned and then looked up at Rachel, her facial expression suddenly changing. "It couldn't be Rosh," she said huskily. "If he'd been the one, they would have found Daniel with an arrow through his heart. Rosh only hunts with a bow, and he never misses what he takes aim at. He wouldn't have needed two shots. You can ask anyone on the mountain. They'll tell you that it's true."

Rachel nodded, not sure if she was disappointed or relieved. "No one told me that Rosh only hunted with a bow. Was he hunting with a bow the day Daniel died?"

"Of course."

"But it wasn't bow season."

"It wouldn't matter to him. Up here, on this mountain, the game wardens rarely come. And if they do, they won't find him. Rosh knows these woods too well."

"You're certain that Rosh doesn't own a gun?"

"*Ne*. No one in that house owns a gun. Rosh's father had a brother who was killed in a hunting accident when he was a child. He's never permitted anyone in his family to touch a firearm."

Rachel glanced away and then back at Mary Rose. "I'm sorry if my questions upset you. I was only trying to help Moses." And that hope was looking dimmer and dimmer every day, she thought. "When I found out that Daniel had hidden his first two marriages from the community, I naturally assumed that you . . ." She didn't finish the sentence. Now she felt bad to have made such assumptions. Relationships were complicated, not just among Englishers but the Amish, too.

"It's all right," Mary Rose said. "My Daniel was a troubled man. I only hope that he has found peace." Slowly, she got up from the floor and looked down at her skirt, stained with water and dirt. "I wanted to help my family, and I fear I've made it worse for them. But I can't be sorry I married Daniel, because my beautiful baby girl came from that marriage bed." She exhaled softly. "It doesn't look good for our Moses, does it?"

Rachel shook her head. "I'm afraid not."

"Pray for him," Mary Rose said. "Pray for us all."

"I will," Rachel assured her.

"And I will pray for you," Mary Rose replied. "For your marriage, that you will find more happiness in it than I found in mine."

Going down the narrow steps, Rachel sneezed and blinked away the dust that had gotten into her eyes. She hoped she hadn't done more harm in coming here. Certainly, Mary Rose had suffered enough. Did she welcome Rosh's attentions? She'd sounded as if she cared for him, and the defense she'd mounted for him would have convinced any hardened jury.

The beginning of a migraine was throbbing in Rachel's head. Where was her migraine medicine? Had she refilled her prescription the last time she'd had an incident? She couldn't remember. But the time to take it would be now, and if she did have any, it was in her medicine cabinet at home. She steeled herself to talk to Alma. Rachel owed her the decency of admitting what she feared most, that Moses had indeed committed the horrendous crime.

Rachel heard the baby fussing before she reached the kitchen. Alma was walking back and forth, patting the little girl's back and trying to soothe her. Rachel went to the woman and held out her arms. Alma passed her the fretting child and Rachel began to pat her back. "Did you try the oil of cloves?" she asked. "Poor little babe. A toothache is the worst." Rachel sat down in a kitchen chair and bounced the baby on her knees. The little girl's mouth and chin were red and chapped from drooling. "Maybe Salome has something that can help her."

"She told me to put a spoon in the refrigerator and get it cold and then let Baby chew on that. And she gave me a bit of coral to hang around her neck. Not as a fancy, but to help the pain," Alma explained.

"Ride a pony, ride a pony, ride him to the mill," Rachel sang to the baby. The teary eyes brightened and a smile stretched across her adorable face. God willing, Evan and I might have a child, Rachel thought. She did want one or two children, but the midwife had been right. She wasn't getting any younger. She tried to imagine what it would be like to have a baby of her own. Sleepless nights, she thought, but oh, the reward of that precious smile.

"You know that I can't go to that place to see my son," Alma said, coming to sit across from her. "To that English jail."

She was wearing a dark-green dress today with a starched white apron and a proper *kapp*. The green did nothing for her complexion. Alma looked bad, her skin color almost gray. Rachel wondered how old she was. If she'd married young and had Moses early, she might not be much older than Rachel herself, but she looked like a woman who had suffered greatly and worked hard. Many Amish women aged poorly, especially those from low-income households. And from what Rachel knew of her, Alma's life had not been an easy one.

"I know I should go. He is my son," Alma went on, "but I can't bring myself to go in there with all those wicked people."

"Not all so wicked," Rachel reminded her. "Moses isn't wicked."

"*Ne,* he isn't. But I'm afraid they will never let him leave that terrible place." She reached for the now cooing baby. "You have a natural touch," she said. "You will be a good mother."

"I hope so," Rachel said. She got to her feet. "I have to tell you, Alma, I'm afraid I failed you. You asked me to help your son and I've done my best, but—" She shook her head slowly.

Alma started to cry. The baby's eyes widened and she started to sob as well.

"He didn't do it," Alma managed. "The police didn't even investigate. They didn't . . . didn't ask so many questions . . . like you. They don't care whether . . . whether my boy is guilty or not. I didn't think it would be this way."

Rachel walked over to stand beside her and put an arm around Alma's bony shoulders. "I'm so sorry," Rachel said. "So sorry. I don't know what else to do."

"Mother?" Mary Rose came into the room. "Whatever is . . . Give me Baby." She took the child from her mother. "Don't, don't cry. Tears will not help our Moses. Only prayer. God must help us."

"I'm so sorry," Rachel repeated. "I've gotten nowhere. And now, I've upset your mother terribly. Forgive me." Still stammering apologies, she found her coat and let herself out of the house. She felt so awful. These women had depended on her and she'd let them down.

Sadly, she walked to her Jeep and got in. She was out of options, and two days from now she'd be married and on her way to her honeymoon. It was over and she'd failed. The taste of defeat was bitter on her tongue. Evan was right: She'd let Alma believe that she could do more than she'd delivered.

And instead of helping, she'd only made things worse.

Chapter 18

❦

"Would you like another poppy seed muffin?" Rachel offered.

"*Ya*, and I definitely need more tea." Mary Aaron carried the electric kettle to the bathroom and refilled it. Because she'd spent the night with her parents at the Hostetler home, she was wearing Amish clothing, minus her prayer *kapp*.

The two of them were having a late breakfast in Rachel's apartment on the upper floor of the inn. Mary Aaron had been up before dawn to help with milking on her father's farm. Rachel had risen at six, but neither had found time to eat.

"Earl Grey?" Mary Aaron asked as she padded back across the rug in her high black stockings. She'd left her shoes at the door. "Or would you rather have the Irish Blend?"

Outside, a blustery wind beat at the old stone house, but the sun had broken through the gray clouds and light poured through the multipaned windows, making the big room cheerful. Mary Aaron's fair hair was pulled back into a bun, though tendrils escaped to spill over her ears and down her forehead. The cold weather had turned her cheeks and her freckled nose a glowing pink.

"Either. I don't care. Just make it strong. I need the caffeine." Rachel, in jeans, moccasins, and a flannel shirt, stood beside a window, trying not to feel overwhelmed.

The room, a combined seating area, bedchamber, and kitchenette, usually neat, was in chaos. The wedding rehearsal was at six that evening and Rachel was still trying to decide what to wear, plus she was in the midst of packing for her honeymoon and trying to pack for a place she'd never been. At least that was what she'd told Hulda she was doing when her neighbor came to take over management of Stone Mill House for the day. In reality, Rachel was contemplating running away to join a Buddhist monastery . . . or maybe a hippie commune . . . with Evan, of course. She wanted to go anywhere she wouldn't be required to add more worries to the ones already troubling her.

The flowered dress that was in first place for the rehearsal hung over the bathroom door; the matching heels were under the bed. Rather, one was under the bed. Rachel couldn't find the second one. Her wedding gown took up half of the closet. The shoes for the gown stood ready on the shelf above. A large suitcase was open on the bed, and Bishop had taken up residence there for the morning, settled contentedly amid the articles of clothing already consigned to the trip.

Evan was working again all day, which was for the best. Because, if she had spoken to him, they would probably quarrel so badly that they would have to back out of the wedding. Rachel's nerves were on edge, so much so that she'd bitten her nails, something that she rarely did. Now she was trying to figure out when she could fit in a manicure.

"Won't you at least come to the rehearsal dinner tonight?" Rachel begged. She'd wanted her cousin to be her maid of honor, but Mary Aaron had declined. She wasn't comfortable taking part in an English wedding, and she certainly wasn't allowing anyone to put her in a bridesmaid's gown. "I'd feel better if I knew you were going to be there."

Mary Aaron measured tea leaves into the teapot. "*Ne,* you'll do fine without me. You'll have Evan and his mother." She made a face and added hot water from the electric kettle to the rose-patterned teapot. "Besides, I don't think I'd like the food. It won't be home-cooked, and it won't be *Deitsch*."

Rachel was afraid that her parents would feel exactly the same way. The rehearsal dinner for the wedding party was going to be at Magnolia, the new little restaurant in town. Evan's mother had picked the place and the menu. Rachel's *dat* was paying for it, despite Rachel's protests, though she knew that he and her mother would not enjoy the evening. Her parents would be on their best behavior, though. Her father would smile and go along with it, but her mother would miss no opportunity to remember each unfamiliar custom and remark and remind Rachel repeatedly of the transgressions at a later time.

Rachel knew what was coming and hadn't the slightest idea how to soften the disaster. She certainly wasn't ashamed of her parents, but she could anticipate nothing but awkwardness for all involved. Evan's mother would gush and Rachel's *mam* would be polite but distant. And Evan, Evan who got along wonderfully with her parents and was adored by his mother, wouldn't have a clue any of it was going on.

Rachel had been born into a conservative and isolated religious group in a house without electricity, a telephone, a radio, or TV. She hadn't ridden on a public bus, in a cab, or on a plane until she was an adult. But sometimes she felt as if Evan was the innocent one, especially when it came to dealing with outward appearances and the undercurrent of emotions involved in the mixing of cultures. Marrying him meant that she was taking on a second mother, and her duties toward his remaining parent would be just as compelling as those she owed her own. It was no wonder that few Amish-born women ever left the faith or married outside it.

"You know, you're supposed to be happy about this wedding," Mary Aaron said, watching Rachel. She dropped her hands to her hips. "You don't look happy."

"I *am* happy. I want to marry Evan." She groaned. "I just wish we didn't have all this other stuff in the way."

"Or your future mother-in-law."

Rachel shook her head. "*Ne,* that's not true. She has a lot of good points. In time, I'm sure we'll become good friends."

"Oh, I'm not so sure about that," Mary Aaron said in a singsong voice.

"My father says marriage is all about learning to put the other partner first. If I put Evan first, then I'll always treat his mother with respect and kindness."

"I suppose." Mary Aaron made a face. "I'm just glad she's not going to be my mother-in-law."

Rachel took a bite of the muffin. It was good, and she found, after the first bite, that she really was hungry. "I spoke to Irene this morning," she said, changing the subject.

"Moses's attorney." Mary Aaron looked up from spreading butter on her muffin. "Anything new? Is he doing all right?"

"Irene thinks he's extremely depressed. He barely speaks, and it looks to her as if he's lost weight. He won't budge from his insistence that he killed Daniel. The hearing is set for next week and I'll be out of the country. I can't even be there to support him and his family." Rachel went to the whiteboard and began to erase the names of the people she and Mary Aaron had talked to over the last two weeks. "I feel like such a failure."

"We tried our best," Mary Aaron said. "And maybe the police are right. Maybe Moses really *did* shoot him, and that's why we couldn't find any proof to clear his name."

"Maybe." Rachel sipped at the remaining liquid in her mug, then finished wiping the board clean. "All this running around, me angering Evan, and I found out nothing."

"Not nothing," Mary Aaron insisted. "You found out that Daniel wasn't the man most people thought he was. Which might be a motive to kill him." She lifted the lid of the teapot to peer in, then looked up. "Oh, I forgot. Jake Sweitzer was visiting for his mother's birthday yesterday. I got him to drive me over to the police station to pick up that police report you wanted."

"I almost forgot all about the report," Rachel admitted. "Thanks for going for me."

Mary Aaron retrieved Rachel's mug from her and poured them both fresh tea. "You wanted to know who found Daniel's body. Right?" She carried Rachel's cup to her, then went to the denim coat hanging on a doorknob and rummaged in the deep pockets. "Here it is." She held up a rumpled but unopened envelope.

Rachel raised both hands, palms out. "You open it. I'm done. It's time for me to focus on Evan and our life together."

Mary Aaron tore open the end and shook out the report. She carried it to the window and carefully read it. "Lemuel Studer, age fourteen, reported finding the body."

"What did you say?" Rachel looked up.

"I said Lemuel Studer. According to the police report, he's who discovered Daniel's body. It's right here." Mary Aaron pointed at the paper. "Lemuel."

Rachel shook her head slowly. "No, Lemuel said he didn't know who found the body. That first day I talked to him after the funeral."

Mary Aaron frowned, looking unconvinced. "Well, the police think he was the one."

"That doesn't make any sense, but . . ." Rachel exhaled loudly, then drew in a deep breath. She cradled the warm cup in her hands and drank slowly, not bothering to add honey or sugar. She welcomed the rich, strong flavor as she considered what she'd just heard. "Well, obviously someone made a mistake. You know how Englishers can be. One Amish man or boy in a black hat and denim coat looks like another."

"Exactly." Mary Aaron refolded the report and slid it back into the official-looking envelope. She dropped it on the table and wandered to the door where Rachel's flowered dress for the rehearsal dinner hung. "This is so pretty," Mary

Aaron said, fingering the soft material. "I can't believe you're finally getting married. Even my mother didn't think you'd ever do it. She kept saying that you were taking so long making up your mind because you weren't sure you didn't want to come back."

"I know," Rachel said. "She told me the same thing."

Mary Aaron's voice grew thick. "Tomorrow, you'll be a married woman, and I'll still be single." She swallowed, and her beautiful eyes glistened with moisture as she turned back to Rachel. "It's not that I'm not happy for you. I am, but somehow, I always thought I'd be the one to marry first."

It snowed in the night, not enough to impede the wedding, but enough to lay a sparkling blanket of snow over the lawns and fields of Stone Mill. That morning, Rachel nibbled a piece of rye toast and sipped at her tea in her room while staring at her beautiful gown. The previous day's rehearsal and the dinner afterward had gone pretty much as she had imagined they would, but there had been no fireworks. Evan's mother and her mother had both pasted fake smiles on their faces and gritted their teeth as they went through the motions. But, on a high note, the food at Magnolia had been good and the waitresses pleasant and competent. And Evan had been wonderful: calm, charming, and so attentive that Rachel had felt as if it really was her special evening.

The day had arrived that so much work and planning had led to. And suddenly the craziness of the last few weeks didn't seem so crazy. It was time that she married, and she could go into this marriage knowing that she'd found someone with whom she wanted to spend the rest of her life. Evan was everything any woman could ask for. He'd been so sweet at the dinner and then he'd called her afterward and they'd talked on the phone until late into the night.

She missed him this morning. Following custom, and interestingly, on the advice of both mothers, they'd agreed not to speak to or see each other until they met that afternoon at the church altar. The idea made sense on several levels. If they didn't talk to each other, there was no possibility of a disagreement before the wedding. And there was a certain excitement about the anticipation of seeing each other that afternoon. But a part of her wished she could hear Evan's voice, share a few laughs and endearments, because the hours between now and the ceremony stretched out like an eternity.

Rachel had planned the morning carefully so she wouldn't feel rushed and now she was almost wishing she'd saved some last-minute tasks for herself. But she hadn't. Mary Aaron was picking up ice and a few final things for the wedding dinner, and she had taken complete charge of the house and the guests today. Everyone had agreed to leave Rachel to herself until it was time to get dressed. And even then, she wanted no fuss.

The reception would be there at the inn, and her mother, her Aunt Hannah, and Ada had the meal arranged down to the groom's cake. They'd all soon be downstairs putting the day in motion. So, it was Rachel's wedding day, and she had nothing to do until it was time to put on her gown.

Debbi from the hair salon had arrived promptly at seven that morning, and the stylist had done her hair there in her apartment so that she wouldn't have to leave the house and chance being seen before the ceremony. Unconsciously, Rachel's hand went to the pins at the back of her head and patted the elegant but traditional up-do Debbi had fashioned. It was fancier than she usually wore her hair, but she liked it and thought it would go nicely with her plain lace veil.

For what seemed like the one-hundredth time, Rachel glanced at her wedding gown hanging in the closet. She loved it, and she hoped Evan would, too. Feeling restless, she got up and went to the gown, brushed a few cat hairs off the protective plastic cover, and lined up her shoes under the dress. Then she wandered to a window and gazed out at the snowy ground below and the sparkling, bare treetops.

She couldn't help wondering what was wrong with her. Mary Aaron was right. She should be more excited than she was, shouldn't she? Were the town gossips right? Did she not really want to marry Evan?

No, that wasn't it. She loved Evan and though it had taken her a few years to get to this point, she was ready to make her vows. That wasn't what was troubling her.

It was Daniel's murder.

No matter how hard she tried, no matter what Evan or Mary Aaron or the police said, she still couldn't accept that Moses had killed him. Yet Moses was facing decades in prison. And she feared he'd never survive, not being the way he was mentally and emotionally. Not being an Amish man in an Englisher world.

Rachel had never been able to tolerate injustice, and that was the problem here. That was what was happening in the case of Daniel's murder. Even with all the evidence, or lack thereof, her gut instinct still told her that Moses was taking the fall for someone else.

But for whom?

After talking with Mary Rose, the same gut instinct told Rachel it wasn't her. She had been too honest with her emotions . . . and Rachel had seen it in her eyes. And the previous day, Mary Aaron had been able to confirm what Mary Rose had said about Rosh, that he and his family didn't even own a gun. That really only left one person. . . .

Could it be possible that Mary Rose's little brother, Lemuel, had murdered her husband? To protect her? To protect himself? To just make the physical abuse stop?

George had pointed out that often the killer was the person who claimed to have discovered the body. Lemuel had told her that he hadn't been the one to find Daniel, and yet that's exactly what the police report indicated. Had a mistake been made in the police report? Because the mistake wasn't hers. She knew what Lemuel had said; he told her he didn't know who found Daniel. Had he lied to her? Had Daniel been murdered by a fourteen-year-old boy? Because if Lemuel had killed Daniel, it all made perfect sense, Moses lying to cover for the person who had actually committed the crime. Especially knowing that his sister and little brother had been abused. Maybe he even feared for his mother and niece.

Rachel sighed and turned away from the window.

She couldn't stand not knowing if Lemuel had lied to her, and she couldn't face the hours of waiting until it was time to dress for the church. She couldn't just sit here when so much was at stake.

Without considering the matter any further, Rachel pulled on jeans, a sweater, and a thermal vest, taking care not to muss her hair. She wouldn't be long. She'd just sneak out the front door, bypassing the kitchen that soon would be a beehive of activity if it wasn't already. She'd drive out to the Studer farm, speak to Lemuel, and be back before anyone realized she was gone. If the police report was wrong, that might make all the difference to Moses's defense. And if it wasn't . . . if it wasn't, then Lemuel had some explaining to do.

Chapter 19

As she drove up the lane to the Studer house, Rachel spotted fresh horse and buggy tracks heading out. So maybe she'd wasted a trip; maybe Lemuel had gone somewhere with his family. She pulled into the yard to find it quiet. The only sign of life was smoke drifting from the kitchen chimney.

Glancing over at the buggy shed, she saw that one carriage was missing, but she wasn't sure if it was Alma's or Mary Rose's. It was possible some of the family members were gone but others had stayed. It was worth knocking on the door to find out.

A dog barked when she got out of the Jeep, but she still didn't see anyone. There was a stiff breeze coming off the mountain, funneling the wind between the barn and house. Fearing damage to her elaborate hairdo, Rachel patted the back of her head, hoping that Debbi had put in enough pins. She paused to inhale deeply again, enjoying the bracing mountain air with its smell of pine, hemlock, and cedar. It was a scent she never tired of, and one she'd missed terribly when she'd lived in the city.

Now that she was here, Rachel felt a little foolish, sneaking out of her house and driving up here on the morning of her wedding. Maybe Evan was right. Maybe she *had* become a little obsessed by this investigation. But a few more words with Lemuel and she was certain she could straighten out the mix-up, and then she could put all this behind her and enjoy her special day. She hated leaving dirty dishes in the sink, and she couldn't abide untidy endings. If the police report was in error, she needed to find out the truth and see that Lemuel's name was removed. And once it was all straightened out as to who actually found the body, maybe—

No. One way or the other, her investigation was ending here today. Now. Because today she was getting married and she and Evan were starting a new life together.

A shovel stood by the back door, and the sidewalk had been freshly scraped clean of snow. More snow was drifting down in big flakes, but Rachel didn't think it would amount to much. The Weather Channel had said that they'd have less than an additional inch today, with more to come the following afternoon. And she and Evan were leaving early in the morning for the airport in Harrisburg, where they'd make their connecting flight in Philadelphia to the island of Provo in Turks and Caicos.

Rachel shivered in the icy wind, glad she'd put on her wool socks and flannel-lined jeans. It was hard to believe that in two days she'd be lying on a tropical beach, listening to the sound of ocean waves and seagulls. Lying on a beach, a married woman . . .

She knocked on the farmhouse door. When there was no answer, she tried again, knocking louder. She was about to turn away and go home, in resolute defeat, when she heard footsteps inside the house. The door opened a crack; Lemuel peered through. When he saw her, he didn't seem surprised. She wondered if he'd been watching out a window.

"May I come in?" she asked. "I won't keep you long."

"Is my brother all right?"

"As far as I know, Moses is well." There was no sense in telling a fourteen-year-old that his brother was depressed.

Lemuel frowned. "Did you come to see Mary Rose? She isn't here." He stood planted in the doorway, his thin frame blocking the entrance.

"*Ne,* actually, Lemuel, I came to see you." She forced a smile. "It's about something in the police report concerning the day Daniel died. I think there's been a mistake."

"What kind of mistake?" he asked.

"Is your mother here?"

He hesitated, then slowly shook his head.

She hugged herself for warmth. The goose down vest was warm, but not made for the only outer layer on a day like this. "It's awfully cold out here, Lemuel. Would you mind if we talked in the kitchen?"

As usual, his straight hair stuck out at all angles. He was not a particularly handsome adolescent, at best. Like many boys, his nose had grown first, leaving the rest of his face to catch up, and he was suffering from multiple skin outbreaks. On top of that, this morning he seemed to have awakened with a cold because his eyes were red, his nose drippy, and the corners of his mouth were chapped. "I told you everything I know," he squeaked. "I've got chores to do."

"This will only take a minute, Lemuel," she pressed.

He exhaled as he opened the door farther and reluctantly stepped aside to let her in.

A half glass of milk and a slice of raisin bread with one bite taken out of it sat on the table beside a jar of peanut butter. Apparently, Lemuel had been having a snack. Behind him, on the stove, a large pot simmered. Rachel smelled ham and cabbage cooking.

Rachel felt more uncomfortable than she had when she'd come to the house before. She wondered where Mary Rose and her mother had gone and wished they were here. Lemuel didn't ask her to sit down, so she stood near the door and did her best to put him at ease. "As I said, this won't take a minute," she repeated, her voice sounding patronizing in her ears. "I just need to know . . . Remind me, who was it who found Daniel's body?"

He looked at the floor and shrugged, his face the typical

teenage mask of indifference. "Not sure." He shrugged again and a bead of sweat formed on his upper lip. "Maybe it was Rosh."

Now Rachel's uneasiness multiplied. When she'd talked to Lemuel before, he'd never impressed her as . . . sneaky. That's what he seemed like today, as if he was hiding something. "Then you have to tell the police detective that, because they think you discovered the body. It's written in their report, Lemuel. I saw it."

"Me?" His face blanched and then flushed. He scratched at an inflamed pimple on his neck and his fingernail drew blood.

Unconsciously, Rachel took a step back.

"It wasn't me," Lemuel protested. "Who told them that?" He glared at her. "That's not true. Did *you* tell them that? That I found him?"

She backed up slowly toward the door. She wanted to question him further, but while she wasn't frightened of this overgrown child, she was suddenly feeling very uneasy. The thought that Lemuel had lied—because he clearly had, she could see it on his face—made her stomach uneasy. Seeing his expression, she realized he may very well have been the one who killed his sister's husband.

The realization that she might be standing alone in a kitchen on an isolated farm with a possible killer hit her hard. This was why Evan had asked her to stay out of the matter. Ultimately, he'd feared for her safety.

"Did you tell them that?" Lemuel repeated, his voice squeaky with anger. His eyes were suddenly no longer those of a child but of a man who'd seen too much.

"No, I didn't tell them you found him. You told me you didn't find him," she hedged. "The police report is wrong, that's all," she backpedaled, knowing it really was time to let the police do their job. "Probably a clerical error." She turned for the door.

"Wait."

"*Ne,* I have to go," she insisted. "I have to be somewhere. You tell the police what you told me, and I'm sure—"

"You shouldn't say that." Lemuel's voice cracked.

Hairs on the back of her neck prickled as she sensed Lemuel's desperation. Abruptly, she grabbed the doorknob and yanked the door open. She rushed through the doorway, babbling something about her cousin waiting for her. Her heart was pounding as she heard Lemuel's loud footsteps behind her.

"*Ne!*" he cried.

Rachel had not taken three steps when she felt a blow to the back of her head. *Oh, no, my hairdo,* she thought, as the ground seemed to shift in front of her and rose. *It will be ruined. I'll have to have it done again before the wedding this afternoon.*

She staggered and fell to her knees. She raised her hand to her head and touched something wet and sticky. She smelled the blood. The stone walkway swayed. *I'm going to be sick,* she thought.

And then the snowy ground came up to hit her.

Someone was crying.

Rachel blinked, trying to fight a wave of nausea.

She swallowed, opened her mouth to gasp for air. What was she lying on? Something scratchy . . . something . . . She smelled hay and dirt. Dirt was in her mouth . . . it tasted like dirt. The sound came again. A baby wailing? *Ne,* not a baby, a *kalb* bawling for its mother.

What was the word in English? she wondered.

She tried to open her eyes, but they felt so heavy; the task seemed impossible.

The back of her head felt as though it were on fire. It was hard to think. She turned her face to the side, feeling the cool earth through the scattered hay beneath her. At least the floor was still and not moving.

The *kalb* bellowed again. *Calf*, that's what it was. The word was *calf*. What was a calf doing at her wedding? She was supposed to be at the church. Evan would be at the church . . . so why was she lying facedown on a barn floor? Her white gown would be ruined and her hair . . .

She tried to push herself up on her hands and knees, but she couldn't get her hands . . .

Panic swept over Rachel as she realized that her hands and ankles were bound with lengths of baling twine. Why was she tied up?

She tried to wade through the fog in her mind. Tried to open her eyes. How had she gotten here? And where was *here*? Was she really in a barn? Was she dreaming?

No, the pain of being bound was real.

She inhaled deeply and sneezed. Definitely a barn. She could smell molasses and hay. She listened, gradually picking out the sounds of horses rubbing against the stall boards and a cow chewing its cud.

Should she call out for help? Where were Evan and the wedding guests? Shouldn't someone notice that the bride was lying on the floor with her hands and ankles tied? How could she and Evan exchange their vows in a barn?

She forced her eyes open and the pain in her head threatened to make her vomit. Her eyelids were so heavy that they closed again under their own weight, but in that brief second, she'd seen the shadowy light coming in the barn window and reasoned that it was still daytime.

"Evan?" she called weakly. "Evan, where are you? I . . . I need . . . you to . . ."

And then the thick snow came down around her, and she fell forward and drifted off into the darkness.

The next time Rachel became conscious, she heard voices and recognized them as Alma's and Lemuel's. She gasped as memories came rushing back. She'd come to the farm to question Lemuel about the police report and he'd turned violent. He'd hit her. He'd knocked her down. The boy had tied her up and left her in the Studer barn.

Lemuel was the killer.

Her head throbbed with pain, a headache like the worst migraine. She wanted to just lie down. Sleep it off, or even sleep into oblivion. Because it was reasonable to think if Lemuel could do this to her . . . if he could kill Daniel, he could kill her, too. But she refused to give up without a fight. She wouldn't be his second victim. She had to find a way out of this before he murdered her to keep her quiet.

The hinges on the barn door squeaked. Then came the sound of footsteps.

After a moment, something nudged the sole of her boot. "Why did you hit her with the shovel?" Alma asked.

"I had to, *Mam,*" Lemuel whined. "She asked too many questions and she figured it out. I had to stop her from going to the police."

Someone shoved her foot again. Alma?

"You hit her too hard," Alma complained. "And now what do we do with her?"

"I'm sorry. I thought—"

"It was wrong. You should have waited and talked to me. I didn't want you in this at all."

"But you said she was asking Mary Rose questions the other day in the attic. Questions that could get us all in trouble."

"I don't care what I said. . . ."

"Alma. Help me," Rachel said, speaking in *Deitsch.* "I need medical attention. I'm hurt. Don't let Lemuel be responsible for two deaths."

"See?" the boy said. "I didn't kill her. She's got a hard head."

Fighting the blinding headache, Rachel tried to open her eyes. "Alma, please. Make him see that this is wrong. He's only fourteen; he won't be held fully responsible. Whatever he's done, we can make this right."

Alma knelt beside her and stroked Rachel's face with a rough palm. "*Ne*. There's no going back now. It's done. You should have let this go."

"But you asked me to—Alma, you asked me to help Moses."

"I thought you were going to make them, make the police let him go. Because he didn't kill Daniel."

Rachel sucked in a breath, trying to ignore the pain and speak rationally. "Moses really didn't shoot Daniel?"

"Of course not," Lemuel said. He sounded like a ten-year-old, but Rachel knew now how dangerous he could be. "He wouldn't do that," he argued. "Moses couldn't do such a thing. It goes against the teaching to strike back, even if it's a bad person and they do evil. You return good for evil. The Book tells us that."

Rachel opened her eyes. Lemuel was standing there in the light from the open door. Behind him, she could see snow falling. The teen looked small and sad, not like a murderer at all.

"Why didn't you send Lemuel away, Alma? Somewhere Daniel couldn't hurt him? Why didn't you send him to Moses?"

"You don't understand," Alma said fiercely, pulling her hand away from Rachel. "It wasn't just Lemuel, it was all of them. All of them to protect. How could I send Mary Rose away from her husband? Was I to tear the baby from her mother?"

"So you let Lemuel stay, and he was so desperate that he shot Daniel?" Rachel tried to lift her head, squinting to see her better. "How could you commit murder, Lemuel?" She tried to sound calm, but her voice rasped like an old woman's.

"He couldn't," Alma said, her tone now flat. Resigned. "My Lemuel? None of my children could do such a thing." She stood and dusted the loose hay from her skirt. "It was me. I had to be the one to make the sacrifice for them. I had to be the one to commit the unforgivable sin."

"*Mam,* don't say that," Lemuel protested, his voice cracking again. "You can do what Daniel did. Repent and be forgiven."

Alma made a small sound of disbelief. "Only if I was truly sorry. But I'm not. I'd do it again."

Rachel coughed, trying to clear the dust from her throat. She rolled onto her side so that she could make out Alma in the shadows. The woman's face was as pale as a ghost, and she looked frail despite her heavy barn coat. She was having a hard time following the conversation. Had Alma just admitted to having killed Daniel? "You . . . you killed him, Alma?"

The old woman's sharp chin bobbed assent.

"Daniel was a bad man," Lemuel said. "He hurt Mary Rose and me, and sometimes Moses, until he left the farm."

"I couldn't keep protecting them, you see," Alma explained. "As mean as Daniel could be, as mean as a copperhead with a broken back, he was afraid of me. Afraid I wouldn't pass the farm on to him and Mary Rose."

The older woman wasn't really making sense. Or maybe Rachel just couldn't make sense of what she was saying.

"Did he hit you, too?" Rachel asked. "If he hit you, killing him might be a kind of self-defense." It was hard to believe what Alma seemed to be saying, difficult to accept that a traditional Amish woman could point a gun at her own son-in-law and pull the trigger. And Alma hadn't shot him just once. She'd shot him a second time when he lay helpless and bleeding on the ground.

"I knew what he would be like when I wasn't here to protect them anymore. I've got this thing, like a crab, growing in me." Alma touched her abdomen. "Just like my own mother and her mother before her. They died of it before they turned fifty, and I'll die of it, too," she murmured. "And when I was gone, what would happen to Lemuel and Mary Rose and the baby? They'd be left at Daniel's mercy. He'd be the head of the family. Don't you see? He had to die. It was the only way."

Rachel took a breath; the stone floor of the barn was hard and cold. The cold was seeping into her muscles, making them stiff and achy. "Did . . . did Moses know it was you who killed him? Did he know and protect you by confessing to the killing?" Rachel asked.

"He didn't know," Lemuel said. "Maybe he suspected, but he didn't know. He asked me if Rosh had done it. Rosh was his friend. He knew Rosh would look after Mary Rose and the baby. Moses thought that, after a while, God would make the police understand that he didn't do it and let him go."

Rachel twisted her neck to look at Alma. "You didn't have to kill Daniel," she argued. "You could have gone to the police."

"*Ne,*" Alma said, closing the man's denim coat she wore. She swam in it. Did it belong to her son in jail, or her son-in-law now buried in the cemetery?

"We don't wash our dirty laundry in front of Englishers," Alma said. "And what would they do? It would be our word against Daniel's. He'd come home and we'd be the worse for it."

"Did you tell the church elders? The bishop?"

"Mary Rose did," Lemuel said. "And the bishop was angry. He told Daniel that it was wrong to mistreat his wife. Daniel just went home and grabbed the baby and shook her until she screamed. He said that if Mary Rose carried tales on him—if any of us did—we'd live to regret it."

"Hush, child," Alma cautioned. "No need to tell her any of that now. It doesn't matter."

But Lemuel wouldn't be silenced. "Rachel has to understand why you did it. She has to see that you had to get rid of Daniel." He dropped on his knees beside her. "Daniel said my mother wouldn't always be around to take up for her, and maybe the baby would just fall against the stove or tumble into the well. He said Mary Rose needed to make up her mind who was boss around here, him or an old woman." Lemuel was weeping now. His nose was running, and he was blubbering but still babbling on. "Mary Rose knew he would kill the baby, but she thought she could change him."

"He might have killed Eliza," Alma said. "Daniel complained that she cried too much and she was just a runty girl. He said next time he'd get a son on Mary Rose, so what did it matter if a sickly girl baby had an accident. One less useless mouth to feed."

"But why then? If all of this had been going on for some time?" Rachel murmured. "Why that day of the hunt?"

"Because he'd hurt Moses and Lemuel again. Because the gnawing in my belly was fierce that day," Alma said in a rush. "Because Salome gave me something for the pain and we both knew that my time was growing short. And because I knew he'd be in that deer stand. And I had to do something before it was too late to save my children."

Rachel blinked, finally realizing what Alma was saying. "You're saying you did it?" Rachel said. "Not Lemuel or Mary Rose? And not Moses?"

"*Ne*. Mary Rose doesn't even know I did it," Alma said. "Nobody knew. Nobody would have ever known if Lemuel hadn't come upon me, coming back through the woods that day."

"I'm sorry, *Mam*," Lemuel whispered, hanging his head.

Alma brushed her fingertips across her son's face. "Wasn't your fault. Couldn't be helped. Just wish you hadn't seen me. Hadn't figured it out."

Rachel's mind was now reeling. Alma had shot and killed Daniel, then Lemuel had accidentally come upon his mother and figured out what happened? If not at that moment, then obviously later when he found Daniel's body.

Rachel looked up from the floor at Alma. "You shot Daniel, not once but twice."

"Had to," Alma insisted. "No more than shooting a rat. Daniel was evil. Evil don't die so easy. He should have died with the first shot, but he started screaming and crawling toward me. He said I'd go to hell. And I said he'd be there ahead of me and pulled the trigger again."

"But you won't go to hell," Lemuel sobbed. "You'll go down on your knees in front of the church and you'll be forgiven."

"*Ne*, that won't happen," Alma said. "It's too late for all that, because I've still got bad things to do to make everything right."

"What bad things, *Mam?*" Lemuel asked.

Rachel held her breath, holding Alma's gaze.

The Amish woman looked away. "I've got to protect you. I'm sorry, Rachel. You seem like a good person, but I can't take the chance that you'll tell the police. You'll tell them that Lemuel helped me hide what I did. He dropped his father's gun down the old well. That makes him guilty, too. And they'd put him in jail like they did Moses."

Rachel struggled against the ropes. "They won't. It's not the same thing," she protested. "Lemuel didn't kill anybody. He's too young to be an accessory to the crime."

"He hit you with the shovel, and he's going to help me get rid of your body," Alma said. "That makes him guilty."

Fear made Rachel's mouth dry. "Alma, please. You don't have to kill me," she begged. "I found a lawyer for Moses. I can convince her to defend Lemuel. So long as you don't hurt me, they'd never put him in prison."

"Don't lie to me. I know about the places Englishers send their children. I may be uneducated, but I'm not stupid. *Juvenile detention centers*." Those three words came out in English, rather than *Deitsch*. "We'll give you a little while to make your peace with God. Pray for your soul and ask forgiveness for your sins. You'll go to heaven when this business is all said and done, Rachel. Even though you left the Amish church, you're a good person. God will understand."

"You don't want to do this," Rachel managed, fighting tears. "Daniel was an evil man. You had to protect your children. But all I've tried to do was help your family. I shouldn't die for it."

Alma shook her head. "They'll be looking for you. We don't have much time to think of the best place to put your body. But giving you time to pray is the decent thing to do. Be at peace. This world is a place of sorrow and pain, and you're better out of it."

"Please," Rachel begged. "Think of what this will do to Lemuel."

"It's Lemuel I'm thinking of," Alma insisted, turning away. "Come, boy. We need to do some praying of our own."

The two of them exited the barn and Rachel was left on the floor wondering why she'd ever left the warmth and safety of her own home.

Chapter 20

Lying there on the barn floor, Rachel refused to wallow in self-pity or sink into a stupor of paralyzing fear as she contemplated her own death. She knew she didn't have much time. Lemuel would do whatever his mother asked of him, and Alma seemed beyond reason.

Frantically, Rachel struggled to free her hands tied in front of her, but the jute twine cut into her wrists. She didn't want to die like this, but worse than the idea of dying was knowing that Evan would be waiting for her at the church. Everyone would stare at him and whisper behind their hands and pity him. They would believe that, as predicted by many, she'd stood him up at the altar.

It would break his heart.

She relaxed for a moment, trying to think. Think her way out of this; it was how she'd managed to get out of situations like this before. The pain in her head brought on waves of nausea, but she couldn't let herself be sick. *Think!* she told herself. Only she couldn't think clearly. The pain was awful, and she was so cold. All she wanted to do was to close her eyes and sleep. If she slept, though, she might never wake. Instead, she concentrated on the twine wrapped around her wrists, working at the knots with her teeth.

If she could get to her phone, she could call for help. But it seemed as if it was a long way away. She'd left her cell in the

Jeep, as she always did when she was visiting an Amish home. Out of respect. She hadn't wanted to disturb Alma's house with a ringing telephone. And she would probably pay for that mistake with her life.

Alma.

Why had she never suspected Alma?

It all made sense now that she knew Alma was ill. Daniel and Mary Rose would have inherited the farm when Alma passed, but Daniel would have been in control. He would have had all the power. Who knows what he would have done to his infant daughter or to Lemuel?

If Rachel had known what was going on under Alma's roof, she could have gone to the authorities. "God forgive me," she prayed.

Part of this was her own fault. Vanity. She'd believed that she could learn the truth and free Moses. Now she might die for her stubborn insistence on interfering where she shouldn't have. She didn't fear death the way many Englishers did because she had faith there was a hereafter. But she didn't want to die yet, not before she and Evan had a chance to marry, to make a life together. She wanted children and the opportunity to grow old with the man she loved. She had to think of a way to get out of this. There *had* to be some way to convince Alma to spare her, if only for Lemuel's sake.

A surge of hope washed over Rachel as she managed to loosen the first knot at her wrists. Warm, sticky blood ran down her neck, coming from where, she wasn't sure. Her head wound? Tied up this way, her shoulders ached and her feet were going numb. She tried to wiggle her toes and only succeeded in causing a cramp in her right calf.

She sucked in a deep breath and tried to hold back a sense of rising panic.

Her mind raced. Odd images rose, becoming vivid flashes of memory . . . the midwife's hearth with its crackling fire . . . a section of cordwood at the instant Moses's ax split through it . . . Chuck's tea mugs and his medal . . . and the red cardinal rising out of the snow in her father's barnyard the day of Daniel's funeral.

"Things are not always what they appear to be," she murmured.

The midwife was no storybook witch. The strange man on the mountain with the barricades and knife was no murderer. The child's lost mitten in the barnyard that day was a bird. And the mother was a murderer.

Rachel's eyelids drifted shut and her head slumped as she lost consciousness to the image of dozens of red mittens swirling through the air like so many crimson snowflakes.

Sometime later a horse whinnied, and Rachel jerked awake. Sunlight from an open door temporarily blinded her vision. She gasped and blinked. Silhouetted against the doorway stood two figures, a woman and a thin boy. The woman had a rifle in her hands. The boy had a rope around his shoulder and was dragging something.

"It's time," Alma said, seeming unaffected by what she intended to do.

"*Ne.*" Rachel shook her head. "For the love of God, Alma, please. Don't—"

"Don't speak to me of God," Alma interrupted. "I'm lost to Him."

"You're wrong," Rachel protested. "God never abandons us. He's here for us when we are at our weakest—when we need Him most."

Lemuel was weeping again, but he dragged the object closer. A large old-fashioned sled built of wood slats on metal runners. "She's trying to get loose, *Mam*," he managed between hiccups. He'd been crying. His eyes were bright, his nose running. "But I tied it good, like you showed me."

"Won't matter." Alma leaned down and jerked on the binding around Rachel's wrists.

Rachel winced.

"God's with you. You keep thinking that, Rachel," the

woman said as she helped the boy drag Rachel's body onto the oversized sled. "I hope it gives you comfort."

Lemuel straightened and wiped his nose with the sleeve of his homemade denim coat. "I don't like this, *Mam*. It's not right. I'll go to the Englisher police. I'll tell them I did it. I'll tell them that I killed Daniel, and Moses will come home. He'll take care of Mary Rose and the baby."

"Hush, *sohn*. This is the only way," his mother crooned. She slowly lifted Rachel's legs, groaning in pain from the exertion. "That old well was a good place for your *dat*'s gun, and it will do just as well for her body. We should have thrown Daniel down there, and then we'd have none of this trouble."

"Lemuel, please," Rachel begged, trying to look up at the boy. "Don't do this. It's wrong. You know it's wrong. It's not too late to stop—"

"No more!" Alma leaned over, and her fingers tightened on Rachel's forearm. "If you don't shut up, I'll take that shovel and finish you off with it now. You should be making your peace with your Maker instead of worrying my boy." She stood upright, breathing heavily. "You'll see, Lemuel," she soothed. "This will be best for all of us. It will soon be over and done and you'll all be safe. Now let's get on with it. The sooner done, the better. And then we'll go inside and have a nice supper."

A sob escaped Lemuel's lips, but he nodded obediently and grabbed the rope he'd used to bring the sled into the barn. The two of them tugged on the rope together and slowly dragged the sled out into the snowy farmyard.

Time had passed. Rachel could tell by the shift in the sun.

Panic seized her. "Help!" Rachel screamed as loud as she could. She rolled one way and then the other, trying to get off the sled. "Help me! Someone! Help!"

Alma dropped the rope and raised the rifle butt over Rachel's head. "I told you to keep quiet," she warned, her voice surprisingly free of rancor. The woman was resolved. She was going to do this. She really was going to kill Rachel.

Rachel stopped moving and clamped her eyes shut, half expecting to feel the wooden stock of the rifle crash into the back of her head. The sled jerked and then slid bumpily over the surface of the snow. She cautiously opened her eyes again as the sled passed the corner of the barn.

The snow had stopped and the temperature had dropped. The sun had come out from the clouds and the late-afternoon light glittered off the snow. It must be after three, Rachel thought. The minister and all the guests would have left the church. Her wedding had come and gone, and she hadn't been there to see it.

She groaned as Alma and Lemuel pulled her through the snow, hitting bumps that sent pain knifing through Rachel's head.

The rifle worried her. Did Alma plan to shoot her before throwing her down the well? It might be better than dying of exposure or drowning in a dark hole, but if they only dropped her in the well, she might have a chance. Evan would come looking for her. Surely he would. Wouldn't he? Or would he believe she'd decided not to marry him and just taken a coward's way out and not told him?

She didn't want to believe that, but why else hadn't he come for her? Hopefully Mary Aaron would know something was wrong. She must have realized she was missing when she went upstairs to help Rachel into her wedding gown. She'd figure out where Rachel had gone and come to the Studer farm.

If Rachel could just convince Alma to leave her alive, she might be able to survive until help came.

There was the sudden sound of splintering wood, the sled shifted, and Rachel slid hard into the cold snow. Her head struck the ground and she gave an involuntary cry of pain. White lights flashed in her head. She heard herself groan, as if she were a distance from her body, and feared she might pass out.

"It broke," Lemuel exclaimed, sounding as if he were about to burst into tears. "Look, that runner's bent under."

Rachel lay in the snow, her back to them, unable to move. Afraid to move and bring attention to herself.

"What are we going to do?" Lemuel fretted. "Carry her the rest of the way? She's too big for me to carry."

"She can walk," Alma said. "Untie her ankles."

Lemuel hurried to obey.

"Lemuel, please," Rachel whispered, peering up at him as he yanked on the twine.

"Leave him alone," Alma snapped at Rachel. "Get up on your feet. You can walk. It's not far."

Rachel rolled on her stomach and made it to her knees before a wave of nausea washed over her. She hung her head. "I . . . I don't know if I can."

It took both Alma and Lemuel to pull Rachel to her feet. She was so dizzy that she could barely maintain her balance. *I wish I could speak to my family one last time,* she thought. *I wish I could tell Evan how sorry I am and how much I love him.*

They walked. She lifted her head to gaze out at the snow and she thought of making a run for it. Of shouldering Lemuel and charging past him . . . of running back to the barn and climbing into the hayloft or making it to the Jeep and driving down the lane. But wishes weren't horses, as her mother had always said. Rachel didn't have the strength or clear head to run. It took every ounce of her strength to put one foot in front of the other. If she tried to flee, she'd be as helpless as a blind kitten. Alma would shoot her, or Lemuel would run her down and knock her to the ground.

She closed her eyes and saw again the flash of red as the mitten turned into a cardinal and flew into the sky. She wished she were a redbird. She'd fly away. Alma let go of her and Rachel fell onto her knees in the snow. A few yards ahead of her, Lemuel began to kick the snow off a sheet of tin. It lay on top of a few rotting beams, just another pile of debris in a farmer's field. If it snowed again tonight, no one might notice it for months or years . . . or ever.

Lemuel lifted another section of metal and Rachel caught a glimpse of mossy fieldstones that lined the inside of the well. She stiffened, thinking of the dank walls and the icy water at the bottom. "Alma, you can't do this," she murmured. "You're condemning your son to—"

A loud metallic click sounded in the still air . . . the sound of Alma cocking the rifle. "I'm sorry to do this to you, Rachel," she said. "But I have to protect my—"

The wail of a police siren drowned out her words. Rachel staggered to her feet. Hope lent her strength and she ran toward the barn. "Evan!" she screamed. "Evan!" Between the barn and the chicken house she heard the roar of the motor and saw the vehicle spin into the yard, lights flashing. A door banged open.

"She has a gun!" Rachel yelled. "Alma has a gun!"

Evan, dressed in his tuxedo, dashed around the barn, gun drawn. Rachel heard the crack of the rifle. Evan got off a shot, but the bullet missed its mark as Alma fired again. The air was filled with the echo of the shots and the smell of gunpowder.

It all seemed so surreal.

Rachel watched, everything seeming to move in slow motion, as Evan crumpled and fell forward. A red stain began to spread across the snow.

"*Mam!*" Lemuel cried.

Behind her, Rachel heard Alma slam another cartridge into the rifle.

Rachel ran toward Evan, screaming his name. Something whined past her head and she heard the sound of Alma's rifle again. Rachel ducked and kept running. She had to get to Evan. Another bullet slammed into the ground beside her. She threw herself over Evan, wrapping her arms around him and trying to shield him from Alma. Evan groaned. "God help us," she managed.

Suddenly, a pack of barking dogs swept down off the slope. A burst of gunfire rang out. "Drop it or the boy dies!" a male voice shouted.

"Don't hurt him!" Alma screamed. "Not my Lemuel." She threw the rifle aside and ran to her son.

"Hands in the air! Flat on the ground, both of you!" Chuck Baker shouted a command to his pit bulls and they closed in on a weeping Alma and the boy. Snarling viciously, the dogs crouched low, muscles tensed and teeth bared. "Don't move or they'll tear you apart," the prepper warned. "If they get a taste of blood I won't be able to call them off."

Tears clouded Rachel's eyes as Chuck snatched up Alma's discarded rifle and strode toward them. He ejected a cartridge and hurled Alma's gun to the ground as he came toward Rachel and Evan, his semiautomatic rifle tucked under his arm.

"How bad is he?" Chuck asked, slicing through the baling twine at her wrists with his hunting knife.

"He's shot," Rachel said.

Gently, the big man rolled Evan onto his back.

Rachel gasped. A neat round hole in Evan's right shoulder was oozing a trail of deep crimson down the front of his tuxedo jacket. "Is he alive?"

Chuck pressed the base of his palm against the bullet wound. With his free hand, he sought for a pulse at Evan's throat. "He's alive," he said. "What about you? That wound on your head looks pretty bad."

"I'm all right," she said. "It's Evan who needs help."

"Good. Then hustle yourself back to that police car and call for an ambulance. Tell them we've got a trooper down and two suspects in custody."

"You're sure?" she asked, tears running down her cheeks. Behind her she could hear Chuck's dogs barking and growling. "You're sure he's alive?"

Evan's eyelids flickered. "I'm alive." He clenched his teeth and inhaled raggedly. "You're late, Rachel. Do you . . . know what today is?"

"I'm sorry," she said. "Oh, Evan, don't die. I love you so much. I—"

"For pity's sake," Chuck exclaimed and rolled his eyes. "Will you two lovebirds quit your cooing and get an ambulance here before he *does* bleed to death?"

Epilogue

The nurse pushed Rachel's wheelchair into Evan's room. One of the four state police officers who were just leaving held the door for her. They greeted her, asked how she was doing, and offered condolences for her injuries. She murmured something she hoped was appropriate to each of them and thanked them for coming to support Evan.

"He's a good guy," Lucy Mars said. In spite of the fact that she was in full uniform, she bent to hug her. "Don't let him get away," she murmured in Rachel's ear.

"I won't," Rachel promised. She still felt light-headed and her head hurt due to a serious concussion as well as the seventeen stitches it had taken to sew up the wound. But none of that mattered. The only thing on her mind was seeing Evan for herself and making certain he really was all right. She'd come so close to losing him the previous day that it was hard to accept they'd both come through the ordeal alive.

"You can only stay for a few moments," the nurse warned. "Officer Parks has been out of recovery less than twenty-four hours."

Rachel nodded and rolled herself forward in the wheelchair. "Evan?"

"Rachel." Evan's pale face creased into a wide grin. "I've been worried about you, darling," he croaked. His voice was hoarse from the effects of the anesthesia, but nothing could hide his pleasure at seeing her. He tried to rise, despite the IVs and heart and blood pressure monitors, but the nurse waved him back.

"You just lay back, Officer," the nurse said, pushing Rachel's wheelchair to the side of the bed. "You lost a lot of blood and you need to remain quiet and regain your strength. You don't know how fortunate you are." She smiled. "Ten minutes. That's all I can give you. And then visiting is over for you until this afternoon." She made a slight adjustment to the IV machine and padded out of the room on soft-soled orange Crocs.

The room smelled like all hospital rooms, of alcohol and cleaning products. One of the machines was beeping rhythmically, and the lights were too bright. It didn't matter. All Rachel could see was the man who'd become the center of her life. He was here. He was alive, and she wasn't riding behind his body in a limousine, in a long line of police cars.

Reaching his bedside, she took Evan's hand in hers and gripped it tightly. "I'm so sorry I messed up our wedding," she blurted. "That was never my intention. I was trying to wrap things up and put the whole mess behind us before we got married."

He offered a wry grin. "I'm sorry I messed up by letting an Amish woman get the drop on me."

She swallowed, trying not to cry. "It isn't funny. You could have died out there. Another few inches and that bullet—"

"Right," Evan agreed, cutting her off. "But it didn't happen. And your weird friend Chuck did a good job of keeping me from bleeding out before the ambulance arrived. He'd make a top-notch paramedic."

"Chuck's outside in the waiting room," she said. "He's been here all night, waiting to see how your surgery went. I asked a nurse to tell him he could go home, then I asked him myself, but so far he hasn't budged."

There was no need to explain to Evan how much of a sacrifice that must have been for Chuck to spend so many hours in a hospital away from the quiet of his mountain. She'd have plenty of time to tell him later. The thought that they would have that time made her chest tighten and she held on to Evan's hand with all her strength. "Nice gown," she teased. It was faded, too small, and covered in purple abstract designs.

"Are you all right, honey?" He gestured to the bandage on her head where her hair had been shaved so the stitches could be put in.

"I'll be fine. All of the Masts have hard heads."

"I was worried about you," Evan admitted. He lifted her hand and pressed his lips to her knuckles.

She raised an eyebrow. "You mean when I didn't show up at the church to marry you?"

He nodded, one side of his mouth turning up in a gentle smile. His brown eyes were bloodshot and cloudy from his ordeal, but she could read the love shining there. "I knew you were in trouble when you didn't come."

"You didn't think I skipped out on you? Like everyone said I would."

"Nope. Not for a second."

She smiled, fighting tears. "But how did you know where to look for me?"

"Guess."

Rachel's eyes glistened with tears. "Mary Aaron."

Evan nodded. "She knew right away that you had something on your mind yesterday morning. Something about the police report. She was certain you'd gone back to talk to Lemuel."

"I'm surprised that when she realized I wasn't home getting dressed, she didn't come looking for me."

"She was really upset about that, so you need to talk to her when you can. She said she knew where you'd gone and had been certain you'd be back in time for the wedding."

"And then I wasn't and nearly got you killed because of

it," she said. "Evan, I'm so, so sorry. I should never have tried—"

"Rachel," he said, cutting her off. "This is as much my fault as yours. I should have believed you . . . trusted in your intuition. Moses is innocent."

"*Ya.*" She stood up, leaned across the bed, and kissed him. "I still should have listened to you. I've made such a mess of things."

"No, you've forced the system to give justice to that young man being held for something he didn't do. You should be proud of yourself."

She shook her head. "Pride is *hochmut*. We're taught not to be prideful."

"Okay." The goofy grin spread across his face again. "Then I can be proud of you for both of us."

"But it's not a happy ending," she said. "Not for Moses or Mary Rose. Certainly not for Lemuel."

"You're certain the widow had nothing to do with it? She didn't know that her mother shot Daniel?"

Rachel shook her head again. "No, Mary Rose didn't know anything. And she and the baby were at the neighbor's when Lemuel hit me with the shovel and her mother tried to kill me."

"You're positive?"

"Absolutely. I told the officers I'd testify that she wasn't on the farm and had nothing to do with it." She thought of Lemuel's face when he'd looked down into the open well and she was filled with sorrow for him. "Will Lemuel go to prison?" She knew that Alma would, for as long as she had left to live, which, if she was as ill as she claimed, might not be long. "He's only fourteen."

"I doubt it. I'm sure Ms. Glidden can convince a judge that he was only trying to protect his mother. That, and she was telling him what to do, making him do it. The court will want him to have treatment, certainly, but I don't believe he'll go to juvenile jail, not if his sister and brother will be willing to be his guardians."

"I'm sure they will. And Moses can move home now to help Mary Rose." She sighed. "Lemuel's been through enough. Without his mother, he'll need his faith and patience."

"That's one thing your people have plenty of," Evan assured her. He looked up at her. "You know, it's funny what comes to your mind when you wake up in recovery. I was thinking about our hotel reservations and that ocean beach. Do you think you could call to tell them that we're not coming? Maybe reschedule for next month?"

"I already have," she said. "And I called someone else as well. Our minister."

"But . . . he was here when I got out of surgery," Evan said. "He's aware of—"

There was the sound of footsteps and a knock at the door.

"I think this is him now," Rachel said.

"Excellent. Two of you finally in one place." The young minister laughed as he came into the room, followed by Rachel's parents, two of her little brothers, Evan's mother, Hulda, Mary Aaron, and Chuck Baker.

"What's going on?" Evan asked.

Rachel studied the crowded room. Her mother and father, Mary Aaron, and the boys were in their best black go-to-church clothes. Evan's mom wore a peach jacket, cream-colored white dress slacks, and beige heels. Hulda and Chuck, in contrast, looked as though they'd been cutting wood: goose down vests, jeans, and hiking boots. Perfect, Rachel thought as she glanced down at the oversized blue scrubs she'd borrowed from one of the techs because her clothes were too bloody to wear and she refused to be seen in a drafty hospital gown.

Evan's eyes widened as Mary Aaron, the minister, and the prepper approached his bed. "Is someone going to tell me what's going on?" Evan asked.

Rachel squeezed his hand. "I love you," she whispered.

"And you know I love you," Evan replied, "but I don't . . ."

"Rachel tells me that you two would like to be married here and now," the minister said. "Since it would be a shame to let that marriage license go to waste, this gentleman and this young woman"—he indicated a smiling Mary Aaron in her black bonnet, and a stern, bareheaded Chuck Baker— "have agreed to be your witnesses. Do you think you're up to it, Evan?"

Evan looked at Rachel. "Do you have any intention of changing your ways?" he asked. "Or can I expect you to keep getting into trouble that I have to get you out of?"

She hesitated, unsure for a moment how to respond. Then she realized there was only one response. "Probably the latter."

"Good." He grinned. "That's my girl." He looked back at the minister. "Here and now," he agreed, holding Rachel's hand tightly. "Marry us now, before she can get away again."

"Rachel?" the minister asked. "Are you certain you're ready to be married?"

She met her cousin's mischievous gaze, and Mary Aaron whispered in *Deitsch,* "Do it."

"We sure are," Rachel said. "In the sight of God and those we love best."

Evan's mother plucked one of his get-well floral bouquets from a vase and shoved it into Rachel's hands. And in the crowded hospital room, amid approving Amish and Englishers, the traditional bonnets and beeping technology, Evan and Rachel finally took their vows for better or worse.

Connect with

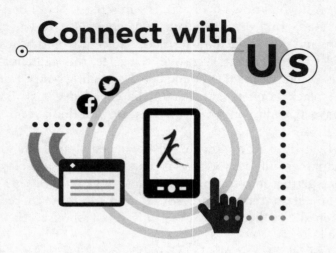

Us

Visit us online at
KensingtonBooks.com
to read more from your favorite authors, see books
by series, view reading group guides, and more.

Join us on social media

for sneak peeks, chances to win books and prize packs,
and to share your thoughts with other readers.

facebook.com/kensingtonpublishing
twitter.com/kensingtonbooks

Tell us what you think!

To share your thoughts, submit a review,
or sign up for our eNewsletters, please visit:
KensingtonBooks.com/TellUs.